Hyder

Advance Praise for *Hyderabad: Book 2 of The Partition Trilogy*

'Hyderabad! A liberation? A tragedy? The result of the Ironman's will and Nehru's vision to build a nation? The daydreams of a Nizam? The diplomatic strategies of Nehru and Dickie? Dreams of a Communist revolution? The common people's struggles and sacrifices for land and a fistful of grain? But everything finally ends with a never-ending, silent violence on women's bodies in the formation of a state. This is well-researched history woven as a thrilling novel by a terrific novelist, Manreet Sodhi Someshwar.'

— **Volga**, author of *Vimukta Kadha Samputi*

Praise for *Lahore: Book 1 of The Partition Trilogy*

'As the men fought over religion and maps, the Partition heaped unspeakable atrocities on women. Manreet's book is a faithful, unforgiving look at what was and also what shouldn't have been. *Lahore* is breathtaking in scope, painful yet gentle to the touch.'

— **Taslima Nasreen**, author of *Lajja* and *Shameless*

'Vivid and atmospheric. By deftly weaving the personal and the political, Manreet Sodhi Someshwar transports us to the uncertain months leading up to the tragedy of Partition.'

— **Aanchal Malhotra**, author of *Remnants of a Separation*

'A timely reminder of what differences and divisions can do ... An engaging read that tries to humanize the politics of the Partition. Current, relevant, and important. This is a voice which makes you question, rethink, and reimagine the past as the future and the future as the past. A voice to pay attention to in these times of rising intolerance and right-wing extremism. A voice of reason and reckoning.'

– **Sabyn Javeri**, author of *Hijabistan*

'Tension pervades this first part of Manreet Sodhi Someshwar's Partition trilogy. It wafts through the corridors of power, penetrates bonds between friends and lovers, and befouls the earth itself. Without releasing the reader from its ominous undercurrent, Manreet deftly weaves the big strands of history with the finer threads of human feeling, reminding us of a calamity that tore apart not just nations and states but also the heart and spirit of a people.'

– **Manu S. Pillai**, author of *The Ivory Throne: Chronicles of the House of Travancore*

'The value of *Lahore* lies in how it does not let the subaltern disappear into the shadow of giants like Jawaharlal Nehru and his socialist dream, Vallabhbhai and his tremendous contribution to the task of the consolidation of the nation, the statesmanship of Lord Mountbatten and the effortless charm of Lady Mountbatten.'

– Scroll.in

'Clearly a passion project, this first book of an ambitious trilogy on Partition is all heart, and brilliantly traces our heritage.'

– *Deccan Herald*

HYDERABAD

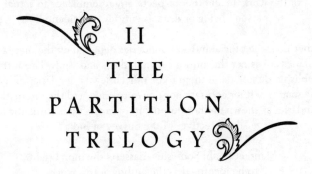

II
THE
PARTITION
TRILOGY

MANREET SODHI SOMESHWAR

HarperCollins *Publishers* India

First published in India by HarperCollins *Publishers* 2022
4th Floor, Tower A, Building No. 10, Phase II, DLF Cyber City,
Gurugram, Haryana – 122002
www.harpercollins.co.in

2 4 6 8 10 9 7 5 3 1

P-ISBN: 978-93-5629-113-3
E-ISBN: 978-93-5629-119-5

Typeset in 11/15 Berling LT Std at
Manipal Technologies Limited, Manipal

Printed and bound at
Thomson Press (India) Ltd

For
Hyderabad,
where god started creating the world

Chityala Ailamma,
the power of one

And Makhdoom Mohiuddin,
aapka saath saath phoolon ka

Is mulk di vand kolon yaaro, khoye tusi vi ho, khoye asin vi haan
Laali akhan di payi dassdi hai, roye tusi vi ho, roye asin vi haan

With partition of this land, friends, you lost, as did we
The redness of eyes chronicles, you wept, as did we

—Ustad Daman

About The Partition Trilogy

Set in the months leading up to and following India obtaining freedom in 1947, The Partition Trilogy is an exploration of the events, exigencies and decisions that led to the independence of India, its concomitant partition, and the accession of Princely States alongside. A literary political thriller that captures the frenzy of the time, the series is set in Delhi, Lahore, Hyderabad, and Kashmir. Covering a vast canvas, Jawaharlal Nehru, Vallabhbhai Patel, and Dickie Mountbatten share space in the trilogy with the ordinary people from the cities that were affected by the partition and the reorganization of the states.

Backed by astute research that ensures the authenticity of the political thread, this trilogy will take readers back into a world of great political upheaval and churn. In its fresh, incisive, and insightful portrayal of a cataclysm that haunts us to this day, The Partition Trilogy is both spellbinding and believable – a remarkable feat.

About The Partition Trilogy

Cast of Characters

His Majesty's Government (HMG)

(London)

King George VI, King of the United Kingdom and British Dominions, and Emperor of India

Winston Churchill, Prime Minister of the United Kingdom from 1940–1945

Clement Attlee, Prime Minister of the United Kingdom from 1945–1951

Lieutenant General Scoons, head of Foreign Relations Office

British Empire in India/The Raj

Lord Louis (Dickie) Mountbatten, last Viceroy of India (1947), and the first governor general of independent India (1947–1948)

Edwina Mountbatten, wife of Louis Mountbatten, and the last Vicereine of India

Pamela Mountbatten, younger daughter of Louis and Edwina Mountbatten

Mizzen, Sealyham terrier belonging to Edwina Mountbatten

Lord Archibald Wavell, second-last Viceroy of India

Arthur Lothian, British resident in Hyderabad

Lionel (Pug) Ismay, chief of staff to Lord Mountbatten

Eric Miéville, Mountbatten's principal secretary

Alan Campbell-Johnson, Mountbatten's press attaché

Claude Auchinleck/The Auk, commander-in-chief of the Indian Army

Major General Pete Rees, Boundary Force commander, head of the Military Emergency Staff

Roy Bucher, general officer commanding-in-chief of Eastern Command

Conrad Corfield, political adviser responsible for the Princely States

Cyril Radcliffe, Inner Temple lawyer, and chairman of the Boundary Commission

Sir Robert Francis Mudie, governor of the West Panjab

General Moore, the military adviser-in-chief

Nizam, His Inner Circle, and Staff

(Hyderabad)

Nizam/His Exalted Highness (HEH), Nawab Sir Mir Osman Ali Khan Siddiqi, Asaf Jah VII

Dulhan Pasha, Nizam's wife

Mir Qamruddin Khan, Asaf Jah I, founder of the dynasty

Prince Moazzam Jah/Shajeeh, Nizam's younger son

Princess Niloufer, Moazzam Jah's wife

Duruu/Princess Durushehvar, Nizam's eldest daughter-in-law

Walter Monckton, Nizam's legal counsel and constitutional adviser

Biddy/Lady Carlisle, Walter's wife

Kasim Razvi, leader of the Razakars

El Edroos, commander of the Hyderabad Army

Brigadier Gilbert, chief of staff of the Hyderabad Army

Nawab Deen Yar Jung, Hyderabad's inspector general police

Nawab of Chhatari, ex–Prime Minister of Hyderabad

Ali Yavar Jung, minister for constitutional affairs

Mir Laik Ali, Prime Minister of Hyderabad

Sir Sultan Ahmed, Hyderabad delegate to discussions on Standstill Agreement

Political Leaders of the Subcontinent, Their Families, and Staff

Gandhi/Mahatma/Bapu, leader of the Indian National Congress

Mohammed Ali Jinnah/The Quaid, leader of the Muslim League, Pakistan's first governor general

Jawaharlal Nehru, first Prime Minister of independent India

Motilal Nehru, Jawaharlal's father, twice president of the Congress

Indira (Indu) Gandhi, Jawaharlal's daughter

Rajiv and Sanjay, sons of Indira

Betty/Krishna Nehru Hutheesing, Jawaharlal's sister

M.O. Mathai (Mac), private secretary to Jawaharlal

Vallabhbhai Patel, deputy prime minister and home minister

Manibehn, Vallabhbhai's daughter, assistant, and housekeeper

Vidya Shankar, Vallabhbhai's private secretary

V.P. Menon, secretary of the States Department

Baldev Singh, representative of the Sikhs to the Viceroy's Executive Council, and defence minister in the interim government

Giani Kartar Singh, Sikh leader

Master Tara Singh, Sikh leader who opposed the partition of Panjab

Maulana Azad, education minister

Rajendra Prasad, Congress president, and president of Constituent Assembly of India

K.M. Munshi, freedom fighter and politician

Brij Krishna, freedom fighter and Mahatma's associate

Colonel Iskander Mirza, secretary of defence, Pakistan

Krishna Menon, president of the India League, and close friend of Jawaharlal

Liaquat Ali Khan, first Prime Minister of Pakistan

N. Gopalaswami Ayyangar, minister without portfolio, and a constitutional expert

Princes

Maharaja Brar, of Faridkot

Jam Saheb, Maharaja of Nawanagar

Maharaja Rao, of Bhavnagar

Hari Singh, Maharaja of Kashmir

Common People

(Hyderabad)

Emily Perkins, Englishwoman, friend of Princess Niloufer

Uzma, companion–confidante of Princess Niloufer

Jaabili/Jagan, peasant woman and Communist

Swami, landlord's son

Lalithamma, bonded labourer

Sithamma, bonded labourer

Jagirdar Vamana Reddy, feudal landlord

Saroja, daughter-in-law of Jagirdar Reddy

Salamma, Sangham comrade

Venkateswara Rao, leader of Sangham

Ali Hassan, Uzma's erstwhile neighbour and student Communist

Afzal, food-cart owner

Lalitha, Sangham comrade

Simha, Sangham comrade

Daniyal Khan, journalist

Khudabax, Daniyal's retainer

Raj Kumar, student activist

Moin/Moinuddeen, clerk in the Nizam's Peshi office

Imrana, female guard of the zenana

Idris, young Razakar

Roger Stetson, BBC journalist

Rustom, owner of Shaheen Irani Cafe

Faqr, student activist

Common People

(Delhi)

Shamsher Singh, Kishan's cousin and chaprassi at Viceroy House

Parminder (Pammi), Kishan Singh's eldest daughter

Beli Ram, Panjabi refugee

Mehmood, coolie at Lahore Junction

Kishan Singh, clerk at Lahore Junction, and a resident of the railway quarters

Others

P.V. Narasimha Rao, student activist

Ailamma, peasant woman who resisted the landlords and became an icon

Khaliq, Jawaharlal's driver

Aurangzeb, sixth Mughal emperor

Nadir Shah, Iranian ruler and conqueror

Ian Fleming, the creator of 007

Sidney Cotton, aviator and businessman

Shah Nawaz Bhutto, dewan of Junagadh

Samaldas Gandhi, freedom fighter and politician

Margaret Bourke-White, American photographer

Padmaja Naidu, freedom fighter and politician

Anthony, servant at Lake View

Christopher Brunyate, solicitor assisting the Nizam

Thomas Elmhirst, commander-in-chief of the Indian Air Force

Albert Kesselring, German general

Hermann Göring, a leader of the Nazi party

Alan Moorehead, journalist

Major Mohsin Ali, commanding officer of Osmanabad district

Map of the Princely State of Hyderabad
(1948)

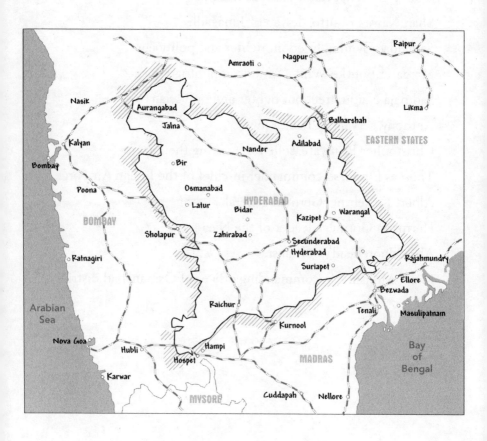

Map of Hyderabad state at present after reorganization into Indian states of Karnataka, Maharashtra, and Telangana (2020)

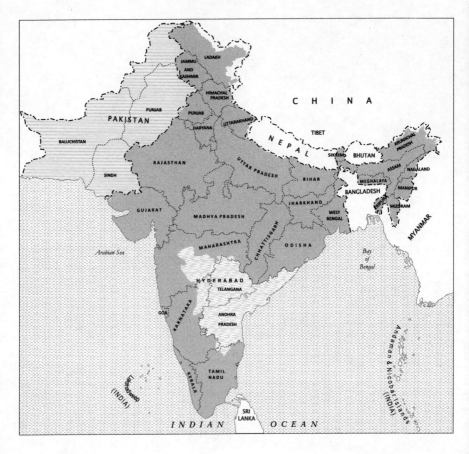

Prelude

Two wars erupted at Independence: one overt, the other covert.

With Jinnah's Kabailis in Kashmir in October 1947, the first Indo-Pak war began barely two months into Independence. Unlike the eighteen-day Great War of Kurukshetra, this fraternal war is into its eighth decade …

The covert war was with Hyderabad, the richest Princely State, ruled by the world's richest man, seventh of the Asaf Jahi dynasty: His Exalted Highness, Nawab Sir Mir Osman Ali Khan Siddiqi. Nizam VII. The 250-year rule of the Asaf Jahis created a state that would be spoken of in the same breath as Mecca and Constantinople in the Islamic world. A magnet for poets after the Mughal court collapsed in Delhi, Hyderabad became a centre of Islamic learning – and a potential Caliphate in the twentieth century. But the state had been firing up the world's imagination for centuries prior.

In 1798, Napoleon, having landed in Egypt, was looking to invade India. Meanwhile, a Russo-French alliance to defeat Britain, and thus secure the Indian goldmine, pivoted over prized Hyderabad, where the Nizam's army was under the command of the French war veteran Michel Raymond. However, Governor General Wellesley was to cannily outmanoeuvre Raymond in Hyderabad. The French loss put paid to Napoleon's plans for India. And what sealed the fate of Hyderabad was the lone foundation upon which the Asaf Jahis had built their rule: loyalty. First to the Mughals, then the British. Such fealty indeed that the First War of Independence – what the British like to call 'The Revolt of 1857' – failed because Hyderabad refused to join the rebellion. Thereafter, the British coddled the Nizams with ever more hifalutin titles as they proceeded with exploiting Hyderabad – a strategy they acknowledged with a winking aside: *Poor Nizzy pays for it all!*

When the time came for the British to depart in 1947, the Nizam – not having learnt from history – reckoned that the Crown would grant Hyderabad independence. He was, after all, 'His Exalted Highness', *facile primus inter pares* – numero uno amongst India's princes. But the sun had set on the British Empire, the Crown would no more honour any treaties with Indian princes, full faith in a feckless ally was never a sensible thing, etcetera. Besides, the British were coveting a bigger prize: that India join the Commonwealth.

Jilted, the Nizam turned to Jinnah. Setting the subcontinent on a year-long rollercoaster ride...

Will Jinnah succeed in his plan for Hyderabad to stay independent, and thus stick a dagger into India's heart? Will the Nizam succeed in his game of pitting India against Pakistan? Will the newly amassed weaponry help Hyderabad hold off an Indian Army vested heavily in Kashmir? Will the average Hyderabadi – caught in the crossfire amongst Communists, Razakars, the State Congress, Arya Samaj, Hindu Mahasabha – get sacrificed in the burgeoning war?

What will be destroyed, what will prevail?

Let's find out ...

1
Hyderabad (July 1947)

'India thinks Hyderabad cannot be independent, landlocked as we are, surrounded by India on all sides.'

'That would be a fair assessment, Your Highness,' Walter Monckton agreed on a nod.

'Fair!' The Nizam harrumphed, slapping a thigh with his right hand. 'You are aware, Mr Monckton, that we once had a seaport? At Masulipatnam? On the Coromandel coast. From where ships set sail for Burma, Bengal, Cochin, China, Mecca … Of course, Asaf Jah II, in his wisdom, rented it out to the East India Company and that was the last we heard of it.'

The eyes of His Exalted Highness, Nawab Sir Mir Osman Ali Khan Siddiqi, Asaf Jah VII, bored into his constitutional adviser with their usual intensity. At such disorienting moments, Walter had a tough time reconciling the sharp knowingness of the Nizam with his general slovenliness. A threadbare sherwani, limp jodhpur trousers, a fez that surely had never been replaced since it first alighted on his exalted head – all encasing a small, spare man with a brush moustache and a mouth full of carious

1

teeth. His first sight of the Nizam in 1936 had bewildered Walter Monckton, attorney-general to the Prince of Wales. Familiar with the British monarchy, acquainted with Indian royalty – be it the Maharaja of Patiala with the Sans Souci diamond glittering on his clothes, or Dholpur in his gold coat studded with pearls – Walter had travelled 8,000 miles from London to offer advice. Surely this unkempt man in slippers, stooped over a crooked stick, with yellow socks adorned with clocks pooling at his ankles, was not the foremost Indian prince exclusively conferred with the 'Exalted' title?

Eleven years on, Walter didn't need lawyerly acumen to deduce that the Nizam of Hyderabad was intent upon being the Wealthiest Shabbiest Man in the world – which could well be another of his titles.

'MAR-magoa?'

The Nizam's high-pitched enquiry snapped Walter to the present.

'HOW are the talks with the Portuguese progressing, Mr Monckton?'

With Indian independence looming, the Nizam had issued a firman of independence on 11 June. Aware of the danger posed to Hyderabad from being surrounded by Hindu-dominant India, he was anxious to acquire a seaport. But the Portuguese, skittish at the ending of British colonial rule in India, were in no mood to sell or lease one of their Goa properties, certainly not a chief seaport. Besides, too much water had flown under that bridge since the Nizam had first initiated the idea. Now India would be independent in the coming month; Paramountcy, that ensured Hyderabad was subject to the suzerainty of the British Crown, would lapse; and the British – much to Walter's chagrin – were abandoning their most faithful ally.

'Your Highness,' Walter began, 'our focus needs to be on ensuring that Hyderabad can remain sovereign after 15 August. As you know, the Plan of 3 June does not clarify explicitly whether Princely States can claim independence. Sir Conrad Corfield of the Political Department was our ally, but the States Department of the Indian government now controls their relations with the princes. And Mr Patel, a most forceful man, is determined to bring the states into India. With the aid of his very supple secretary, V.P. Menon.'

The Nizam waved his right hand in the air, his slender fingers plucking at some unseen chords. 'I have written to the Viceroy, reminding him that after a century of faithful alliance, I should certainly be able to remain within the family of the British Commonwealth.'

The Nizam's stentorian voice filled the room, making him appear larger.

'Even Jinnah says the states are FREE – free to join any dominion they wish, or stay independent!' At his raised voice, a couple of heads thrust out from behind a heavily curtained doorway. With their dark features, fierce eyes, and bristling weapons, the Nizam's Arab Guards impressed Walter with their power and savagery. Wholly devoted to their master and his fabulous wealth – the Nizam's annual income was purportedly 3 million pounds a year, tax-free – they added to the air of stealth and intrigue that pervaded the ill-lit room.

'Your Highness, strictly speaking, the Princely States were never part of the Dominions of the Crown. They were in treaty relations to the Crown and under its protection—'

'Protection the Viceroy will NOT provide! So we must deal with half-penny, two-penny Indian politicians.' The staccato bursts kept the Arab Guards' ferocious heads buoyed within the curtain folds.

Walter resorted to a study of his surroundings, an old ploy he'd developed to allow time for the Nizam to finish venting. The room was redolent of cigarette smoke. Through a stained-glass window dim light, filtering through monsoon clouds, picked up dust motes in the room cluttered with furniture and bric-a-brac. A Victorian statuary of a mother and child was an incongruous sight. Walter couldn't see what the Nizam saw in the rather deplorable piece, but it was placed in proximity to the Nizam's chair ... The Nizam's thinking on the lapse of Paramountcy couldn't be faulted. When he himself had first heard of the creation of the States Department, he had remarked to Corfield: 'Patel intends to inherit the rights, but not the obligations of the Paramount Power.' However, what could also not be denied was that a storm was headed their way. A majority of other Princely States had read the storm signal and had scurried for safety – to India. It was Walter's duty to assist the Nizam in reaching the best possible conclusion for Hyderabad. Clearing his throat, he sought the Nizam.

'I think I can claim that, as a result of discussions I have had with the Viceroy and his staff, we have at the moment open to Hyderabad an offer of accession more limited than could have been expected before, and more favourable to Hyderabad than we can expect again after 15 August when the British have gone.'

From his pale, thin face, the Nizam's eyes stared at Walter. His brown moustache quivered with some emotion. Walter's legalese had not found favour, clearly. He was looking to simplify the thrust of his earlier argument when a titter sounded, before it erupted into loud laughter. The Nizam's spare frame rocked with jollity in his chair, the crooked stick tapping a brisk tempo on the floor.

'Mr Monckton,' the Nizam shook his head, 'that was no poetry, even you will admit. No Shakespearean iambic pentameter; no da-DUM, da-DUM, da-DUM. Tell me, when you enter law school in England, do they leach you of all poems? What are the views of the Crown on poetry?'

He continued laughing and a small smile escaped Walter. They were an ill-assorted pair, as Dickie Mountbatten had remarked. What the Viceroy did not know was the multitude of oddities the Nizam carried within himself. Besides being a world-class miser, who resided in the decidedly unlovely King Kothi when the grand Falaknuma Palace was available, the weird old fellow was a poet in Persian and Urdu, the founder of the great Osmania University, and the restorer of the ancient artwork of Ajanta. Yet, here they sat, the floor patterned with stubs of cigarettes the Nizam puffed like an engine, His Exalted Highness chortling while urgent matters regarding the fate of Hyderabad—

'In Islam, Mr Monckton,' the Nizam resumed in brisk fashion, 'the ideal ruler should be a master of the pen as well as the sword. A poet is always appointed to teach his royal pupils the art of poetry. The Asaf Jahis, we have produced four poet Nizams!'

Walter acknowledged this with a slow, deep nod. 'Your Highness, I believe, writes in both Persian and Urdu.'

The Nizam beamed. Walter recalled an anecdote he had heard. The Nizam had published his anthology at a young age. Despite its exorbitant price, it sold out immediately. None wanted to be seen as lacking in loyalty to the young ruler.

Now, the Nizam urged him with one hand. 'Perhaps not poetry, but try simpler language.'

The sound of rain lashing against windows picked up. The room had grown even darker. Walter felt like he was in an intimate mushaira with the Nizam, His Highness presiding as he spun legalese into couplets for an ashrafi, the gold coin inscribed with the image of the Charminar.

'Your Highness, Hyderabad's claim to dominion status has been disposed of by the Viceroy. And Britain will not preserve Hyderabad against democratic India, despite the treaties, "inviolate and inviolable" as the wording goes, between the Crown and native princes. My advice therefore is that we sign a treaty with India rather than signing the Instrument of Accession. This sends a clear signal that the two parties are equal. We surrender only the three main subjects – defence, foreign affairs, and communications.' Walter adjusted his glasses. 'I have even secured the Viceroy's agreement of Hyderabad's neutrality if Pakistan becomes involved in a war with India.'

'Ah! Pakistan.' The Nizam leaned forward, his eyes alight. 'Jinnah says that Hyderabad could give a lead to other Princely States by declaring independence. With Mysore and Travancore, we form an independent block to defend ourselves against India!'

Walter was aware that Mr Jinnah was writing to the Nizam in most honeyed tones, requesting HEH not to take any decision without his concurrence and knowledge. Having taken Hyderabad's case to Mr Jinnah earlier, Walter was not sanguine about the leader of the Muslim League. Of course, it would be to Pakistan's advantage to leave India with multiple stab wounds, one for each Princely State if possible …

'Jinnah,' the Nizam intoned, 'is a friend of the Mussalmans of Hyderabad. Soon, I am sending a delegation under Kasim Razvi to meet with him.'

The mention of the rabid leader of the leading Muslim party in Hyderabad gave Walter pause. An image of the fiery man with flashing eyes popped up in his mind's eye. Best, however, to stick to the agenda on hand. 'Well, it's perfectly understandable for Hyderabad to want to be closer to Pakistan, but there is the matter of geography. A large swathe of India between—'

The Nizam had begun shaking his head, his right index finger oscillating in the air. 'Not so soon, Mr Monckton, not so SOON. Junagadh will join Jinnah; so say my spies. How far then will Hyderabad be from Pakistan? From Karachi to Veraval to Marmagoa is our sea link. Junagadh will be a good base for planes as well. Now, I know we don't have a seaport yet, but Jinnah will help us gain an outlet to the sea if it's to his advantage.'

Junagadh joining Pakistan would be a master stroke for Mr Jinnah. A short distance separated the south-eastern corner of Junagadh from the western tip of Hyderabad. Additionally, it would rile up Mr Patel – a beachhead of Pakistan in Gujarat, his home state! Still.

'Your Highness,' Walter spoke forcefully, 'we *have* to consider the full picture. In the eventuality that Junagadh does join Pakistan, India could still blockade Hyderabad. Will Pakistan guarantee to supply Hyderabad with food, weapons, troops? And if India foments an internal revolt amongst Hyderabad's 85 per cent Hindu population, will Pakistan still come to its aid? These are important considerations—'

Abruptly, the Nizam had stood up and was tottering to a table littered with papers. 'Write to Jinnah, Mr Monckton! Get me ANSWERS!'

It was not the first time HEH had switched from mirth to anger. Walter watched him pluck a crumpled ball of paper and hold it up like it were some totem, his left hand bearing down upon the crooked staff. In the thin light, a cobweb's slim finger dangled above the Nizam's head. The old lion roared.

'From Aurangzeb to now, Asaf Jahs have ruled for three centuries. Hyderabad will remain FREE!'

2
Hyderabad (July–August 1947)

It was time to quit the heroics, really!

Walter was trying to preserve the integrity of the greatest state in India, despite the Nizam's maddening preoccupations with unreality. Berar, Masulipatnam, Marmagoa … This was not the time for acquisition of ceded territories or new ones, however advantageous they might appear on paper. Walter had explained at length to Dickie Mountbatten that the Nizam would not compromise his independent sovereignty and personal prestige. 'Instead of talking of "accession" or "adherence", could not an agreement be made?' he had pleaded. 'Such language would be more acceptable to His Exalted Highness.'

But Mountbatten had stayed firm. And the Nizam was failing to grasp the seriousness of India's intent. It did not help that a coterie of men was bent upon guiding the Nizam to great divergence from his own advice. Two men especially – the militant Kasim Razvi and the inspector general police, Nawab Deen Yar Jung. In a normal situation, the former should have been put in jail by the latter, but the objective of Azad Hyderabad had united them.

As his car wound down the well-paved road, Walter mulled over his last discussion with the Viceroy, who was assisted by Conrad Corfield and V.P. Menon. The sky had stopped leaking, the public park was bursting with magenta bougainvillea. Hyderabad's extraordinary cleanliness had astonished him on his first visit, such a contrast to the cities of British India. As was the side by side existence of Muslim mosques and Hindu temples. The car started to slow down; the road ahead had sprung an unruly throng. Men jostled about waving green banners. 'Long live King Osman!' Cheers rang out followed by a lusty, 'Free Hyderabad for Hyderabadis!'

Walter watched as a group of men, likely college students, passed handbills out. He instructed the driver to get some.

The script was mostly in Urdu with some English ... 'No pact with Indian Union!' It was the handiwork of the Majlis-e-Ittehad-ul-Muslimeen, the Council for the Unity of Muslims, Kasim Razvi's party.

Razvi had created a paramilitary wing of the Majlis called the Razakars, volunteers, which he'd organized on the model of Hitler's Brown Shirts. The resident estimated they were 1,00,000 strong. Apparently, the man had risen to prominence after a mob burnt down Shah Manzil, the official residence of the Nawab of Chhatari, then president of the Nizam's Executive Council! With that show of strength by the extremist faction of the Ittihad, the rogue had inveigled his way to the Nizam, and was now a close adviser ... Walter shuddered to think what the Razvi-led delegation to Jinnah might yield. The next instant, he was jolted out of his rumination as shots rang out!

Instinctively clutching the car seat, he ducked, cautiously scouring the crowd outside. Some scruffy-looking men, silhouetted against the dark sky, were firing guns in the Arab manner. The driver caught his eye in the rear-view mirror and apologetically offered, 'Just some celebration, saar, for the coming freedom.'

A while later, having left the demonstration behind, the car headed towards Hussain Sagar Tank. As they drove past the heart-shaped lake, Walter determined to write to Mr Jinnah right away. Later that night, he had a dinner invitation to the British resident's house, a tranquil refuge from the din of the city, and he was looking forward to some convivial chatter with Arthur Lothian to take his mind off the Nizam. Besides, the date for his second wedding was set, 13 August. A smile crept up his face, dissolving the owl-like demeanour. Walter couldn't wait to start married life anew with Biddy. Both their divorces had come through and they had managed to conduct their affair discreetly, without embarrassing the Viceroy.

Lady Carlisle, Biddy to friends, was the director of the Women's Auxiliary Corps in India, when he first met her in Delhi in May 1946, and promptly fell in love! Walter was staying at the Nizam's splendid guest house and had invited her over. The planned dinner on the lawn was upset by an abrupt storm. Nonetheless, in the hurly-burly, as they scurried for cover, he pulled off a proposal.

ॐ

The evening air smelt of moisture and jasmine. Walter would have liked a gentle breeze, but in its absence, the cooling air of the Residency would do. Built like a palace, on the scale of Blenheim almost, complete with Corinthian columns, a flight of granite stairs, flanked on either side by a gigantic lion, the Residency oversaw the Musi river which divided the city. The trill of birds filled the vast compound that was dense with banyans, peepuls, tamarinds and mahogany trees.

'It is not unusual, you know,' Arthur, the resident mused. 'A sudden romance in the tropics!'

Walter had just finished recounting the story of his quick engagement to Biddy.

'I was taken by surprise myself.' Walter's eyes twinkled. He was relishing the fine single malt the khidmatgar had served.

'I know the feeling, old chap,' Arthur winked. 'But … there's something about the tropics …' He gazed off into the distance, lips pursed in thought.

Walter sipped his malt, enjoying the birdsong. The wedding was to be held at the Residency and all arrangements were taken care of. He hoped Biddy would like Lake View, where he was staying. The house was cool and white with views of the Hussain Sagar—

'Look,' Arthur urged, 'look around you.' His right hand, clutching a crystal glass of whiskey, swept the lush garden complex that flowed outwards and came to a stop at the vibrant canna lilies in the nearest flower bed. 'There's a lushness, an intensity, a … a swiftness to this place …' He shrugged, quaffed the whiskey and nodded. 'You'll learn. Whatever you estimate, approximate, calculate, whatever – the result will always exceed it. Tropical volatility!'

&

Jinnah's response arrived in the first week of August. Walter re-read it, focusing on significant text.

… *the State must earn its own independence by standing on its own feet and making all sacrifices, even, if necessary, the abdication of the Nizam.*

The Nizam would be surprised at the betrayal, in such sharp contrast to the honeyed letters he'd received thus far. Walter was not. The Nizam was incapable of seeing shades of colour, except black and white – Mr Jinnah was all grey. What was he playing at though …

The Hussain Sagar Tank glittered in the afternoon sun. As he sipped his tea, Walter watched a kite float past. With abdication out of question, it would be back to Delhi. Mr Patel would suspect the temporary cooling of relations between the Nizam and Mr Jinnah, and drive a hard bargain. Walter must focus on Mountbatten. On 15 August, the Viceroy would become governor general of India. He would continue to take part in the negotiations between the Dominion of India and Hyderabad, but in his new role. The time to get concessions for Hyderabad was *now* – when Mountbatten was still in a stronger position to persuade the Indian leaders.

3
Delhi (August 1947)

'You must understand, Sir Walter, that it is impossible to make any sort of Standstill Agreement unless Hyderabad first accedes to India.'

V.P. Menon gazed intently at the Nizam's constitutional adviser. He had lost count of the number of times he had reiterated that one simple criterion to Walter Monckton since their negotiations began. He was also aware that the distinguished lawyer was not to be blamed. His client, the Nizam of Hyderabad, in the clutches of fanatical Muslims, had seemingly lost all sense of reality.

Dickie watched Walter Monckton swing his head from VP to him and back to the sheaf of papers in front of him. He was hopeful he could still coordinate with Monckton to bring the Nizam in. Indeed, he had offered to fly down to Hyderabad if that would help. But the Nizam appeared reluctant ... And the Viceroy couldn't afford a rebuff. Hence, the parlous state of affairs.

'Sir Walter,' Dickie sallied forth, 'the Nizam's got to make terms with Congress some time – his kingdom is plumb in the heart of India, and transfer of power is five days away.'

Monckton clasped his hands above the papers. 'Accession to India is not a precondition as per any British pledge. This coercion must stop.'

Menon cleared his throat. 'The Indian government does not consider itself bound by any such undertaking.'

'That's preposterous!' Monckton threw his head back, yelling almost. 'Mr Patel is already threatening an economic blockade against Hyderabad ...'

The temperature within the Viceroy's study must have risen for the air conditioner roared in syncopation. Dickie gazed at the serene Mughal Gardens unfurling outwards from his study. The sailor-blue room, which he had got redone as soon as Wavell left, amidst the lush greenery, was his oasis. One in which he had fought, and won, many battles since he began the work of Viceroy in March. Hyderabad though was a tricky beast. Much like Bhopal – a Muslim dynasty ruling a largely Hindu state – except Hyderabad was better equipped to go it alone in genuine independence. In the English lawyer, whom Dickie had known for many years, the state had a formidable ally. Dickie returned his gaze to the study and locked eyes with his chief of staff. The bulldog jaw, which had lent the nickname 'Pug' to General Hastings Lionel Ismay, made his manner appear lugubrious. Now Ismay turned his head to Monckton.

'Sir Walter, Congress will never again offer such good terms as we should get now—'

'Perhaps it needs reminding,' Monckton fumed, 'that the Nizam enjoys the backing of Mr Jinnah, and that – if Congress continues to bring pressure on Hyderabad – every Muslim throughout the whole of India will rise as one man to defend the foremost Muslim kingdom.'

Pug Ismay probed his chin. 'Sir Walter, that would satisfy nobody. Hyderabad, as you are aware, is militarily defenceless. And afloat in the sea of India, its chances of joining Pakistan are well-nigh impossible. Besides, what of the 85 per cent Hindu majority? What are their views at the prospect of accession to Pakistan?'

'Gentlemen!' Monckton slapped his palms on the table. 'Hyderabad is *not* acceding to Pakistan or India. The Nizam has already written to the Viceroy that he cannot contemplate bringing Hyderabad into organic union with *either* of the two dominions. He is prepared, however, to enter into a treaty with India.'

'Which is not acceptable to India,' Menon pointed out flatly.

They had gone a full circle. 'Sir Walter,' Dickie spoke firmly, 'one must face the facts.'

With a flourish, Monckton withdrew several sheets from his sheaf of papers. He passed a set each to Menon, Ismay, and Dickie, tap-tapping the sheaf with a brisk index finger as he spoke, 'I was anticipating this line of argument. Precisely why I have drafted this letter – a copy of which is with each of you – to Churchill. I intend to dispatch it immediately if the improper pressure on Hyderabad is not relieved.' Then he sighed and sat back in his chair.

Dickie read the letter.

... It may well be that you will not hear from me again upon this matter apart from a short message to let you know that the German tactic on the old European model has been adopted in India. But I rely on you in the name of our old friendship to see to it that if this shameful betrayal of our old

friends and allies cannot be prevented, at least it does not go uncastigated before the conscience of the world.

Dickie fingered the cuff of his shirtsleeve as he recalled his last interaction with Churchill. The ex–Prime Minister had regarded his Viceregal appointment a personal as well as national betrayal, dismissing it as 'Operation Scuttle'. He could not fathom why Dickie was lending himself to its execution. 'The whole thing wears the aspect of an attempt by the government to make use of brilliant war figures in order to cover up a disastrous transaction,' Churchill had railed.

Adding further injury to Churchill's wounds, Dickie had brought along as his chief of staff, Pug Ismay – one of Churchill's favourite generals. A letter such as this reaching the Conservative leader would do no good. Steepling his fingers, Dickie looked serenely at the men seated around the table. What VP and Ismay knew, but Monckton did not, was that Dickie had already concluded there was no chance of gaining Hyderabad's accession by 15 August. He needed more time to persist with the negotiations. Suggesting to both Mr Patel and Jawahar that an extension would be helpful, he had offered his services in future talks. He expected to get two months.

Sir Walter looked like he could do with a stiff drink. Dickie was in full sympathy with him, but he also believed that Princely States would be better off negotiating now than after the transfer of power. Surely the esteemed lawyer understood that if a treaty was unobtainable, accession on favourable terms might prove a lesser evil than its alternative?

Dickie would not call his bluff. Best to let Sir Walter stew.

4
Hyderabad (August 1947)

As Uzma gathered the dessert bowls, she watched Miss Emily Perkins screw up her nose. 'This is one ugly palace, Niloufer! I much prefer your Hill Fort residence.'

Miss Emily glanced at the hallway leading from the zenana to the courtyard. 'And what's with the "KK" everywhere?' She tapped at the letters inscribed on the glass windows.

'King Kothi,' Niloufer said, adjusting the pallu of her blue chiffon sari. 'KK.'

'Yes,' Miss Emily said, 'but why?'

'Oh, that's because it was given in nazar to Abba by one of his courtiers – a man called Kamal Khan, I believe. Since his name was scribbled all over, Abba decided it was easier to name the palace King Kothi.'

Miss Emily tossed a knowing head. 'Isn't nazar the business of acquiring goods the Nizam likes without having to pay for them?'

Uzma watched Niloufer shrug as she stepped away from the mirror and studied herself. The rich gold brocade border of the sari was threaded with blue, which matched the sapphire necklace and drop earrings she wore. With her hair up in a bun – *chignon*, Niloufer liked to correct Uzma in her fancy French accent – that accentuated her lily-like neck, she looked the most beautiful woman in the world. As she caught Uzma nod approvingly, Niloufer tossed her an air-kiss.

'Main qurbaan,' Uzma answered, furling both hands to the sides of her head.

Watching which Miss Emily copied the gesture, then scooted to the mirror and continued twirling her hands as she repeated, 'Meh coor-bey, meh coo, meh ... Whatever!'

Uzma stacked the dessert bowls as Miss Emily traipsed around the room, walking on her toes, her arms extended. She looked like a grasshopper. 'Okay, what are we doing for entertainment? That dessert was dreamy but so-ooo rich that it's glueing my eyelids together.' By the time Uzma could finally flee Iram Manzil, even the mention of khobani ka meetha would make her gag. But in her years of royal service since, she had trained herself to excise Hyderabad's famous dessert from her murky past: It was just another sweet.

'How do you even make it?' Miss Emily had paused to query.

Gathering silverware, Uzma elucidated. 'The secret, Miss, is the milk. It comes from buffaloes fed with pistachio, almonds and other such nuts. How can the milk not be creamy then?'

'Buffaloes that eat nuts! You know, in London we can't get decent milk even now?' Emily Perkins threw her hands up in the air.

'I was thinking of taking you shopping to Charminar.' Niloufer slid bangles on her wrists before holding them up. 'You wanted these?'

Emily Perkins wagged her head, an index finger leading her as she approached. 'Princess Niloufer,' she bowed in an exaggerated manner, before stabbing her finger on the choker that nestled on the neck of her friend, 'what I really, really want is this wee gem. Which will see me till my dotage.'

'My dear Miss Perkins, you haven't seen anything yet! There's a reason I brought you here to KK first. Follow me.' Niloufer ran ahead. At the doorway, she turned and beckoned Uzma to follow.

Leaving the tray on the carved walnut side table, Uzma followed her mistress down the corridor. Fifteen years they had been together, since the fifteen-year-old Niloufer, a princess of the famed Ottoman Empire, had come to Hyderabad as the Nizam's daughter-in-law, married to his second son. Teen Uzma was hired as maid, tasked with tasting the first morsel of every food meant for Niloufer. The British resident had heard rumours that the mother-in-law intended to poison the young bride. Dulhan Pasha, the Nizam's waspish first wife, had intended to choose brides for her two sons. But the Nizam, keen on an alliance with the Caliph, had married his two sons to the daughter and niece of the exiled head of the Ottoman Empire and Muslims worldwide. In the fifteen years since, Uzma had graduated to being a companion–confidante of Princess Begum Sahiba Niloufer Khanum Sultana. The girl with dimpled cheeks, violet eyes, and blue–black hair had grown into a woman whose beauty the world raved about. Uzma remembered the first time Niloufer was invited to the Residency. A visiting Angrez officer, old enough to be her grandfather, who was seated beside Niloufer at the dinner table, forgot to eat as he stole looks at her all through the meal! A wide-eyed Niloufer had recounted this to Uzma later. And the Nizam looked so happy, like he had become the Caliph already—

Uzma steadied herself as her foot snagged against a crooked floor tile. Bending over, she plucked the cigarette foil stuck to her slipper. Stubs lay discarded in the corners and against the walls, and the floor was thick with dust. King Kothi had always had the air of an old whore – ugly even in her youth. Now it smelt like her ancient armpits. Uzma shook her head. So much time had passed since that dinner at the British resident's … The Nizam had not become the next Caliph, his first wife had gone mad, his kingdom was in great danger—

'Uzma!' Niloufer beckoned at the head of a staircase. 'Hurry!'

Uzma snapped out of her reverie and sprang to action. Down the stairs the three women went, Niloufer with an index finger to her lips. The air was musty, the stairs filthy and endless, as they wound down until they reached a vault. The Arab Guards, with kohl in their eyes, having perked up at the sounds of their imminent arrival, bowed deep as Niloufer swept her way towards them. Past the guards, they had entered a secret cellar. Niloufer kept moving forward until the space opened up into what appeared to be a very large underground parking, filled as it was with trucks and lorries.

'Really, Niloufer,' Miss Perkins said with brows raised, 'a garage?'

Niloufer winked and sped forward to the nearest lorry.

As her eyes adjusted to the partial light, Uzma realized that the cloaked lorries had flat tyres, the ground beneath them cracking with weight.

'Uzma, help me,' Niloufer said as she tugged at the tarpaulin covering a small lorry. Dust rose into the air and made them cough as the two women pried apart the thick cover. Emily Perkins hovered, waving her hands to clear the air, before she gasped. 'Lordy lord!' Uzma was just as shocked at what lay exposed. She had heard rumours, but here was the proof. The Nizam's treasure of gems and pearls and gold was reputed to be more than one could dream of, let alone hoard. And yet, here it was, stored in trucks for hauling Allah knew where for the vehicles had sunk into the ground waiting ...

Miss Emily ran to the next truck, clambered up, tugged at the tarpaulin, letting off more dust, and peered inside. Shaking her head, coated in dust, her mouth still unable to close, she chanted, 'Rotting jewel lorries! Rotting. Jewel. Lorries. Jewel ... lorries!'

The three women wound their way back up the stairs, dust on their clothes and sparkles in their eyes. Miss Emily could not get a handle on herself. 'What in god's name did I just see?'

Gaily, Niloufer said, 'I promised you an adventure!'

'But, why?' Miss Emily pleaded.

'Apparently, Abba suspects he's going to be robbed of all his va-a-a-st treasure. Either by some revolutionaries, Commies, or Hindu India ... Which is why the treasure is all packed to go.'

'Go where? Those lorries aren't driving anywhere!' Miss Emily was still shaking her head in wonderment. In the corridor, kicking a half-smoked cigarette away, she asked no one in particular, 'Is that why the whole palace is submerged in dirt? Imagine cleaning it, and accidentally revealing all those hidden treasures?'

5
Hyderabad (August 1947)

E mily Perkins declared the Charminar as 'magnifique!'
    After buying an armful of bangles and vials of attar, she expressed a desire to see the wild countryside. As the Buick headed towards Banjara Hills, Niloufer yawned, her head lolling on the cushioned leather seat. 'Damn that khobani ka meetha, I can't keep my eyes open!' Beside her, Miss Perkins was curled up, her mouth open as she dozed. A breeze flitted in through the sun-dappled convertible, lulling the occupants in the rear seat. In the front seat, Uzma watched the streets get less crowded as the car purred on.

'Uzma!'

She turned to look back where Niloufer had sprung upright. 'Begum sahiba?'

'Driver, stop the car!' Niloufer ordered, then pointed to the building across. Shaheen Irani Cafe. An airy place packed with patrons, voices and music spilling out of its large windows that opened onto the street. 'Uzma, let's get some Irani chai; it's sure to wake us up.' Niloufer beamed.

'Ji, begum sahiba,' Uzma replied as she arranged her sari pallu to cover her head.

'I wish I could come inside with you,' Niloufer sighed as she gazed longingly at the cafe. The Nizam allowed his two daughters-in-law all sorts of liberties – no purdah, the freedom to go everywhere, clubs included, to party even – but eating out in public, that too at the dens-of-Communists Irani cafes would be a sacrilege. Uzma stepped out.

The manager seated at the door of the cafe had seen the cream Buick and stood up at Uzma's entrance. He took the order and shouted it in the direction of the kitchen, 'Teen pauna', holding three fingers up for emphasis. Uzma patted her pallu, aware that the manager's enthusiasm had drawn eager glances in her direction. With lustrous long hair that skimmed her hips, and skin the colour of golden jaggery, Uzma drew the male gaze like a sugarcane press did flies. There were so many men seated at the wooden tables, slurping tea and talking loudly, that her eyes glazed over. She kept her sight above their heads as she surveyed the cafe, normally forbidden territory. Amidst the hubbub, the sound of ghazals filtered through. Likely from that jukebox where two young men stood. She inhaled aromas of tea and cigarette smoke, fried oil and caramelized sugar—

'Uz-ma aapa?'

A young man stood a short distance away, studying her intently. 'Are you Uzma Ikram Ghani, daughter of Inayat Ghani of Faizpur?'

Uzma's eyes narrowed. A decade-plus since anyone had reminded her of the past. A past she had buried long back.

'Forgive my manners ... You ... you are the exact copy of your mother – if, that is, you are who I assume you are.'

Disappointed with the way his tongue had coiled all over itself, the young man shook his head.

'And ... *who* are you?' Uzma enquired guardedly.

'Ali Hassan. I'm a student at Osmania University.'

Ali Hassan ... The toddler at the neighbour's ... From aeons ago ...

He smiled slightly as her eyes widened in recognition.

'So what are you doing here?'

Ali Hassan gave a boyish grin. 'We,' he turned to point to a table where three young men sat on rickety chairs, and were in the midst of animated conversation over tea and cigarettes, 'are all students. It's our adda. A place to meet others and discuss social issues.'

'Hmm ...' Uzma noticed his almond-coloured eyes, the shock of thick, wavy hair, his Adam's apple at his scrawny neck. 'Do you go back ... to Faizpur?'

He nodded. 'Family is still there, same house.' He paused. 'I assume you don't? We haven't seen you ...'

The server arrived with three ceramic cups and saucers on a tray and a plate laden with Osmania biscuits. Especially crafted to meet the demands of Nizam Mir Osman Ali Khan for a snack that was a little bit salty and a little bit sweet, the biscuits had become a Hyderabadi staple now.

'Not these, please,' Uzma indicated the biscuits.

'Complimentary,' the manager said, right hand to his chest. 'Please, a small token,' he gestured to the gleaming Buick across from the road in which the sunglasses-wearing princess in her blue shimmery sari sat upright, a radiant sapphire set in gold. When Uzma made to pay, the manager declined assiduously.

Ali Hassan watched the Buick and nodded. 'I'd heard you were in the Nizam's employment.' He was not smiling any more, his eyes full of meaning.

The server had stepped out and stood waiting for her. Uzma locked eyes with Ali and said softly, 'You know where to find me.' She nodded at the manager and exited the Irani cafe.

∽

Banjara Hills was studded with giant slabs of rock that were strewn at such precarious angles that it seemed the legend was true: God began creating the world in Hyderabad. This was the ancient quarry from which all mountains in the world were made – only some rocks left behind as evidence. With the rains, green shoots had sprouted on the red soil. From where they stood, the women surveyed the city of Hyderabad sprawling below them.

'This,' Miss Emily spread her arms out wide, 'this vista reminds me of the moors back home. Only, it's even more wild and desolate … but enchanting, definitely enchanting.'

Uzma sat on a flat boulder and studied her surroundings. The defining colour was red – red soil, reddish boulders, wild red flowers. So much blood had spilled that the soil could hide it no more. So much blood was being squeezed that it was leaking out onto the contours of the land. She probed the red soil, digging her fingers into it. The grainy, wet coolness was refreshing, she let her hand stay buried.

Damn that Ali Hassan! With hair thick enough to weave a mat out of. She gave him haircuts when he was a toddler … How old would he be now? University, so twenty or twenty-one? She was how old? Thirty or thirty-one? She didn't know exactly. When she joined princess Niloufer, she was considered similar in age, but mature, far more mature. The princess was a nubile girl; Uzma's body had carried a child … Uzma twisted her mouth, hiding it behind her hand atop which she rested her chin. To distract herself, she watched Niloufer weave flowers into Miss Emily's short hair. They had the intimacy of women who had known each other as girls, who were students together once. Ali Hassan was a student who went to Irani cafes. Was he one of those Communists who were leading a People's Struggle in the countryside, whose members were revolting against the Nizam's police, whose flag was red …?

∽

Uzma's mood had not lightened as they headed back, passing dilapidated thatched huts with skinny children and barns housing skinnier cows. Past wagons drawn by worn oxen, past over-burdened donkeys, past men whose ribcages threatened to explode out of their thin hides. The car slowed down as a cow lay in the middle of the narrow street. A peasant, its owner likely, sat beside it on his haunches, head clasped in his hands. Uzma exchanged looks with the driver, who braked and honked. The man looked up, misery etched in the furrowed face, but did not move. The driver stopped the Buick and stepped out. He returned after a conversation with the man. The cow was dead; it had collapsed on the road.

'Why?' Miss Emily asked. For an educated, grown woman, she could be quite dense.

'No food,' Uzma said. The cow looked like it had been decaying for years.

Emily Perkins sat up and studied the spectacle. 'Honestly,' she exhaled, 'I don't know who looks more sickly: the dead cow or the poor man. While some buffaloes get to eat nuts …' She grabbed the plate of Osmania biscuits they hadn't touched, stuffed as they were from the meal, dessert and milk-laden tea. Opening the car door, she marched to the peasant, plate in hand. Uzma decided to follow.

As Miss Emily held the plate out to the man who looked befuddled, a clutch of children swarmed out of nowhere, their bellies protruding, knees knocking, bones jutting. In bare clothes, festooned with snot and flies, they clamoured for the biscuits. A confused Emily Perkins tried to ration the biscuits, one to each child whose fist was pummelling the air, when the plate got knocked out of her hand. It rose in the air, raining butter-laden Osmania biscuits onto the soil. The children dived to the ground, snatching, grabbing, hitting, wailing, gobbling, gobbling, gobbling.

Once the women were back in the car, the driver reversed and took another route. After a long silence, Emily Perkins spoke to no one in particular. 'Why am I reminded of the French Revolution ...?' She twisted her mouth and looked ahead. Niloufer sat with a resigned air.

Uzma had learnt English from the princess, enough to understand and speak some. She knew a smattering of French too. Niloufer had grown up in a place called Nice on the southern coast of France. C'est la vie! J'adore. But Uzma didn't know about the French Revolution. She must ask Niloufer about it.

'Remember our history lessons, Nilou?' Miss Emily tossed her chin. 'This is some weird time travel, but Hyderabad in monsoon reminds me of Versailles in spring.'

They passed the maidan, where men were playing polo against a horizon of gently sloping hills. Beyond lay Faizpur, her poor wretched village ... Uzma could not shake off the desperate children shovelling around the dead cow as if a plate laden with gems from one of the Nizam's lorries had upturned, and not one piled with Osmania biscuits.

6
Delhi (August 1947)

Jawahar took a deep breath that filled his chest, lifted his heart and, temporarily, shook off his unease. With firm hands, he tugged the halyard, raising the tricolour higher and higher until it soared – orange, white, and green fluttering above lakhs of free Indians. A cheer swept up from the crowd, breaking into full-throated cries.

'Pandit Nehru ki jai!'

'Hindustan zindabad!'

'Raja Nehru zindabad!'

From the raised platform upon which the flagpole stood, he watched his fellow-countrymen and -women, their faces upturned. Behind them, the regal Red Fort stood in its sandstone splendour, witness to the passage of power from Shah Jahan to the British, and now to the Indian people. An expression of the multiple traditions of India – Islamic, Persian, Timurid, Hindu – this symbol of power was just the right place to raise the flag of newly independent India. He recalled hoisting the tricolour for the first time in Anand Bhavan, seventeen years ago, on 26

January, an act which was replicated across India, the hope for purna swaraj rippling across the country. Now, on 16 August 1947, that cherished future had arrived.

'Jai Hind!' Jawahar began his address.

'We have gathered here on a historic occasion at this ancient fort to win back what was ours. This flag does not symbolize the triumph of individuals or the Congress, but the triumph of the whole country.'

People surged forward, closing the distance between the dais and the grounds. He had wanted this to be less formal than the flag-hoisting ceremony yesterday at Princes Park with Lord and Lady Mountbatten. He had switched his white sherwani for a fawn khadi jacket. In the gathering, he could see the saris of some women were the colours of the tiranga.

Smiling, he continued, 'The free flag of India is the symbol of freedom and democracy, not only for India but for the whole world. India, Asia, and the world must rejoice on this great day.'

Joyous shouts rose from the crowd as he talked about his duty to the nation and the people, calling himself their pratham sewak. In a sober voice, he recalled Netaji Subhash Bose, whose dream it had been to see the tiranga unfurled at the Red Fort. Netaji was no more, but his dream had been achieved.

Jawahar paused as the gathering roared. Tomorrow, the Radcliffe Award would become public, revealing the final contours of India and Pakistan. The twins were still conjoined, their final separation just hours away. Unease flooded him. Happenings in Panjab were already infecting Delhi ... Firming his jaw, Jawahar continued.

'The government faces many challenges as our new nation begins its journey. But the first challenge will be to stop all acts of violence. Brother cannot turn against brother. India is responsible for protecting Muslims on its side of the border, and India will do so.'

A murmur arose. Before it could gather momentum, Jawahar thundered, 'We will ruthlessly suppress all sectarian killings!'

∾

That afternoon, Claude Auchinleck, the long-time commander-in-chief of the Indian Army, arrived at the renamed Parliament House. As he updated the leaders on how independence had been marked in Panjab, Jawahar's unease ratcheted.

'Several eastbound trains full of Hindu and Sikh refugees from Lahore were attacked by Muslims, the passengers hacked to death. A mob burned down the gurudwara of the sixth Sikh guru on Lahore's Temple Road—'

'But the Boundary Force has been constituted to prevent exactly this kind of violence,' Jawahar interrupted.

Straight-backed and soldierly, the Auk, as he was popularly called, surveyed his audience with keen blue eyes. 'Boundary Force commander Major General Pete Rees rushed immediately to Amritsar, hoping to pre-empt any retaliation the Sikhs might plan in revenge. He was too late. Dozens of Muslim women had been stripped naked and paraded through the city streets. Many were raped and killed. Some did manage to get shelter in the Golden Temple, the Sikhs' holiest shrine.' His eyes rested on the defence minister.

Baldev Singh turned to the Prime Minister. 'I'm in touch with Tara Singh … He agrees matters have gone too far.'

'*Too* far …' Jawahar muttered, his face pale and drawn.

Buntings hanging gaily in the corridors were a reminder that Independence was just a day old. Everywhere, Jawahar could smell the musky marigolds gracing doorways, the air fragrant with cardamom from too many celebratory sweets and the fresh paint from newly coated walls. Yet, it was all souring so quickly ... The Maharaja of Faridkot, who had bankrolled many Sikh jathas marauding the countryside, was in Delhi seeking asylum at the US embassy, he had heard. After setting Panjab on fire, he was looking to buy a ranch in California! With barely controlled fury, Jawahar turned to his defence minister.

'Tara Singh must call off the jathas now! And he, along with Giani Kartar Singh, must travel through Amritsar and speak with Panjabis.'

Baldev Singh nodded. Tara Singh had wept openly at the recent outrage in Amritsar. But surely the Akali leaders knew when egging on the jathas that blood would spill? The Sikhs had lost so much with the partition of their beloved Panjab, but a civil war was not the answer.

Jawahar had turned to the supreme commander of the British forces in India and Pakistan. Surely the general who had defeated Rommel in WWII could conquer this scattered aggression ...

'Clearly, we are inadequately prepared. So my question is: How do we stop this madness?'

'In theory,' Auchinleck spoke with authority, 'a show of force by mixed Sikh, Hindu and Muslim units under British officers should ease fears in the border areas and prevent an exodus. In theory, we were to have a Boundary Force of 50,000 soldiers – the largest peacekeeping force ever assembled. In theory, a military comprising diverse elements from across the subcontinent can be partitioned. In *theory*!'

'Can you spare more troops to Panjab?' Baldev Singh asked. 'Concentrate them in the cities of Lahore and Amritsar. Hopefully, their presence will deter the biased policemen as well.'

The Auk stood akimbo, his gaze directed at the floor. He had got his soldiering start in Panjab, spoke Panjabi fluently, and knew the tall, macho men whom he had commanded for the greater part of his life. He had trained them to fight wars; now they had turned their inextricably mixed communities into combat zones. 'An army built on non-communal lines is being divided on the basis of religion. At a time when the country needs it most. The atmosphere is most vitiated.'

An army is a single entity with a single brain, a single heart, a single set of organs, the Auk had complained to the Viceroy, Jawahar knew. But ...

'I understand your distress, but Mr Jinnah was adamant that unless he had his own army under his command on 15 August, he would refuse to take power. So we have to deal with the situation as is.'

Auchinleck raked his reddish hair, his eyes steely.

'A mixed squadron, probably Gurkhas and Madrasis,' Baldev Singh suggested, 'who are not bound by the fear of firing on their co-religionists.'

There had been enough talk. Jawahar stood up, palms planted on the table. 'I will take that as a yes, Commander. Meanwhile, I will convince Liaquat to tour the sensitive areas with me. And Baldev will get the Akalis to call off the jathas. This outrage cannot continue!'

∞

At York Road, the tents housing the refugees in his garden now covered every square inch of land. How could he prevent people from leaving their homes? It was the one question on his mind as he toured West and East Panjab with Liaquat, both Prime Ministers showing a joint front in the face of the escalating civil war. They had chastised Muslim leaders in Lahore, laid into the Akalis in Amritsar, but discerning their sullen faces and grim jaws, it was difficult to determine if the tour would have any good result ...

'Papu,' Indu tapped his forearm from the chair where she sat at the dining table with him.

'Hmm ...'

'You're not eating.'

Jawahar pushed his plate away. 'I don't have any appetite left.'

Indu sat upright, hands folded in her lap. 'Well, you shouldn't go touring affected areas if you're going to be thus afflicted.'

Jawahar turned to her with surprise and, watching her stern-matron persona, chuckled. 'The children take up so much of your time, you speak to everyone like they were Sanjay or Rajiv!'

'Well, stop behaving like a child then.' Indu moved the plate of food back to Jawahar. 'Besides, you won't be any good as a sick Prime Minister.'

Hearing which, Jawahar sighed and tried to stick some food in his mouth. But the images from the Panjabi countryside clouded his brain and clogged his food pipe. He sniffed; there was nothing wrong with the dal. The stench was lodged deep in his nostrils. He could try, like Lady Macbeth, to out the damned spot, but he knew he would inhale rotting carrion as long as he lived. Exhausted, he slumped back, letting his head hang on the back of the chair.

Governor Mudie, in West Panjab, was of the firm belief that the first priority was to swiftly evacuate minorities from Amritsar and Lahore. Together, Hindu–Muslim–Sikh were tinder. But Jawahar could not let himself believe that. Wasn't Bapu disproving Mudie's hypotheses in Calcutta? Hadn't he made people see sense in Bihar? Mudie didn't even want Jawahar touring Lahore, fearful what the presence of India's Prime Minister might invoke. Lahore was Jawahar's nanihal, the city his mother grew up in – its summers had let him run with abandon in the barest of clothes, its winters had warmed his toes around bonfires, its residents had cheered him on when he was elected president in the 1929 Lahore Congress session—

'Here!'

He opened his eyes at Indu's voice. She had switched his dinner plate with a bowl of sweet.

'Eid seviyan,' Indu grinned. 'Home-made. Khaliq brought them.'

Jawahar smiled. He had been eating the sweet dish every Eid since Khaliq had worked – first for Motilal Nehru, now him. Visiting Lahore on the holiest day in the Muslim calendar, with a chance to greet his Muslim brothers, had been one benefit of his two-day tour. He spooned the thick creamy vermicelli, hoping the end of Ramzan—

A commotion sounded. Excited voices erupted outside. Abandoning the table, Jawahar and Indu rushed to the window that looked onto the driveway. Some of the refugees were hurrying from the garden towards the gate.

'Maro, maro!' Kill them, kill them!

A high-pitched scream shattered the air.

They sped outside. Jawahar scraped his way through the people who blocked the road to the gate. Screams and scuffles rent the twilight. A crackling sound, the smell of petrol, then a combustion and screams, screams, screams. The crowd began to melt away. The sight at the end of the driveway squeezed Jawahar's heart. His crazed eyes scoured the surrounding for a blanket, a sheet, a cloth … a bucket of water … Behind him, Indu was whimpering, stuffing a fist in her mouth.

'WATER, WAT-er,' Jawahar shouted, his voice hoarse, 'a chador, sheet … anything! Help!'

'Hindi, Hindu, Hindustan! Hindi, Hindu, Hindustan!'

The dhoti-clad men, their faces covered, raised their fists and shouted.

'Akhand Hindustan!'

A cry ripped his throat as Jawahar lunged forward. The men scampered away. In the gathering darkness, he saw them clamber atop a tonga, which trotted away briskly. In front of his gate, the burka-clad woman, whom the miscreants had doused in petrol and set afire, had stopped writhing and gone silent. Her charred limbs, splayed on the ground, still appeared to be fighting off her attackers.

7
Hyderabad (August 1947)

M ir Osman Ali Khan puffed another Charminar cigarette, gazed at the gardens and pondered. A shayr hovered at the edges of his mind. Leaning forward, he took a sip of thick demitasse coffee. In the cocoon of heavy monsoon air, laced with acrid smoke, his mind felt unusually sluggish. The affairs of the state were at odds with the concerns of a poet, and his mind was conflicted by the daily back and forth with two-penny Indians, who, come Independence, seemed to have risen in their own reckoning. Nevertheless, he drew on the filterless cigarette, trying to still his mind and coax the couplet back. His eyelids felt heavy. Perhaps it was the opium that he had taken – more than his daily 11 grams.

In the shaft of weak morning sunlight, fumes curled and wafted. From a mounted portrait on the wall, a man stepped out. Sharp nose, pointed beard, bejewelled dastar, a white angarakha overlaid with pearl necklaces up to his waist. The man had a story to tell. An ancient story, much recounted, one that Osman knew. Yet, the man beckoned and Osman tipped his head forward ...

In the year 1700-something, matter not the exact year, Aurangzeb was the Mughal emperor in Delhi, when Qamruddin was returning from a hunting trip. He came upon a fakir begging for food. From his saddle bag, Qamruddin pulled out seven loaves of bread and offered them to the holy man. Grateful, the fakir blessed him: Qamruddin's family would rule for seven generations.

Who would have thought: One measly loaf could fetch a generation of rule? Eh? That was not all though. Like all good stories, this too had versions and variations. In another, it was Qamruddin who was desperately hungry and the fakir fed him. Satisfied by the seventh kulcha, he stopped. For dessert, he received the same blessing, one kulcha, one generation of rule.

There existed another version, less popular – but closer to truth, perhaps?

Osman bent forward, his stick creaking.

In this story, the fakir was the one starving and Qamruddin was too miserly to offer more than seven kulchas from his abundant stock. Instead of a blessing, he got a curse. Qamruddin's dynasty would end with his seventh generation!

Osman felt a jolt down his spine. The man from the portrait was gazing in the distance. He was lit by the sunlight. In his gossamer angarakha, he tread air, not ground. Turning to Osman, he asked: So who was this Qamruddin?

Osman had some idea, but before he could dredge it up through char and tar, the man had floated ahead.

On his father's side, Qamruddin traced his lineage back to the First Caliph himself, Abu Bakr. He took the saddle as soon as he could walk. When he was six, emperor Aurangzeb said of him: The star of destiny shines on his forehead! In time, he became Aurangzeb's Viceroy in the Deccan, with the hereditary title, Nizam ul Mulk, Regulator of the Realm. He was crowned Asaf Jah: the Equal to Asaf, the Grand Wazir in the court of King Solomon. So successfully did he build his power base in the Deccan that he outlived eight Mughal emperors in Delhi. How did he do it? Hmmm.

The man had locked gaze with Osman.

He had great ability, Osman thought. And was an outstanding soldier ... and—

He had greater cunning! the man finished. *Think*. In a time with Persian invaders, French freebooters and British mercenaries, how does the acolyte of a crumbling Mughal empire hold on to his fiefdom? Let me illustrate. When the feared Nadir Shah ransacked Delhi and strew its streets with corpses like fallen leaves in autumn, emperor Muhammad Shah summoned his aide for help. Nizam ul-Mulk, bare-headed, his sword hanging around his neck, presented himself before Nadir Shah and, in supplication, quoted the great Persian poet Hafiz.

> Oh, King, your anger has killed so many men,
> If you want to kill some more, bring them back to life again.

Long story short, Nadir Shah was moved enough to end the massacre. Nizam ul-Mulk returned to the Deccan, trailed by exiles fleeing Delhi for his Mohammedan kingdom. He was the first Asaf Jah. You, Osman Ali Khan, are the seventh. And the question is, which version of the story of seven loaves do you believe? Blessing, curse or is there a third story you wish to tell?

The man from the portrait – Qamruddin, Nizam ul-Mulk, Asaf Jah I – had gone absolutely still. Even the dust motes were trapped in light. Vivid images flashed before Osman. A child astride a horse. A boy swordsman locked in fierce battle. A man holding up a severed head. A resplendent court. A dark soil replete with diamonds. A flag with a kulcha as emblem. The Portuguese, Dutch, French, and British, in capes and frock coats, at their trading posts along the coast—

The court in Delhi has shifted, a new government is at the helm.

The man in the portrait barely moved his lips, but his voice boomed across the room.

What will *you* do, Osman Ali Khan, seventh Nizam of Hyderabad? This ancient land, hedged by its great mountains on east and west, the vast plateau bridging India's north and south, the land where I founded the Asaf Jahi dynasty and claimed my kingdom. Blessed, cursed – will you go begging to prevent the sack of Hyderabad? Or will you, the ruler of the greatest Mohammedan power in India, craft your own story?

Feet padded into the room. Seven salaams later, a stack of morning newspapers appeared on the table in front of the Nizam. The bearer disappeared. Even Qamruddin had vanished, back to the portrait of Asaf Jah I on the wall. Osman blinked, his daydream over. The cigarette in his hand was a smouldering stub. Flicking it away, he lit another, puffed, and reaching for the newspaper on top, *Waqt*, glanced at the headlines. He frowned. Discarding the paper, he grabbed the next one in the stack. His frown deepened. He tossed the newspaper, grabbed the next, read and scowled.

Walter Monckton, along with the Nawab of Chhatari and Ali Yavar Jung, the men negotiating with India on his behalf, were conspiring against the state, all the newspapers had headlined. They had … He frowned at the Urdu text …

held secret meetings with Pandit Jawaharlal Nehru …

sold themselves to Sardar Patel …

framed a letter conveying the terms of surrender …

'SUR-render!' the Nizam denounced, hurling the newspaper across the room.

8
Delhi (August 1947)

Trust the British fair play, Vallabh mused wryly.

Radcliffe had displeased everybody equally. Liaquat was outraged over the grant of Gurdaspur and Ferozepur to India; Vallabh was incensed over the Chittagong Hill Tracts being awarded to Pakistan. And the cleaving of Panjab had sent kafilas in both directions, east and west. People pouring into Delhi, seeking refuge in the homes of Jawaharlal, Maulana, his … Purana Qila … were threatening the calibrated balance of the city. Jinnah was fortunate that Karachi was far enough from West Panjab, but the capital city of the new Indian state could not afford to be swamped under. Delhi must hold if the Government of India was to hold.

A knock and Vidya Shankar, his private secretary, popped his head in. 'Sardar, the governor general is here.'

Lord Mountbatten entered, his hand extended. Since 15 August, the last Viceroy of India had transitioned to his new position as the governor general of the dominion of independent

India. In which position he was still pursuing the prickly Nizam of Hyderabad.

'I'm afraid I bring bad news, Mr Patel,' Mountbatten said as he sat across from the desk.

'Five days since Independence, Your Excellency, and bad news is spreading like invading locusts. What can be worse?'

'Walter Monckton has resigned.'

Vallabh raised his brows in surprise. 'Despite the two-month extension?'

'No, different matter altogether. Apparently, local Hyderabad newspapers are full of scandalous reports of how the English lawyer is selling off the kingdom to the Hindus.'

'Razvi is behind this. He cannot stomach the thought that the Nizam, under Mr Monckton's guidance, might take a decision that benefits all Hyderabadis.' Vallabh bunched his mouth in displeasure. Walter Monckton drove a hard bargain, as any barrister worth his wig, especially one who had advised a King on abdication, but he kept the Nizam tethered to reality. Without him, Kasim Razvi would mount Osman Ali on a winged horse and send him flying. 'We have a huge problem. Who will give sane advice to the Nizam, already off his rails? You're aware, Your Excellency, what El Edroos is up to?'

'Major General Peter El Edroos?'

'Selfsame. The Hyderabad army commander is in London looking to buy arms from whomever will sell it to him on the open market. My sources tell me that he had a meeting with Czech arms suppliers for 3 million pounds worth of orders.'

With the successful birth of independent India and Pakistan, Dickie had assumed they had already crossed the Rhine. He and his staff were plain exhausted. Recent illnesses – Miéville with thrombosis, Ismay with dysentery – and the long hours in the run up to 15 August had left him with little appetite for fresh crises. But here it was: El Edroos planning to stockpile weapons could only mean he was readying Hyderabad for a war!

'Those are grim tidings, Mr Patel. I'll have to convince Sir Walter to stay on, if only to provide a steadying hand to Hyderabad as the Nizam's coterie continue to stir up eddies.'

Vallabh nodded briefly. The success of their joint mission – securing a majority of 565 Princely States to India by 15 August – owed a lot to Lord Mountbatten's royal charm and soldierly tenacity. 'That would be very helpful, Your Excellency. There is no limit to the extent to which Kasim Razvi will not go. As you know, Muslim refugees are pouring into Hyderabad from Central Provinces. Razvi's plan is to get so many of them into the state that the ratio of 15 per cent Muslims begins to improve.'

'The man's fanaticism borders on frenzy!'

'One hundred percent. As we say, in Gujarati, sau feesdi.'

A knock on the door, and a bearer entered with a tea tray. As he set about pouring tea, Vallabh glanced around his new office. Located in North Block in the erstwhile Secretariat and the Council Chamber, now Parliament House, it was spacious and spare, the way he liked it. Mani wanted to add some potted plants, which would be good. Plants recalled to his mind some of his earliest memories, of working in the field with his father. It was a tough life, burdened by debt, but the physical labour had toughened him. His older brothers teased him and called him 'mad bull'. At the recollection, Vallabh smiled inwardly. The bearer placed the teacup in front of him, its aroma drawing Vallabh back to the present. He noticed a film of perspiration on Mountbatten's face.

'Perhaps the air conditioning needs an increase, Your Excellency. I told Shankar to set the temperature such that I don't catch a chill!' Vallabh laughed.

Mountbatten dismissed it with an airy wave of his hand.

'A summer cold may not be the best thing to catch in the current climate.'

The two men sipped on their tea. Vallabh marshalled his thoughts. The bull was ageing, the rage of his youth condensed into steel. No more the need to paw up dust in a display of threat. Instead, the patience and wisdom of Nandi, the guardian of Kailasa, was required.

'The Nizam is like a lone leaf on a tree, blowing in every which direction. With Razvi's exhalations, with El Edroos's forays, Monckton's counsel ... Our goal, Your Excellency, is to guide the leaf onto our palm, so we can land it safely in the soil of Mother India. The Nizam might forget, but Hyderabad is more than just the princes – there are 16 million people who must get to enjoy the fruit of a free India.

'Besides,' Vallabh continued, depositing the cup back on the saucer with a rattle, 'how can the belly breathe if it is cut off from the main body?'

9

Hyderabad (September 1947)

I will not be a concubine, I will not.

Fiercely, Jaabili muttered it over and over as she cleaved a coconut against the sickle-shaped blade, repeating it with every stab the knife made in tender flesh – chanting as if she were the temple priest at his daily japa and not the young girl from a bonded family. A hillock of coconuts to be dehusked, chopped, grated, which shielded her from cooks and other workers engaged in preparations for the celebratory dinner. Jagirdar Vamana Ramachandra Reddy had married off his third son and added another wing to his already massive mansion. The kitchen had been readying for the joint celebration for a whole week now, the duration of Jaabili's stay in her new 'home'. Jail, really, for she had been sent here against her will, a parcel that accompanied the bride from her parents' home. Jaabili's parents were bonded to the bride's parents, and Jaabili was the adi bapa gift: Her duty was to tend to her new mistress and provide sexual service to the master.

Jaabili shifted on the plinth, the narrow wooden frame was not meant for crouching upon for endless hours. Tucking a stray strand back with her right wrist, Jaabili wished she had allowed Swami to have his way with her. When exactly had play turned into dry humping and stolen kisses, she didn't recall. But at sixteen, he wanted more and Jaabili knew that could be dangerous. Hadn't Lalithamma been beaten with tamarind birch by her own mother and promptly dropped her baby? An unwed mother was a criminal thing. Sex before marriage was dangerous. Sex after marriage could kill you in childbirth ... But being a virgin was dangerous too. If Swami had taken her virginity, she would not be fit for concubinage – his grandfather, the deshmukh, would have chosen another girl from the families of his bonded labourers.

Alas! Jaabili sighed and tossed the shell onto the mountain of eviscerated coconuts. She had seen the groom. Not only was he shaped like a pestle – a man with a woman's ass – his breath smelt of sour kokum. She pinched her nose in recollection. Jaabili was helping the bride dress up when he had passed by, pinching her bottom and winking as he went. Really, a man with such generous buttocks should help himself to his own, no?

'Aye, Jaabili! You will take a lifetime to get through a sack of coconuts, eh?'

Nodding to the cook, she doubled down and pretended to make haste. But really, how fast could she go? The sickle had taken the fingers of many women.

'Grate me some, fast!'

Grabbing a half coconut, she scraped it against the serrated fan at the end, grating the white flesh. But how was she to get herself out of this particular pickle? Would tonight be the night? The bride had dutifully lain in bed with her husband for a full week now. She was sore – anyone could make out from her gingerly walk – but Jaabili knew from helping her with the daily bath ritual. She had bite marks on her breasts, her thighs ached and her lady parts were as tender as raw meat.

'Okay, enough now,' the cook hailed. 'Bring the plates of grated and chopped coconut, quick!'

Jaabili stood up, brushed the crumbs off, smoothed down her sari and, with a plate in each hand, walked to the cook. Enveloped within aroma-laden steam clouds, glistening with sweat and oil, the cook grunted at her offering. 'Here,' he indicated the large ladle, 'keep stirring. Do not pause for a single moment. If my koora is ruined, that will be the end of you.'

Diligently, Jaabili began to stir. The ladle was large, the wok commodious enough to curl within, the curry spitting up regularly. She used both hands and shoulders to keep rotating the thickening curry like it were a slumbering beast.

The cook returned from his toilet break, shouted brisk commands to some of the other workers, then waved for her to give way. A couple of stirs later, he grunted his satisfaction, then indicated a mound of red chillies. 'I want them pound fine.'

By now, her shoulders and her bum were sore. The chillies would make her cry.

She started to pound, sniffling and wiping her eyes as she went. Back home, pounding turmeric and chillies was the task assigned to her younger sister. Jaabili had feigned fear of them like Sithamma, one of the other bonded women. Her mother had spanked her. Sithamma had a reason, what cause did Princess Jaabili have? But Jaabili had stuck to her act, despite several thrashings, until her mother gave up and assigned the work to Saroja, the younger girl. Jaabili was not afraid of chillies; she just hated the burning smell of them in her nostrils. As for Sithamma, it reminded her of her punishment.

The chilli powder was almost done, but the pungent fumes were working their way through the thin cotton edge of her sari that she had wrapped like a veil. Blinking her eyes, she sniffled as Sithamma swam into her mind. The poor woman was thrashed, then chilli powder was splashed onto her wounds. Because she had left work briefly to breastfeed her baby.

Jaabili sniffled, wiped her eyes and peered at the mortar. The fiery red chillies had yielded a bright-red powder, a pinch of which would set a tongue afire. Just the sight made her eyes water … A thought came to her. It seized her with its sheer brazenness. *Could* she? Dare she? A shiver ran down her spine in the hot, humid kitchen. They would skin her alive! Besides, where would she run to? She could not return home, unless she wanted to make them all suffer …

A red flag fluttered in her mind. The Sangham was asking for volunteers, women even, to join their efforts to rid peasants of the tyranny of vetti. No more compulsory services and exactions to the jagirdars and deshmukhs. It was a struggle that her family and other bonded workers had ignored. But Jaabili need not. Between concubinage and freedom struggle, she knew what she wanted.

She sniffle-smiled at the fiery chilli powder.

10
Hyderabad (September 1947)

It was his first time meeting the Nizam. A great honour indeed – one that could have been bestowed upon the commander-in-chief of Hyderabad's armed forces earlier perhaps?

What were those piled-up jars doing in the corridor? Covered with cobwebs too ... The floor was dusty ... pockmarked with pigeon droppings ... On the wall, a portrait of the Nizam, dripping in jewels, his turban ornament sparkling with diamonds. A full-length mirror in a gilded frame adorned the wall across. The strange mix of soiled and splendid was disorienting. He squared his shoulders, waiting to be summoned.

Catching his reflection, Major General Syed Ahmed 'Peter' El Edroos stooped, steadied the dastar upon his head and fidgeted with the bagloos at his waist. The stiff-backed army veteran of two world wars had discarded his uniform for the mandated attire to be worn in the presence of the Nizam. The headgear and elaborate belt were unfamiliar encumbrances, yet essential reminders of court protocol: Stand with hands folded and head bowed in the presence of HEH, renounce any presumption of a seat. The rumour went that when Jinnah visited, he crossed his legs and proceeded to smoke whilst conversing with His Highness! In Hyderabad, it was permissible to stab a person in the back, but to be rude to him? Jinnah's first visit to the court was his last.

El Edroos cleared his throat and focused his mind on the meeting ahead. The Nizam would seek his opinion and the general had to deliver it without alienating the reclusive ruler. Like all his predecessors, the Nizam had surrounded himself with a coterie. However, Mir Osman Ali Khan was virtually a prisoner in King Kothi, seldom venturing out to inspect what was actually happening in the state. Intrigue, which hung heavy in the palace, like the velvet drapes and musty air, had begun to leak out, pitting Hyderabadis against one another in paranoia. Razakars versus Communists, the Ittehad versus the Hindu Mahasabha, native Mulki versus non-Mulki—

It was time.

He followed the retainer who, upon entering the room, bent low at the waist and proffered seven deep salaams to the Nizam. El Edroos gave a smart salute. 'Your Highness.' The retainer exited without turning his back. Osman Ali Khan was shorter than El Edroos's mental image of the Nizam and ... Was his sherwani *torn* at the collar? The general, who prided his ability to size up people in one glance, was dismayed at the sight of the general decrepitude. Hyderabadi custom battled with soldierly forthrightness within El Edroos as he struggled to reconcile the slovenly creature in day-old clothes and a dirty fez with His Exalted Highness Nawab Sir Mir Osman Ali Khan Siddiqi, Asaf Jah VII. So confounded was he that he sat in a chair without registering the honour he had been bestowed with.

The Nizam blew smoke as he sat in his own ornate chair and regarded the general. 'The army minister tells me you've returned empty-handed from London. Why?'

'Your Highness, the purpose of my visit was to purchase arms for Hyderabad, whichever I could get, mainly automatic weapons and anti-tank guns. On my way back, I visited Switzerland and the factory where six-pounder anti-tank guns are made. In Prague, I visited the famous Skoda Armaments factory. The Swiss and the Czech are willing to sell, but will not take responsibility for delivery. In London, unfortunately, I had no success.'

El Edroos paused, remembering the summons he'd received from the head of foreign relations in London. Lieutenant General Scoons, under whom he had served in the 4th Corps in Burma, had heard of his UK mission and was categorical in his instruction: *Stay out of it, Peter!*

'It appears impossible to purchase arms and ammunition from abroad as Hyderabad is not recognized as an independent country.'

The Nizam grunted and exhaled smoke. A bitter smell hung in the air. He fixed his eyes on the general, who was built like one of his Hashemite Arab Guards: tall, broad-shouldered, handsome.

'The ones who will sell, the Swiss and the Czech ... Why can't we arrange delivery?'

'Even if we purchased arms and ammunition from Europe or the Middle East, it will be impossible to import them into Hyderabad. Bombay, Madras and other seaports are all closed to Hyderabad traffic.'

'Goa?' the Nizam rasped.

'The land route between Goa and Hyderabad is under Indian surveillance.'

Osman Ali Khan tossed the cigarette to the floor, which was littered with butts. He watched it smoulder before stubbing it viciously with his toe. 'The Hyderabad Army contributed three quarters of its military force for service abroad in World War II, which helped the British WIN! Why will London not come to our aid now?'

In silence, El Edroos watched the Nizam rant. Surely he was aware that not only could they *not* make fresh purchases, but even their troops were returning from overseas *without* their equipment? The original equipment with which the Princely States' Forces had been sent abroad was paid for by the respective states. However, the troops returned without any equipment because the understanding was that they would be re-equipped at the cost of the Government of India. But Hyderabad was sitting on the fence with regards to accession to India. El Edroos had taken up the matter with General Moore, the military adviser-in-chief, and Baldev Singh, the defence minister of the then interim government. Now with the Nizam keeping a foot each in India and Pakistan, no one was willing to re-equip the Hyderabad Army. An army without arms may well be staffed by toy soldiers.

The general squared his jaw and refused to play ball with the Nizam, who had started to pace the sparsely furnished room, tapping a crooked stick as he went.

'The Ittehad can arrange weapons for its volunteers but a general cannot? You expect the Razakars to do the job of the state's army?'

Kasim Razvi certainly seemed to believe so. The leader of the Razakars called himself 'field marshal' and had clearly convinced the Nizam that his ragtag group was organized on military lines. Sticks, swords and some Sten guns did not qualify for arms – how was El Edroos to disabuse the Nizam of this notion?

'Your Highness, the Razakars have a role to play as supporters of the Muslim cause. However, they must refrain from wearing military uniforms and holding parades as if they were a parallel armed force of the State of Hyderabad—'

'WHY? Why not?' the Nizam shrieked.

—and terrorizing non-Muslims, the thought continued in El Edroos's mind.

'Even Deen Yar Jung tells me that the Razakars are doing valuable work keeping a check on the Communists, the ... the Hindu Mahasabha, Arya Samajis! The commissioner of police does not share your concerns, General. And you know he has spies everywhere who give him information from ground up.'

El Edroos had a distinct feeling of encirclement – the Nizam surrounding him with increasingly outrageous offensives. Except, the Nizam should know that the commander-in-chief was not his enemy. And if he was keen on an independent Hyderabad, surely the viability of its army to defend the state against the might of the Indian Army should be a major concern?

A rustle of feet as the retainer entered again, his arm lashing out in salaams. He had barely finished announcing Kasim Razvi when the Razakar chief strode in and greeted the Nizam like he were an old friend. Noticing the general, Razvi gave him a perfunctory nod. His eyes were like burning coals, the fez worn at a rakish angle, his beard like that of a mid-career maulvi's. Razvi flitted about the room. From what El Edroos had heard, the bird-like man had been declaiming that the Asaf Jahi flag would soon be flying from the ramparts of the Red Fort.

El Edroos was aware that Deen Yar Jung paid a daily morning visit to the Nizam. A motley crew of beggars, thieves and layabouts served as his spies, and were the basis of his intelligence briefs. Now the militant Razvi too seemed to have familiarized himself with King Kothi.

The Nizam looked pointedly from Razvi to El Edroos. There was only one guest chair in the room.

El Edroos stood up, saluted and exited.

11
Delhi (September 1947)

Dickie Mountbatten had brought down the shutters on 150 years of British rule in India. He had done that in less than five months through relentless toil. Now, having officially transferred power to both dominions, he was ready for some rest. 'Lazed in bed all morning,' was his diary entry at the start of his holiday in Simla. Dickie and Edwina had come there directly from Lahore after a Joint Defence Committee meeting agreed to disband the Panjab Boundary Force on 29 August. Both Jinnah and Jawa were equally convinced that the force favoured the other side. Well, that was that. Dickie had shrugged off the demise of his last operational responsibility and embraced the break from work.

But the birth of fraternal twins had become a messy postpartum affair. They had split, officially, but behaved as if they were conjoined at the chest, refugee kafilas departing and arriving from West and East Panjab. Many kafilas terminated in Delhi, the heart of India and its capital. The refugees carried little with them except their tales of woe – of how Hindus and

Sikhs had lost everything to Muslims. Over 2,00,000 of them had poured into the city of a million people, clamouring for home, food and water, but above all, revenge.

Echoes of the uproar in the dusty plains had reached the verdant hills of Simla. A bomb had exploded in Fatehpuri Masjid in Chandni Chowk, the locus of old Delhi. Not content, a horde had gathered to hurl bricks at the mosque. In a local high school, children sitting for their matriculation examinations were interrupted when goondas stormed in and butchered the Muslim students. Sword-wielding gangs had taken over Delhi streets, dragging out and killing Muslims. One particular echo reverberated in the ears of the Mountbattens. On 31 August, they had held a farewell party for an aide-de-camp who was returning to England. His train was stopped and all the Muslims on board were butchered, except for one: his bearer, cowering under his seat.

Breakfast in the lawns of the Viceregal Lodge on the morning of 4 September was a sober affair. News had just arrived that their treasurer, in Viceregal service for thirty years, and his wife, had been murdered in another train to Delhi. In contrast to the desultory tapping of their cutlery, a drongo was chirruping animatedly.

'We're needed in Delhi.' Edwina sipped her Darjeeling with concentration. 'With an estimated half-a-million refugees on the move, I need to set up facilities for their relief and welfare.'

As he applied butter on toast, Dickie nodded. 'You are the person most skilled for the task. With your Red Cross and war work … undoubtedly … I am not sure what service I can provide, or *should*.' He locked eyes with his wife. 'Just three weeks since I handed over reins to the new government, I cannot be seen interfering with it now.'

Edwina surveyed the gardens, the distant blue hills cloaked with mountains, the dewy grass beneath her feet. When they had last visited in May, Jawa was their houseguest. Her eyes swept to the cypress tree at the far end of the lawn, conversing under which she had felt a real connection with the man who was now India's Prime Minister. She recalled his profile against the Himalayas, the ridge of his high cheekbones, his aroma of crushed rose and cigarettes. Edwina exhaled. Jawa was far from his beloved mountains, fighting to save Delhi, trying to inject sense into fiery crowds, consoling refugees ... She had seen him walk amongst them, place a comforting hand on someone's shoulder, listen attentively to the story of another, reiterate, 'I know, mere bhai, I know; it is my sorrow too.'

Placing her cup back in the saucer, Edwina extended her arm and touched Dickie. 'I'm going back to the capital.'

Before Dickie could reply, a bearer hurried over with a telegram. Which Dickie read and passed to his wife.

'Looks like we both have reasons now.' Edwina folded the telegram.

But Dickie looked uncertain. 'Because VP says that the situation is completely out of hand and that I am needed in Delhi?'

'V.P. Menon won't send this telegram without the blessing of his boss. Which means Sardar Patel wants you, and Jawa will welcome your assistance, of course.'

The drongo's chirps sounded like a spirited echo of *of course, course, course* ...

Dickie sighed and sat back in his chair. 'How far can I go in gripping matters for them instead of making them do it themselves? Is this a matter of stage fright, you think? First time facing the footlights, etcetera ...'

Edwina shrugged. 'They could do with your support, but ... you must not *appear* to be gripping matters yourself. Think you can do that, darling?'

✅

Back in Delhi on 5 September, the Mountbattens caught up with the Prime Minister and deputy prime minister. Delhi was afire with widespread arson and murder. Offices and streets were empty, hospital mortuaries packed to capacity.

'The British press is having a field day, for sure,' Jawa grunted as he indicated a news item.

... half a million people fighting in the blazing streets of Delhi ...

'Delhi has caught Panjab's infection,' the Sardar said grimly.

Jawa looked immeasurably sad and his deputy, angry. Well, this general mood of dazed bewilderment had to go. Dickie squared his shoulders and dove in.

After several hours of consultation, he proposed setting up an Emergency Committee, reporting to the Cabinet, to deal with the troubling situation. When Jawa suggested that Dickie be the chairman, he accepted on one condition. 'The fact that the governor general is chair should not be published.'

'Time spent in Raj prisons has not equipped us for emergency administration, Your Excellency.' Jawa shrugged. 'Getting the governor general, with his extensive war record, to oversee this effort is a practical objective.'

Thereafter, Dickie swung into his new role with the ease of the erstwhile SEAC commander who had taken the Japanese surrender in WWII. For permanent members of the committee, he enlisted Jawaharlal Nehru and Sardar Patel, along with ministers Baldev Singh (defence), John Matthai (railways) and

K.C. Neogy (in the newly created post of Refugees). He would co-opt other members as required. He summoned Pete Rees, whose Boundary Force Command had closed down, to head a small Military Emergency Staff operating inside Government House. Pamela, who had experience assisting with medical and welfare efforts, was to be Reese's personal assistant. Ismay was recalled from Kashmir where Dickie had sent him to help the Maharaja make up his vacillating mind. Edwina took charge of Refugee Relief and Welfare.

Just as in the days of war, Dickie set up a large Map Room in Government House, outfitted with maps, telephones and staff. Not a day late. On 6 September, news came of a bomb thrown into New Delhi railway station, packed with fleeing Muslims. Police had to fire at the mob of Hindus and Sikhs, amassed despite a curfew. To add to the cauldron, Jawa and Patel had very different notions of how to handle the communal violence in Delhi. A memory surged in Dickie's mind from a recent meeting of the Emergency Committee, when the home minister had updated them on the security and food situation.

§

'I have issued a shoot-at-sight order to Delhi police.' Vallabhbhai cast a look around the table, his face serene, eyes sharp. 'Some Sikh and Rajput soldiers attacked Muslims instead of protecting them. They have been replaced with the Madras regiment. I called a meeting of Sikh leaders and have threatened to set up concentration camps to put all Sikhs in them, unless the violence is immediately leashed. All weapons have been banned, except Sikh kirpans—'

'Tch!' Jawaharlal expressed his annoyance.

'—which are to be *sheathed*.' Vallabh's eyes flashed. 'A particular concern is the security of Mahatma Gandhi. We are also trying to provide Bapu with cover, but he refuses. As you are aware, he is visiting camps, which are dangerous places nowadays. People rush to him and in all that crowd ...'

'Communal feelings have so destroyed the fabric of Delhi,' Maulana waded in, 'that protests are being raised at the recitation of the Koran at Bapu's prayer meetings.'

Jawaharlal gripped the table with both hands. 'It is imperative that we control the communal elements. The RSS and Hindu Mahasabha *must* be banned. Their presence is like fuel to the raging fire in Delhi. And the Sikhs have to be restrained, their kirpans banned.'

On a shake of his head, Vallabh said, 'That will amount to discrimination. A kirpan is a mandatory article of their faith—'

'Are we going to justify murder in the name of religion?'

The meeting was heading for a meltdown. So Dickie decided to referee with a hair-raising tale about the Pakistan high commissioner.

'He absconded to the airfield to catch the next flight to Pakistan. You can all imagine how Jinnah would have blown a fuse upon his arrival!' Having got the attention of both Jawa and Patel, Dickie held out both hands in an expansive gesture. 'Thankfully, we got whiff of it in time and I sent a member of my staff to kidnap the commissioner right back!'

∽

Dickie shook his head to clear his mind. The incident had reminded him of the Pakistan High Commission's complaint about their perilously low food supplies. Immediate restocking was imperative, lest Jinnah too, joined the fray between Patel and Jawa in the capital city.

On that grim thought, Dickie decided he would open the day's Emergency Committee meeting with a salvo of his own.

'Gentlemen, if we go down in Delhi, we are finished.'

12
Hyderabad (September 1947)

When Jaabili was summoned to the groom's quarters, she went with her fists clenched.

He patted the bed on which he sat. She approached slowly until she stood right in front of him. Her boldness surprised him, he gave a delighted chuckle. Like a snake, his right arm whipped out and grabbed her breast. It was in that moment that Jaabili's arms swung up to his face and her fists squirted their contents into his eyes. Before the rest of his pestle-shaped body could register his stinging eyes, she had grabbed a sheet off the bed, and started to maniacally wrap it around his head and chest, muffling his shrieks and pinning his arms. Then, she ran.

She had come to the house with nothing; she left with nothing. Except the red-chilli powder in a pouch tucked into the waist of her sari. She stayed off the road, hurrying through the scrubland, staying in the cover of boulders, skirting the thick forest teeming with jackals, leopards, bears, pythons ... Her feet stung, her breath was short, her heart was in her mouth. They would already be on her trail, on foot, on vehicles, a swarm of men armed with spades, crowbars, muzzleloaders. If they caught her, the only mercy would be a swift death.

Jaabili ran, skidding over wet grass, plunking into puddles, grabbing tall bamboo for support. Around her, the jungle hummed and rumbled. She passed her village, but did not stop. The hamlet of Koya tribals lay ahead. They had overthrown their corrupt leader with the help of the Sangham, planted red flags in their fields, and taken up sticks and slings to defend themselves. Sweat clouded her eyes, slicked her limbs, but the red flag fluttered in her mind, propelling her on.

∽

Salamma gave Jaabili refuge in her house where, after muttering her request to join the Sangham, Jaabili fell into an exhausted stupor. When she awoke, it was midday, rain knocking on the house of wood, palm leaves and grass. Since Jaabili was keen to join the Sangham, Salamma had sent word. All she could do was wait and stay hidden. News of an attack on the jagirdar's son had filtered to their hamlet. Jagirdar Reddy's men were roaring up and down in their vehicles.

'Eat,' Salamma handed her a bowl of rice and chaaru. She had thick, capable hands, her skin was leathery, lined, her eyes as sharp as nettles.

The peppery vapour reminded her of home. 'Did they,' Jaabili swallowed back the lump in her throat, 'go to Purnali? My village.' She tossed her head to indicate it was in the neighbourhood.

Salamma nodded. What she did not mention was that the police had raided Jaabili's house, thrashed her father, crushed her mother's breasts with forceps, stripped her siblings naked and bound them up with chameleons tied to their thighs. Watching Jaabili's mouth wobble, she only urged her to eat. Later, she handed her a tin of cibazol powder and some clean rags. 'This will keep your wounds from getting infected.'

As Jaabili cleaned her torn feet and legs, wincing where the cuts were deep, Salamma kept asking her questions. All same questions, just asked differently each time. *Jagirdar Vamana Ramachandra Reddy's second son, eh? Third son, you said, ah? Why had she stayed for five days and not escaped earlier? What, ten days, you said? Ah* ... Jaabili knew what the older woman was doing – checking her stories for inconsistencies. For it was entirely possible that Jaabili was a spy sent by the enemy. The police had burnt entire villages to get information on the whereabouts of the Sangham, its leaders and supporters.

For three days, Salamma fed Jaabili and questioned her. In that time, Jaabili had emptied out her entire life story to the matron, even the incidents of her canoodling with Swami, the landlord's son. All she learnt was that Salamma was the leader of the hamlet. And the Sangham had plucked the palm leaves, that kept her house dry, directly from the groves of landlords.

By the time the return message came from the Sangham, Jaabili had recovered.

'You will need it,' Salamma said as she packed a cloth pouch with fried chana and jowar rotis. 'The trek is long and through the jungle.'

∽

Venkateswara Rao, the leader of the Sangham, looked like a school master with thick black glasses, watchful eyes and a nose large enough to support those glasses. The rest of his face was lost in facial hair, dense as a jungle. He even sat behind a narrow wooden table. He spoke with Salamma first while Jaabili waited outside his room. They were meeting in a low-roofed house which had the appearance of a hut from the outside, located in a dense grove of teak trees. Several men with guns patrolled the surrounding area. It was all was very quiet, except for birdsong.

Salamma and Jaabili had walked for eight hours and reached by twilight. During the trek, Salamma walked in front at a visible distance and Jaabili followed. The matron was alert to every sound and when she halted, she raised her left fist – a signal for Jaabili to stop and stay silent. Once, Salamma left the track and veered off. When she returned after some time, Jaabili noticed the revolver in her right hand, which she then tucked into her waist cloth. They were dressed identically, brownish saris tied dhoti-style skimming their knees, the pallu secured firmly at the waist. There was no talking.

Before they started their trek, Salamma had asked, 'Have you ever seen a sloth bear in the jungle?'

Jaabili shook her head.

'Leopard? Jackal? Wild boar?'

To Jaabili's nos, Salamma replied, 'Good. Through this trek, you must be like those animals who live in the jungle without being seen by men.'

Now, Salamma beckoned to Jaabili. Venkateswara Rao seated Jaabili at the table on the single chair, clasped his hands behind his back and started to ask her questions. About her village, her family, their landlord, about Jagirdar Reddy, his sons, his third son, the bride, adi bapa, why she had escaped, how she had escaped, how she knew about Salamma's hamlet, how she knew how to find Salamma, why the Sangham, what did she know about the Sangham …

Jaabili's throat and head had started to hurt. She was never at a loss for words, but this line of endless questioning was too demanding. However, Rao just kept walking back and forth in the small room, unfurling a string of questions like it was Hanuman's tail, in his clear, quiet voice. Just when Jaabili thought she would fold upon herself and slide in a heap to the floor, he asked, 'What can you do for us? Can you fire a gun?'

Jaabili shook her head.

'Nurse wounds? Give injections? Know medicines?'

Again, Jaabili shook her head wordlessly.

'Do you read or write?'

Jaabili sat like a mute.

Rao came to a halt and shrugged. 'What *can* you do? Cook?'

The tone took her back to the Reddy kitchen, where the cook was berating her for taking too long with grinding the coconuts.

'I can cook, but I don't like to and I don't want to. I can run fast, I know the jungle, and I am not scared.' Jaabili tilted her chin defiantly. 'I want to join the Sangham because the red flag says women are equal to men.'

Rao's eyes had widened behind his glasses. He studied Jaabili directly. She held his gaze. Then Rao turned to look at Salamma, who had been sitting on the mud floor cleaning her revolver. Their eyes met.

Salamma gave a final wipe down to the revolver with the edge of her pallu before tucking it at her waist. 'We need a courier, Comrade Rao. Someone to fill Lalitha's position.'

The unspoken interaction between the two intrigued Jaabili. 'What does a courier do?'

'Carry messages, ferry comrades, gather information ...' Rao removed his glasses to polish them with his shirt. 'A Sangham is only as good as its couriers. We have begun training women couriers because the police do not suspect them. Therefore, they can go to places male couriers cannot.'

A courier sounded good; a courier sounded important. But Jaabili felt like she was seeing a partial picture.

'However,' Rao held up his glasses to examine, 'you are new and untested—'

'Test me then,' Jaabili said, sitting upright, her exhaustion having evaporated at the prospect of being able to do real work – work that would help smash the jagirdars and deshmukhs, feudal landlords who regarded peasants as their slaves.

Again, Rao scrutinized her. 'Okay,' he said finally. 'We can begin your training from tomorrow.' He waved a hand to indicate that she could leave and dipped his head at a map on the table.

Jaabili nodded and headed out. At the door, she paused. 'What happened to Lalitha?'

'The Razakars caught her. She refused to reveal any secret, so they shot her,' Salamma said dourly.

Rao threw her a quick glance. 'After they had plucked out her nails and hung her upside down for hours.'

13
Delhi (September 1947)

The western coastline of peninsular India, starting at its southern tip on Cape Comorin, ascends in a broad north-westerly direction until it reaches Kathiawar. Here, it begins to flounder. The ditzy, undisciplined dance results in another peninsula, one that resembles the open maw of the mugger crocodile the region is famous for.

Since time immemorial, the maw has swallowed the Arabian Sea and spewed it back, alongside spices, textiles, timber, traders, marauders. At this western tip of India, the entire subcontinent appears ready to plunge into the deep blue expanse. Any wonder then that this is the land of lore: where Krishna departed for his heavenly abode, where Agastya drank up the entire ocean, where Ghazni rode on horseback to sack Somnath ...

In the year of our reckoning, 1947, when a schism in the subcontinent has created a new nation, only salt marshes separate India's prized peninsula of Kathiawar from Pakistan. Verawal, Kathiawar's famed port from where ships have sailed for Zanzibar and China for a millennia, is within sneezing distance of Jinnah's Karachi. Somnath, home to the iconic temple, is still sore with stories of Ghazni's raid of 1024. Complicating matters further, both Verawal and Somnath are part of the Princely State of Junagadh, predominantly Hindu but ruled by a Muslim Nawab.

On 15 August 1947, as Prime Minister Jawaharlal Nehru had proclaimed India's tryst with destiny, Viceroy Lord Mountbatten had scrambled to deliver to the deputy prime minister the promised basket of 565 apples. Short by three: Two large and rosy – Hyderabad and Kashmir – the third small, yet of sizeable heft – Junagadh. And on 15 August, Junagadh had announced its accession to Pakistan; India be damned.

Junagadh's attitude was perilously unsound, considering it was one of 300 Princely States in Kathiawar and Gujarat, all of which had acceded to India. What gave the tiny state such temerity? Its prized seaboard and the guiding hand of Mr Jinnah was what. The act was a guaranteed red flag to the professed 'mad bull' responsible for integrating the Princely States in independent India.

As a native Gujarati, Vallabhbhai took Junagadh's betrayal personally.

༄

The telegram of 13 September bothered him terribly, Vallabh admitted. His colon had flared up in sympathy, he noted wryly. Casting aside the newspaper he was reading, he removed his semi-circular glasses and gazed at the veranda which opened onto the lawn. The sky had darkened with rain clouds ... Perhaps the much-awaited monsoon would arrive? They could do with a respite. He sighed. Junagadh's accession to Pakistan was the first danger sign for splitting India again. Having got his Pakistan, Jinnah wasn't content with one Partition ...

Manibehn entered, a servant with the tea tray behind, the door held open by Vidya Shankar.

'Ah, Shankar,' Vallabh beckoned from the chair where he was reclining, 'come, come. We have much to discuss this afternoon.'

His private secretary nodded. In the year since he had started working with the home minister, teatime was the period when Shankar updated the Sardar on the day's developments and they discussed important issues. In a year of upheavals, bad news had arrived with regularity as had stakeholders with differing views. The man with the high forehead, broad nostrils and piercing eyes, listened to all sides without giving any clue to his own thoughts.

Vidya Shankar settled on the sofa, depositing the folders he had carried for discussion by his side.

With his chin, Vallabh indicated Junagadh's telegram lying on the table. 'Your thoughts?'

'Looks like Mr Jinnah has decided it's time to put Junagadh to use. If the Nawab of a Hindu-majority state can accede, why not the Nizam of Hyderabad? Also, Jinnah's smarting from Maharaja Hari Singh's refusal to grant his request for a two-week vacation in the Valley.'

'Hmm ... Junagadh, the pawn. Kashmir, the Queen; Hyderabad, the King.'

'You think so, father?' Manibehn asked as she served tea. She placed the usual platter of biscuits and savouries on the table. 'Why not Kashmir as the King?'

Vallabh sipped the fragrant hot tea. His colon would complain, but really, the last time he gave up tea was in jail when trying to follow Bapu's lemon-based concoctions. The dark cloud on his forehead matched the one outside, for the room had darkened abruptly. Shankar rose and switched on a tube light.

Having finished his tea, Vallabh reclined in his chair. 'Jinnah knows he can claim Kashmir for Pakistan as a Muslim-majority state. Hari Singh's vacillation is slowing Jinnah's cart. But Hyderabad … India's largest Princely State, and its wealthiest, with a Nizam who is the richest man in the world – now *that* is a King worth acquiring. Except, Hyderabad is Hindu majority, locked in the belly of India.'

'And Junagadh is the wedge,' Shankar said. 'Jinnah can connect Karachi and Verawal, and have his navy ships docked in India practically.'

In his mind, Vallabh saw the unusual geography of Junagadh – fragments of other states embedded in it, as Junagadh butted an arm into the state of Baroda. At the Princely States' conference in July, Junagadh's representative had told Mountbatten that he intended to advise the Nawab to accede to India. However, Nawab Mahabat Khan had temporarily absconded to Europe, leaving charge to his dewan, Shah Nawaz Bhutto, a Muslim Leaguer from Karachi. Additionally, Vallabh had learnt that Junagadh had secretly recruited Baluchis and Hurs from Pakistan to the state forces.

'You know, father,' Manibehn said, as she placed her empty teacup on the tray, 'if you draw a straight line connecting Nadiad to Porbandar, Gondol will be on that line.'

Vidya Shankar frowned.

Vallabh sniggered. 'Mani sounds cryptic, Shankar, but it's really quite simple. Bapu was born in Porbandar, I, in Nadiad, and Jinnah's family hails from Gondol. All Gujaratis.'

'All lawyers,' Manibehn added.

'All Congressmen too, until …' Shankar shrugged.

'So how many Gujaratis does it take to partition India?' Vallabh leaned forward in his chair.

He sounded jocular, but Shankar had learned to read that implacable face.

On a grimace, Vallabh turned his head towards the dark exterior where fat raindrops were bouncing off the veranda floor. A shower, finally. The birds trilling loudly in the afternoon had anticipated it. He could smell the wet earth, something his peasant heart rejoiced at. He brought his gaze back to the room. 'One partition is all we will allow, no matter what Jinnah anticipates.'

Vallabh stood up and started pacing the floor. Vidya Shankar readied his pencil and notebook. In the sudden hush, he was aware of the spatter of raindrops, the whirr of the ceiling fan and the rhythmic slap of slippered feet.

Manibehn smoothed her khadi saree and followed her father's progress. Since 1928, she had been his full-time caretaker. Homemaker, secretary, nurse, companion, she had accompanied him to jail at times. Some days, she could even read his thoughts.

'Junagadh is the joker in the pack, father.'

'Sau taka!' Vallabh swivelled and gave one of his rare smiles. 'You play bridge, Shankar?'

Shankar answered with a wordless shake of his head.

'Bridge is a game of skill, not luck. In bridge, there is no bad hand. The cards you have are not what decides the winner. What matters is how well you play against other players. Let's see if we can play the wild card of Junagadh better than Jinnah.'

Vallabh resumed pacing the drawing room. 'Here's what we will do. A multi-pronged approach.'

Shankar began to take notes as Manibehn listened keenly.

'Junagadh's action has aroused resentment amongst the Hindus of Kathiawar and their rulers. The chief princes, Maharaja of Bhavnagar and the Jam Saheb of Nawanagar, have been in touch with me. Let's use them to put pressure on Shah Nawaz Bhutto ... Next, there are Junagadh's feudatories: Mangrol, Manavadar and Babariawad. While lawyers debate whether these feudatories can accede independently of Junagadh or not, I want V.P. Menon to proceed immediately to meet each of them for accession. Third, let's dispatch a brigade of Indian troops and soldiers from some of the Kathiawar states to be positioned near Junagadh's frontiers. Finally ...' Vallabh paused. 'Get Samaldas Gandhi on the line ...'

Shankar waited for the Sardar to complete his thought. Samaldas Gandhi was a relative of Bapu's, he knew, based in Bombay?

'Surely,' Vallabh resumed pacing, 'the disgruntled residents of Junagadh and other parts of Kathiawar want to express their dissatisfaction with the dewan and his accession to Pakistan by setting up a provisional government? An Arzi Hukumat? Based out of Rajkot, with Samaldas Gandhi as its president?'

Shankar nodded, smiling to himself. Vallabhbhai epitomized a shayr Shankar loved.

Brave men do not turn their faces against the flood of troubles
a lion swims straight when he enters the flooded waters.

Junagadh's dewan and eccentric Nawab would live to regret the betrayal.

14
Hyderabad (October 1947)

Emily Perkins had a book in her. And what better subject than the Princely State of Hyderabad in the throes of Indian independence? What a lark then that her best friend from school days in Nice had become Princess Niloufer, daughter-in-law to the Nizam, the richest man in the world! And, Emily beamed, conditions in Hyderabad were so like the dawn of the French Revolution, she might just get a *Tale of Two Cities* saga out of it.

As Uzma arranged tea ware, Miss Perkins's excited voice floated in from the terrace where the two women sat. By now, Uzma had learnt about the time when the French common people had rebelled against their King and stormed his palace. Liberté, égalité, fraternité! Any other maid could prepare tea, but Niloufer was picky and preferred Uzma to serve her morning and afternoon tea. She liked the tea leaves brewed to just the right honey colour, like sunshine in a cup. Uzma stepped back and examined the serving tray. The porcelain blue-and-white teapot, teacups with saucers ... Ah, the strainer. Plucking the silver strainer and bowl from the shelf, she placed it beside the sugar pot. Uzma couldn't understand what Emily Perkins was getting so excited about. Nobody was going to storm the Nizam's King Kothi Palace. He was their Nizam ul Mulk. Though, if they did, and each person took one of a jewel or gem or pearl or gold bullion, how different would their life look!

She took a deep breath and shook her head at her fanciful thought. From the paper bag, she extracted the Osmania biscuits Miss Perkins had requested, which the driver had driven to Shaheen Irani Cafe for. She arranged the biscuits artfully on a china plate, the aroma of sweet butter in her nose, powdery semolina on her hand. Licking a fingertip, she set the tea pan to boil water. Miss Perkins was keen on further sightseeing and Uzma was to accompany her. Niloufer had a social to attend with Prince Moazzam.

Uzma tipped the boiling water into the kettle, closed the lid, and let it seep. Tidying up, she shook the paper bag, removed the bill, and scrutinized it. Princess Niloufer was firm that no purchases were to be made without proper payment. The reputation of Dulhan Pasha, her mother-in-law, preceded her and she was determined to establish a clear break from the practice of walking into stores, buying whatever, and leaving shopkeepers scrambling to send bills for payment back to the palace. About to discard the receipt, she turned it over and frowned at the scrawl. *Osmania University.* Below which were the initials: *A.H.*

Ali Hassan. The university student who spoke to her during her visit to the Irani cafe. The memory of that encounter returned to her with a sharp pang. Did he *live* in the cafe? How did he manage to catch the princess's takeout? And what was the meaning of this coded message?

Uzma paused to process what she was feeling. Not pleasure, not pain, but more like an exhausted relief at having been discovered at the end of a very prolonged game of hide and seek.

Uzma walked to the terrace with the laden tray. Hill Fort Palace perched on Naubat Pahad. A stunning vista of emerald green unfurled in front of them.

'... what tosh, Nilou! You're no Marie Antoinette, but you have to admit the circumstances are pure Dickens!'

The princess laughed gaily and Miss Perkins waved her cigarette-holding hand in the space between them. The ceiling fan spun the air, stirring the potted lilies and the pallu of Niloufer's chiffon sari. Miss Perkins lounged in her chair, knees tucked up, blowing curlicues with her slim cigarette. As Uzma served her tea, she asked, 'So, where do we head to after? Golconda Fort or Osmania University?'

The answer rose to Uzma's lips from somewhere.

∽

At Osmania University, Uzma thought she had arrived at the grandest of the Nizam's palaces. A long driveway flanked by tall palm trees, a fountain in the centre, and a stately monument of pinkish stone set in an endless garden. Emily Perkins and she mounted the steps to the arched entrance from which spread out pillared hallways with rooms, rooms and more rooms! In contrast, the entrance to King Kothi was called Purdah Gate because a musty tarpaulin covered it!

She knew the Nizam had founded the university by issuing a firman, Miss Perkins had told her, and it was the only place where students were taught in their language, Urdu. But walking down the cool hallway, Uzma couldn't understand why the Nizam would want to gift a palace to students.

Miss Perkins was expected by the principal, so Uzma took leave and decided to explore the vast gardens. She could see mostly male students, dressed in sherwanis, and a clutch of female students in burkas. She stopped at the seal of the university. The Nizam's crown at the top, radiating sun rays, atop which sat three words: *Noorun Ala Noor*. Knowledge is Light. Students, young enough to be her sons, craned their necks as she walked down the steps. She was wearing one of Niloufer's less ornate hand-me-down saris – maroon crepe with a border of embroidered booti. Perhaps she should have worn her burka? But Princess Niloufer insisted that, as her personal attendant, Uzma need only cover her head. Keeping her head erect, Uzma walked past the sentries towards a tree in the gardens. In the distance, a dog ambled. Suddenly an extended arm was handing her a pamphlet. Taken aback, she grabbed it and hurried towards the lawn.

Finding a secluded spot in the shade of a tree, Uzma read the pamphlet. A bold headline:

Join Indian Union!

It was followed by text in Urdu and Telugu.

15 August ... independence of India ... thrown off the shackles of imperialism ... join free and independent India ...

She could see the pamphleteer in the distance as he handed out the sheets. He was dressed similar to the other men, in a sherwani, pyjama and fez, but he must be Hindu. The Muslims wanted the Nizam's rule to continue because with the proclamation of Ani'l Malik, sovereignty vested not in the ruler but in the Muslim community. With the Nizam as head, all Muslims were rulers – even the beggars in the streets – and therefore superior to other Hyderabadis.

'*Should* Hyderabad join India then?'

Startled, Uzma looked up at the man who had slunk up behind her. He grinned and dipped his head in adaab. That thick head of hair reminded her of the boy she would scare into sitting still with the threat of nicking his ears whilst administering a haircut. She didn't know whether to be pleased or annoyed … So she spoke gruffly.

'Do you make a habit of slinking up behind women?'

Shaking his head, Ali Hassan pinched the skin at his neck. 'Forgive me, aapa. But I am glad you came.'

Uzma frowned. 'What makes you think I came to meet you?'

'I didn't say that. I'm glad you came to the university.' His eyes studied her.

A parakeet tweeted. Uzma steadied the sari drape over her head and handed the pamphlet to Ali Hassan. 'What do *you* think?'

Calmly, he tore up the paper. 'Hyderabad should not join India or stay under the Nizam. It should be a free state run by its people.'

Uzma frowned as if she had heard Farsi. Seeing her confusion, Ali said, 'See, if Hyderabad joins India, nothing will change. Now the Nizam makes all the money; in a free India, it will be the wealthy elites. Nothing will change for the *people* of Hyderabad – poor now, poor then.' He tossed his chin towards the ground, 'May I?' At Uzma's nod, Ali sat on the grass, crossing his legs.

Resuming his thread, he explained, 'The state Congress wants us to join India, the Razakars want the Nizam's rule to continue. The Hindu Mahasabha, the Arya Samaj, the Ittehad-ul-Muslimeen … all are bent upon distracting us. Hindu–Mussalman is not the issue; the issue is the exploitation of the masses. Does poverty stop at the doorstep of a Muslim peasant?' Sweat beaded his face, his almond-coloured eyes had darkened.

'There is truly only one alternative: The Communists. Our struggle is against landlords, against inequality, against the feudal system.'

'You wear the crown of knowledge?' Uzma muttered her doubt aloud.

'You do too,' Ali Hassan said on a defiant nod. 'You don't need a university education to know that. Just think back on Faizpur and your childhood.'

Uzma's mouth tightened. She didn't need reminders of her past.

'Think, aapa. You were sent away from home because your parents couldn't afford to feed you. And why was that? Because the system of jagirdari had crushed your peasant father. With no money left—'

'I was sent off to Iram Manzil because I was a *girl*!' Uzma spat out. Her chest heaving with emotion, she glared at Ali Hassan. 'When the drummer came to our village that summer, I was the liability my parents were happy to have taken off their hands. Not their precious sons, their old-age insurance.'

Uzma's eyes moistened at the memory that had sprung up after ages. Once a year, the drummer would go round the jagir, calling out for those who wished to give up their children, rounding them up for Iram Manzil. She was one in the cartload that was deloused upon arrival at the red-painted mansion. Her clothes burnt, she was bathed and clothed, and assigned her work. Labour for livelihood, life in the interstices.

Ali Hassan's Adam's apple was bobbing as he searched for ways to break the impasse. A parakeet was screeching above them now.

Uzma made to get up. Emily Perkins would begin searching for her.

'Aapa,' Ali tried to get her to stay.

'I'm happy where I am, Ali,' Uzma said softly.

'I'm glad things worked out.' Ali rose with her. 'But if they hadn't? What if your father was able to till his land without the chokehold of the jagirdar? He would never have had to send you away.'

Uzma folded her arms across her chest. 'But he did. And here I am. End of story.'

'But don't you want things to change?'

'Why should I care?'

A commotion sounded. They turned their heads. At the stairs leading up to the grand entrance, a scuffle had broken out. Some men had surrounded the pamphleteer and were snatching his papers. Shouts rang out.

'*Long live, King Usman! No pact with India! No, no, no!*'

Ali Hassan glanced from the commotion to Uzma, hopping on his toes. 'You should care, aapa, for the little Uzmas still out there.' Saying which, he sped off towards the pink stone monument, a moth hurtling towards light.

15
Hyderabad (October 1947)

The weather had cooled down enough to leave the bedroom window ajar. With luck, a breeze from the lake would add splendidly to the comfort. Walter and Biddy had retired to bed with that plan; Walter, particularly, needed a restful sleep after the relentless back and forth between Delhi and Hyderabad. Now, they were close to reaching an agreement, which both the Nizam and the Indians were ready to sign on. Amen.

Their peaceful slumber was sundered by a tumult of voices, a shrill din that rose from the street in front of Lake View, ballooning into a downright racket as it poured through the open window. Walter and Biddy sat up in bed, Biddy wondering if she was back in London during the Blitz. Walter reached for his glasses on the bedside table and, thrusting the round-framed spectacles on, padded to the window. A throng of men clustered at the gate, arms flailing, throats rippling. In the dark, he tried to ascertain their number – it was growing steadily.

On a shake of his head, he latched the window shut, muffling the noise, and drew the curtains. The foreboding he had been carrying with him was a tart taste on his tongue.

'It's 3 a.m.!' Biddy exclaimed, as if there was a proper time when such things ought to be conducted.

'Do you want to go back to bed, love? This racket will stay.'

Biddy shrugged one shoulder. 'Beastly hour. What time do you fly to Delhi?'

'Never.'

Walter rubbed his unshaven jaw, wrestling with the tiny bristles as the dismal realization dawned upon him. 'I don't think I'll be flying to Delhi, Biddy. The,' he swivelled his eyeballs towards the window, 'reception committee outside is meant to ensure that.'

Biddy's hand flew to her mouth in alarm. Walter joined her on the bed, one foot on the floor. She plucked the hand that was resting on his thigh and folded it between hers. 'I'm sorry, love. At dinner yesterday, when you were lost in thought, I'd asked if it was the curry, and you'd said no. What niggled you was why the Nizam had delayed affixing his signature on the agreement two days in a row.'

Walter sighed. 'Yesterday, he checked the agreement personally in the presence of his delegation. *Again*. Yet, he promised to sign it today morning and have it sent to me by 8 a.m., so we could leave for Delhi by air at 8.30 a.m. Not the best solution, but acceptable. Finally, I consoled myself, the Nizam is being realistic. He realizes how vulnerable Hyderabad is … and this is the best he can hope to get from India … But the one condition to the agreement? Immediate acceptance. To be signed, sealed, and delivered to Dickie Mountbatten today, Monday, 27 October.'

Biddy's eyes widened. 'Which is why the crowd at our doorstep. To prevent you from leaving!'

⁓

Walter instructed Biddy to telephone Christopher Brunyate of Coward Chance, the firm of solicitors working with Walter on the Nizam's behalf. When he didn't answer, she rang Brigadier Gilbert, the chief of staff of the Hyderabad Army. Reinforcements would arrive within half an hour. Meanwhile, the brigadier would give orders to the military guards and police at Lake View to fire if anyone dared enter the compound. Thereafter, Biddy rang for Anthony. The servant arrived with tea soon enough and withdrew to draw Walter a bath.

Morning tea was on the balcony normally, with its restful vistas of terraced gardens and the abundant blue of the Hussein Sagar shimmering in the sun rays. Walter and Biddy sipped their Darjeeling to the uneven chorus of protesters. 'I've known the man for ten years ... You'd think it gets easier. The medieval intrigue that hangs in his court isn't anything like the stratagems of European courts ... It's sheer rascality, of the kind,' he tilted his head, 'we are witnessing outside.'

As the wartime commander of the women's services in India, Biddy had learnt a thing or two about India. She had had a tough time with recruitment, coming up against restrictions she'd never considered – of caste and community. Castes did not mix, and Indian women did not mix with men, socially or at work. So Biddy had turned to the Anglo-Indians to operate the women's auxiliary corps. The Nizam had turned to Walter for superior advice, but his community appeared to have other ideas ...

Biddy nibbled on an Osmania biscuit, the buttery flavour so reminiscent of shortbread. 'How would you describe your relations with the Nizam?'

Walter was about to pour himself another cup. Abandoning that, he sat upright, put on a sombre face and began to speak like a doctor. 'The prognosis, I'm afraid, is not good. The client appears to be a difficult child with suicidal tendencies. He might have asked for a solicitor, but what he really needs is a nurse ... whose main task is to prevent or postpone the suicide.' Calmly, Walter resumed pouring tea as Biddy guffawed into her teacup.

⁓

Walter had a leisurely shave, then bathed. Through the windows, he kept an eye on the throng outside. It had multiplied. As the light grew, he saw men jostling against the gates as if on a tide, throwing themselves periodically against the boundary walls of Lake View, and being pushed back by guards with sticks. What unnecessary melodrama!

Walter was trying not to be bitter, but his estimate of the Nizam had plumbed. A stray remark from an ex-resident came to mind – 'His tactics resemble those of an octopus: to smother his opponent in a cloud of inky fluid ...' Harsh, but valid. The Nizam was a master of obfuscation. The ungainly display of force outside could not occur without Osman Ali Khan's concurrence. The goons outside were definitely Razakars, sent to Lake View on Kasim Razvi's orders. A call, like that of a muezzin, rode the air. Walter peered outside. Daybreak. One of the men had given a call to prayer. As he watched, the men dropped to the ground as a single unit, bowed their heads, and started to pray.

Two lorries packed with sepoys arrived from Brigadier Gilbert. Walter and Biddy were escorted out of Lake View by grinning soldiers who had seen action in Burma and were amused by the theatrical display of force on the street. The soldiers rode in front, smiling, bayonets sticking out of the lorries, as they ferried the Moncktons to Brigadier Gilbert's house.

Gilbert informed Walter that the men who had staged the protest at Lake View had done the same at the residences of the Prime Minister, Nawab of Chhatari, and of Sir Sultan Ahmed. All on the orders of Kasim Razvi, who had decided upon direct action after hearing of the agreement being sent to Delhi.

'A coup d'état.' Walter nodded grimly.

As Biddy conversed with the hostess, Walter took a walk to clear his head. The morning was crisp still, the susurrus of daytime had not drowned out birdsong. Because of slanders against him, he had earlier resigned from the Nizam's negotiating committee. It appeared his role as the Nizam's adviser was coming to an end as well. This coup had demonstrated what Lord Mountbatten, V.P. Menon and Mr Patel had stoutly maintained throughout the negotiations: The Nizam is *not* the master in his own state.

A patch of red canna lilies caught his eye, bringing with it a snatch of a prior conversation ... something the resident had said about 'tropical swiftness' ... the pace of things ... The Nizam might stay cooped up in his ivory tower of King Kothi within his manufactured reality, but the ill-will from rest of India would buffet him soon enough.

An excessively mean and squalid little room with two decrepit swivel chairs floated into his mind. Peshi office. Where HEH, owner of several splendid palaces, insisted on conducting daily meetings. The only other furnishings in the Nizam's Peshi office were piles of dusty letters and documents, one wooden cupboard and an assortment of cobwebs. Tea, when it arrived, was accompanied by one single biscuit. Unconsciously, Walter pressed the small of his back, which ached at the end of every meeting.

He drew himself upright and breathed in the air. He would give the Nizam one final chance to disown Razvi. Failing which, time to resign and get back to Blighty.

Biddy beckoned him from a first-floor balcony. Looking forward to a full English breakfast, Walter took the steps two at a time. Gilbert's living room was airy and spacious, the air chiming to the tinkle of cutlery. Walter felt simultaneously light and lugubrious.

16
Hyderabad (October 1947)

The Nizam was aggravated, tapping his crooked stick to some internal turbulence. Before the stick snapped, sending the ruler into a paroxysm about what the newspapers were calling the 'October coup', he decided he must put the ruler's mind at rest. Kasim Razvi cleared his throat. He had taken care not to sit. The Nizam was a stickler for propriety and generally preferred to be the only one sitting or smoking. Razvi's standing position confirmed to the Nizam that he was in charge.

'Your Excellency,' Razvi said, 'India is occupied. Their troops flew into Kashmir yesterday. Very good for us because their attention is diverted. Why should we not use this window that has newly opened, to renegotiate?'

'Hunh!' The Nizam snorted loudly before eyeing Razvi sideways. 'Jinnah was blindsided.'

Razvi listened attentively.

'When you met Jinnah yesterday, he was still thinking he would be able to control Kashmir and Hyderabad, eh? Two of the richest kingdoms in the Quaid's pockets, Pakistan secured

... So he thought. Now look: India has Srinagar, India has Kashmir.'

Razvi kept his voice calm to counter the Nizam's shrillness. 'Your Excellency, Mr Jinnah is a friend of Hyderabad—'

'Of the Ittehad, you mean!'

'The Ittehad was born to serve the cause of Hyderabad. And with India's independence, the Ittehad's role has only grown. We Muslims rule because we are more fit to rule! But Hindu India doesn't want to accept that basic fact. So the Ittehad must rally to defend the Asaf Jahi kingdom for generations to come.'

Osman Ali Khan contemplated Kasim Razvi before turning his head away. Would Ittehad-ul-Muslimeen be able to cancel out the Pir's prophecy that the Asaf Jahi rule would end after seven generations? Through scheming and cunning and cross-border alliances ... Certainly, Jinnah was willing to lend an ear to them. Just yesterday, he had met Ittehad emissaries in Lahore and counselled them that the Nizam must not sign any agreement with India. Obviously, that was in Pakistan's interest. What was an infant nation's first need? Money! Which Hyderabad could provide. But the Quaid had underestimated India ...

'The signed agreement was to reach Delhi today. WHAT is to stop Patel from sending troops into Hyderabad tomorrow?' The Nizam finished with a flourish of his stick in Razvi's direction.

Kasim Razvi threw his head back and laughed. 'The Dominion of India cannot afford a war on two fronts. Patel and Nehru can't manage Delhi right now. Refugees from Panjab are arriving by the trainload. From what I hear, the capital of India is looking like Kurukshetra!' Razvi slapped his hands together. 'Then, there is the Junagadh trouble. And Kashmir will take a long time because Pakistan isn't going to roll over and let India walk all over it!'

Nehru and Patel, the devils! Osman felt an urge to smoke. He reached for the crushed packet of Charminar on the centre table, which wore a thin rain of ash and stains of coffee, found one last cigarette, lit it and puffed hungrily. The devils spoke of democracy, of fair play, then why not allow Hyderabad to sign a Standstill Agreement with Pakistan as well?

'India is weak,' Razvi was continuing, 'why should we sign anything with them right now? Let them come with a begging bowl, then we see. Azad Hyderabad rahega, Lal Quila par chalega!' Razvi beamed as he slipped into his street-protestor mode.

The Nizam grabbed his stick and banged it hard against the floor. 'Where do you THINK you are? WHAT behaviour is this?'

Razvi bowed deep. The Nizam was a boy in a lion's costume. Kasim Razvi must look appropriately fearful of Hyder, the Lion. But he must not forget the boy within, who could not be reasoned with, but needed direction and counsel and eulogies.

'Your Excellency, forgive me for I got carried away. But my blood boils that yesterday's jailbirds think they can harass noble princes! Here in Hyderabad, we have a royal line of three centuries blessed by Allah. The rogue Indian government can't lord over us. Our plans are bigger, more ambitious. The foamy waves of the Bay of Bengal shall soon caress the feet,' he paused to catch the growing gleam in the Nizam's eyes, and started to rack up the appellations, 'of our beloved Rustom-i-Dewan, Arastu-i-Zamon, Lieutenant General, Muzaffar-al-Mulk, Wal-Mumaik, Fateh Jung Sippah Salaar Mir Osman Ali Khan Bahadur Nizam-ul-Mulk, Asaf Jah. The waters of the Arabian Sea shall wet the golden sandals of our beloved Nizam. The sacred Asaf Jahi flag shall fly over the ramparts of the Red Fort at Delhi.'

The vision was impressive, Osman agreed inwardly, but wasn't the clever Razvi trying to distract him from more pressing issues?

'Walter Monckton is threatening to resign!'

'Which will be a gift just in time for Hyderabad Day! I would like to tell our people on 1 November that, inshallah, Hyderabad will remain independent.'

'AND the Nawab of Chhatari!' the Nizam thundered on. 'The Razakars went too far, TOO far this morning.'

Razvi gave a beatific smile. 'Your Excellency, *your* Razakars showed great discipline. Not one act of violence. A peaceful protest – one even Gandhi would approve of,' he sniggered. 'And it got us result. The agreement is the death of Hyderabad. We will now reopen negotiations in what are more favourable conditions. With one leg in Kashmir, India can hardly stand upright in Delhi! Time to dissolve the old delegation and appoint a new one. One that will forcefully press Hyderabad's case and not prostrate at the feet of *Lord* Mountbatten like *Sir* Walter did.'

The Nizam glowered at Razvi. 'Watch your tongue! Hyderabad has been a "Faithful ally of the British Government" … The substantial contribution we made to the war effort granted them victory.'

'Exactly! And yet, where is the special consideration Hyderabad deserves from the British?'

Razvi's eyes were challenging the Nizam. The forty-four-year-old graduate from Aligarh, a lawyer by profession, knew he was on solid ground. The British were a perfidious people who had ruled in India by coddling the princes while extracting wealth for themselves. Their treachery in Awadh was legendary. Wealthy Awadh, with its control of the Doab, the fertile plain between the Ganga and Jumna, was looted by the East India

Company to finance the Raj. And the Raj's stranglehold over Hyderabad was as old as the Asaf Jahs, the British resident overseeing the process of succession from the time of Asaf Jah II. In effect, the Nizams paid the British to lord over them. What was the popular British inside joke? *Poor Nizzy pays for it all!* Now the British had left and the ex-Viceroy had cozied up to the dung worshippers!

Osman Ali Khan blew smoke to the ceiling. He knew what Razvi was alluding to. Mountbatten was paying no attention to Hyderabad's special status, browbeating Sir Walter even. When he had issued the firman of Hyderabad's independence, the Hyderabad State Congress had counter-attacked him, claiming that the right to determine the relationship of Hyderabad with India belonged to the people, not the Nizam. Tirtha, its president, had asked for a plan of action against the firman! That ungrateful wretch! He was running free because of the Nizam's charitable nature. But the Ittehad, under Razvi's leadership, had supported his firman and protested soundly in the streets! Razvi was a scoundrel, but a useful one. Osman rounded upon him angrily.

'WHAT is your suggestion? Considering,' he slapped his thigh, 'your little meeting with Jinnah didn't pay off exactly?'

Kasim Razvi probed his wispy beard. Jinnah's portrait hung in his office. The Quaid had succeeded in creating a separate homeland for Muslims; he was an inspiration. Razvi hoped he could do something similar for Hyderabad's Muslims ... The Nizam was handy in such an enterprise. Ittehad's slogans said it best: Free Hyderabad for Hyderabadis! Long Live King Osman! The Nizam's desire to be in control was a garden that Razvi tended to with great care. An idea that he wanted implemented, he seeded in the Nizam's mind days in advance. He nurtured it with whispers, guided it with cues and, when the moment arrived, the Nizam announced the selfsame idea like it had sprung from HEH's mind.

'Mr Jinnah's advice is sound: We don't give an inch. No agreement to be signed for the time being. Let's watch India settle the issue of Kashmir.'

The Nizam nodded his head in synchrony with his tapping stick.

'Mr Monckton, Your Excellency will agree, was not demonstrating enough ambition for Hyderabad. As per the agreement he negotiated, we will not be at liberty to purchase arms. And we will need the consent of the Government of India to increase the size of the Hyderabad Army? Why, I ask? How do we defend ourselves?'

Razvi paused. The Nizam held onto a glowing stub and inhaled deeply. Razvi tried not to show his disdain. Given a free hand, he would rip down the heavy curtains of the airless room, throw open the windows and set the entire palace staff to scrubbing the floor. Then he would march the Nizam to his weekly bath – Nawab Deen Yar Jung, who met HEH daily, quipped that the incessant smoking did not mask His Excellency's body odour – attire him in a new sherwani and fez, and take him on a victory ride through Hyderabad on 1 November, showering ashrafis on people who hailed, 'King Osman! King Osman!'

The Nizam stubbed out his cigarette. 'NEW agreement, NEW delegation!' He flounced around in his chair.

Razvi's eyes flashed. Monckton and Chhatari had to resign, having failed to deliver the agreement to Delhi. 'Exactly! We need new men to negotiate for Hyderabad. Men unafraid of any sarkar – British or Hindu.'

Razvi massaged his beard. Of such suitable men, the Ittehad-ul-Muslimeen had several.

17
Delhi (October 1947)

Along the banks of the Ravi river, one of the five that merge into the Indus, sits Gurdaspur. In 1947, little distinguished the district from other nondescript Panjabi ones. But, like the alluvial plains on which it lay, several substrata of history undergirded it.

Nanak, the founder of Sikhism, married into a Gurdaspur family. After his peregrinations, which took him from Mecca to Nepal preaching the oneness of man, he settled on the northern bank of the Ravi in 1515, ploughing the fields and setting up a revolutionary kitchen for all: the langar. It was where he breathed his last. Muslims regard him their Pir, Sikhs their first Guru, and Hindu households raised their first sons as Sikhs. Guru Nanak changed the course of the subcontinent.

Near the southern bank of the river, a brick platform – dusty, unadorned – stands amidst fields. They call it Takht-i-Akbari. Hastily constructed in 1556, it is the spot where one of India's greatest emperors (to be) was crowned by Bairam Khan, the regent nervous at the untimely death of Humayun and its ominous repercussions for the nascent Mughal empire. The thirteen-year-old boy-King would go on to such success that historians routinely refer to him as Akbar, the Great. Jalaluddin Muhammad Akbar changed the course of Indian history. For an insight into him, you must skip the splendours of Agra and the ruins of Delhi, and trek to Gurdaspur, instead, where it all began.

Nestled at the foothills of the Himalayas, its mango orchards and cool breezes made Gurdaspur the summer residence of favour of Ranjit Singh, the Lion of Panjab, who established the first Sikh empire in 1799. Beating back the Afghans, he reclaimed the precious Kohinoor from a Durrani scion, kept the British at bay, and restored the Golden Temple. With his secular, liberal outlook – a Muslim wazir, French and Italian army generals, a no-conversion policy, generous grants to temples – the Maharaja established a modern empire of toleration.

In 1947, on 17 August, as the Radcliffe Line became public, Gurdaspur shot to fame again. A subdivision of Lahore under the British, with a narrow Muslim majority, Gurdaspur might well be deemed Pakistani. Along with another narrow Muslim-majority district of Ferozepur. But a slight complication ...

Amritsar sat in the middle of Gurdaspur in the north and Ferozepur to the south. Whatever Radcliffe knew or didn't, he was aware that Amritsar was the Sikhs' Vatican. If he gave Gurdaspur to Pakistan, Amritsar would be encumbered by Pakistan on east, west and north. If he gave Ferozepur to Jinnah, Amritsar would be in Pakistan's palm in the south. Even ex-Viceroy Wavell, in his prospective plan for Pakistan in February 1946, had assigned Gurdaspur along with Amritsar to India.

In the end, Radcliffe gave Gurdaspur to the Sikhs, thereby offering to India the possibility of Kashmir. Because the only tract connecting Kashmir to India passed through the slim neck of Gurdaspur. And, once again, history changed course in the ancient alluvium.

∽

Jawaharlal Nehru, a Kashmiri Brahmin, was a product of a mixed Hindu–Muslim culture. You could say he was its secular embodiment. Ten generations prior, his ancestors had descended to the plains of United Provinces from Kashmir. Yet, the Himalayas kept their hold on him. During his jail term in Dehradun, with no interviews, no visitors, even when he could not see the Himalayas from his cell, he was comforted by them. They looked down upon him with the wisdom of a million years, mocked at his varying humours and soothed his fevered mind.

Late September 1947, Jawaharlal consented to plebiscite on Junagadh to Liaquat Ali Khan in the presence of Dickie Mountbatten. Liaquat jumped at the chance, aware that similar terms would apply to Kashmir. Vallabhbhai responded that a plebiscite in Kashmir was conditional on one for Hyderabad.

Jinnah, ballistic at the Radcliffe Award, had put Junagadh to play, but the pawn didn't work as planned. When volunteers of the Arzi Hukumat government entered the state, the Nawab decamped to Pakistan with the state treasury. The parlous food situation that followed forced Dewan Shah Nawaz Bhutto to request Samaldas Gandhi to take over governance. Stung, Jinnah then began a blockade of essential goods to Kashmir, since those usually arrived via western Panjab. Vallabhbhai, earlier indifferent to the notion of Maharaja Hari Singh acceding to Pakistan, had been incensed by Pakistan's acceptance of Junagadh's accession. He sent crews to make a motorable road from Gurdaspur to Kashmir, one that would traverse the tributaries of the Ravi and climb 9,000 feet to the Banihal Pass. Meanwhile, Srinagar airport was equipped with wireless equipment to increase its viability in the coming winter.

Maharaja Hari Singh, however, with royal hubris, wanted both the head and tail of the accession coin: to join India, but not relinquish any of his privileges. Jawaharlal insisted that the Maharaja release Sheikh Abdullah as a first step towards establishing a popular government. Jinnah – damn due process – had already despatched Kabailis, a legion of rough-and-tumble Pashtuns from the North West Frontier Province region of Pakistan, who were making their way into India along much the same trail used by past invaders such as Alexander in 325 BC: following the course of the Kabul river, crossing the Indus to enter Taxila, 20 miles northwest of Rawalpindi. Under the onslaught of the Pathan guerrillas, the Maharaja's army crumbled. On 24 October, a desperate Hari Singh sent an envoy to India with two letters: a plea for help and an accession to India. That evening, Srinagar plunged into darkness. Kabailis had seized the power station on the city's outskirts. Srinagar could fall any moment.

In Delhi, Jawaharlal convened an urgent meeting of the Defence Committee to consider Hari Singh's twin requests. Barely two months after Independence, the first Indo-Pak war had begun. And the subcontinent would never be the same again.

∽

What started in the Himalayan kingdom in 1947 is reverberating to this day.

The story of Kashmir is ancient and current, layered and complex, deep and unsettling. It needs all the love and care and attention to detail a storyteller can possibly give. What the story deserves, in the least, is its own book. That is my promise to you, dear reader.

So, for now, we return to Hyderabad and the Nizam and his ongoing mushaira with India ...

18
Delhi (November 1947)

The Map Room was really a War Room.

For waging a war on the ongoing crisis. Through information, plans, conferences. All available walls in the room were papered over with maps, most tables dotted with telephones, many unmanned. Full staff was yet to arrive. General Pete Rees, who had won his chops in Burma, was heading the Military Emergency Staff. A few of his former subordinates – two British officers and four Indian – had also arrived. As had Pamela, who was doing her first 'job' that Daddy had suggested. Answering telephones, compiling lists and notes, sending messages – being, in essence, the general dogsbody.

Work was from 9 a.m. to 1 p.m. and 2 p.m. to 6 p.m., including Sundays. Her fingers were a wee sore from typing and Pamela was looking forward to lunch hour. Mummy had the entire estate on rations and really, between spam and bully beef, Pamela was happy to give both a miss at lunch. A leisurely walk was what she had in mind. The sky was blue with nary a cloud and a prickly sun.

She would have to get lucky to find a shaded path to walk on, the estate was housing so many refugees who just kept pouring in from Panjab ... Panditji and Mr Patel kept clashing over the refugee crisis; Daddy was struggling to contain the violence while Mummy was tearing around hospitals arranging guards, food—

A chaprassi in scarlet-and-white uniform greeted her with both hands in a wordless namaste.

'Shamsher Singh,' Pamela inclined her head. 'I've been meaning to meet you. How is your niece doing?'

Raising his hands skywards, the chaprassi said, 'By god's grace, Miss Sahib, Pammi is ... better ... than when you saw her.'

Shamsher Singh had been expecting relatives from Lahore. But Partition had upset his plans terribly and it appeared that the family had perished in the Lahore riots. Except for the oldest daughter, who had found her way to a refugee camp where Pamela had ended up meeting her. That coincidence, a miracle almost, had led to Pammi uniting with her uncle.

'It's only been a few days,' Pamela said encouragingly. When faced with situations beyond her, she found herself mimicking Mummy, which was not bad by half. 'Perhaps I can meet her?'

As the chaprassi looked uncertain, Pamela showed the purse she clutched in her left hand. 'It's my lunch hour and I have some ointments she could use.'

With the Map Room keeping her busy, Pamela had not been able to the visit the clinic where she volunteered. Viceroy's House, now Government House, had a large staff, and a school and a clinic therefore for the families. Both were under the Vicereine's office and Pamela was a regular, but with the curfew there were very few patients.

Shamsher Singh seemed to swallow a lump in his throat. Next, he extended his right arm for Pamela to proceed, and followed one step behind.

⁂

She had found herself some shade. In the covered porch of Shamsher Singh's tiny house where a bountiful money plant's tentacles framed one arch. Pamela and Pammi sat on two rope chairs, a low wooden table between them. On the table were glasses of tea, a plate of samosas and another of a sticky brown sweet. Pamela's unexpected arrival had sent Shamsher Singh's house into a tizzy. His wife had rustled up the spread and his children crouched behind the doorway, spying. Food was in short supply and Pamela felt guilty, but Shamsher Singh had insisted the girls eat.

'Go ahead,' Pamela urged in Hindustani as she held up the savoury plate to Pammi. 'Take one, otherwise I can't.'

Hesitantly, Pammi took one samosa which then sat cupped in her hands in her lap. She looked wan and listless but washed, and was dressed in a fresh salwar kameez, which was two sizes too large for her, and a wool shawl. The long sleeves kept her arms covered, shielding from view the vile items that had been tattooed on Pammi's arm. The one she was scrubbing determinedly when Pamela had encountered her. To chase away that horrible image, and to encourage Pammi to eat, Pamela tucked into a samosa. By god, it was delectable! After meagre, repetitious meals of minced beef, the fried pastry with spiced potatoes was pure heaven. The battle between guilt and desire was settled. 'Go on!' Pamela urged as she licked her lips.

Pammi glanced up, then took a small bite.

After wiping her hands on a kerchief, Pamela removed some ointments from her purse. 'These will help with the cuts and bruises.' She placed them on the side of the table near Pammi who glanced up at them briefly. Her right eye was half shut, the eyelid purplish. A crow flapped to the porch entrance, and a child darted out and chased it away. Just as quickly, the boy dashed back to his post behind the door. Pamela grinned. Pammi, meanwhile, had swallowed her pastry.

'Fancy a walk, Pammi?'

Shamsher Singh followed them at a discreet distance, keeping Miss Sahib and his niece in sight. Pamela understood his nervousness, the estate was teeming with refugees and there had been one stabbing incident. At the Mughal Gardens, the chaprassi took leave. Pamela had a quarter of an hour left. She promised to bring some books for Pammi to read the next time. Bright-yellow chrysanthemums made for a happy splash as they walked. At least Pammi's head had stopped examining the ground. The extensive gardens had caught her attention as she gazed at the geometric flower beds, the water fountains, the endless stretch of green grass—

A commotion made the women swivel their necks. A gardener with long shears in one hand was waving his other arm at something. Or someone. As the women neared the scene, they sighted a grubby man standing in a pool of pink beneath a bougainvillea tree, gesticulating at the branches laden with flowers. Some of the other gardeners had also arrived at the spot now.

'What's the matter?' Pamela asked.

Sighting her, the workers bowed and looked to each other before one of them spoke up. 'Miss Sahib, this man here break into Mughal Gardens ... and just speak to trees.'

'S-*peak*?'

'Ji, huzoor ... Miss Sahib ... speak–speak, all the time, to trees ... As if they are people. Tch! We remove him, he again return.' The gardener twirled an index finger at the side of his head before tossing his chin at the man beseeching the bougainvillea. 'Mad.'

Likely a refugee, from one of the tents on the estate. As Pamela wondered how she could help, Pammi had moved closer to the man who was carrying on his monologue without any heed to the audience he had gathered. Her left arm extended, she mumbled something, then spoke louder. 'BELI Ram?'

The man swung his head around as if whiplashed. His eyes grew wide, his mouth opened, the words retracted. Dressed in a filthy kurta and loose pyjama, his hair spiked with dust, he was a picture of grime. But a smile was splitting his face. Which made Pammi light up hesitantly. Like when the early morning rays crept into a dark room. As the man blundered towards her, the gardener with the shears shouted and lurched. Pink petals floated from the bougainvillea tree. The man clutched Pammi's outstretched hand. Big fat teardrops spilled on his face, cutting clear tracks through the grime.

∾

'Bapuji,' Pammi repeated, 'Bapuji', as if it were a mantra, her mouth wobbling, her face swollen, her eyes blank. Tears escaped every now and then. She would embalm their charred bodies with her tears ... Bapuji, Narinder, Surinder.

Bapuji wouldn't flee Laur without his beloved Pammi, Beli Ram had recounted in a quiet voice. What Beli Ram didn't know was that Bapuji had forbidden her from leaving home. But she had ... she had disobeyed her father ... and she had killed her family – serious scholarly Surinder, naughty Narinder, whom she had raised after Mataji passed away and Bapuji became their mother. Bapuji with his gentle eyes and soothing hands and soft voice and patient loving ways ... no more.

'Let's ...' Beli Ram urged as he led her towards a fountain, 'let's wash your face.'

The white memsahib had questioned how they knew each other. Beli Ram was a coolie at Laur Junction, he had explained, where Kishan Singh was a railway clerk. Satisfied, she had left Pammi in his care with instructions to the gardeners to let them linger. Moistening one end of her chunni in the water, Beli Ram dabbed Pammi's eyes and cheeks gingerly, then let go and stood by awkwardly. In the distance, a bird chaser yodelled as he swung a large cloth. Encountering Pammiji was the stuff of his dreams, something Mehmood took great pleasure teasing him about. Now look. Here they were, together, but each yearning to go back to Laur of old ...

'Nobody goes back!'

Beli Ram whirled around. In the gulmohar tree, a woman had thrust out an arm and was shaking her hand at him, her bangles clinking. He hurried to talk to her.

'I've been here for 200 years, ever since Nadir Shah's qatl-e-aam. Nadir Shah, don't know? Another invader. His soldiers killed so many people that corpses carpeted the streets. On that cursed night, I died in childbirth. Since then, I have made my home in the trees. Not just me,' she swept her arm, 'you can see the others.'

Sure enough he could. He was getting to know them, the women in the trees, some in salwar kameez, some in lehengas, some in sarees, some brazen, some modest ... They spoke to him, relieved there was someone on ground who could hear them. Some had been in the trees for so long they spoke a different tongue which Beli Ram didn't understand. Still, they spoke. Other refugees were calling him mad. But even in Laur he could see the churail in the big banyan tree in their gali when no one else did. And the night Mehmood rode him out, Beli Ram saw Billo too had ascended the banyan. What did the gardeners and other folks know? He had to get back to Laur. Then he would tell Mehmood about all the churails he had met. Mehmood would believe him. The only other person who would believe him was the old woman who had scolded the men in the kafila. What had she said …?

What do you expect? All those women who have died giving birth to Pakistan! They squeezed it out of their bodies, didn't they? Now their souls are strung on the trees of Panjab …

Not just Panjab. If Beli Ram met her, he would tell the matriarch that women's souls were strung in Dilli too—

A hand on his elbow startled him. 'Beli Ram?'

Pammiji was by his side, watching him.

Beli Ram waved a reassuring hand. 'I'm okay. See, see there … You see?' He indicated the woman in the gulmohar who was sticking her tongue out. 'No need to be rude,' he scolded her.

'Beli Ram,' Pammi asked with concern, 'whom are you talking to?'

Beli Ram exhaled like a balloon deflating. 'You don't see them either?'

As they walked back to Shamsher Singh's house, Beli Ram told Pammi of his ability to converse with churails. Since leaving Laur, he had frequently sighted churails perched in trees. Some spots though were thick with them, Dilli the densest. He asked the churails why. They snorted and called him an innocent. 'Know how many Kings and Sultans have fought over this city? And when men go to war, who do you think is the battlefield?' '*Who* or what?' Beli Ram had debated. 'Who!' the women thundered in unison, and answered: 'Us!' When Beli Ram still didn't get it, a kindly woman gave a lopsided smile and said: 'What are men but overgrown babies? When they go to war, it's women's bodies that form the battlefield.'

Beli Ram was going to make his way back to Laur soon. He intended to check out its trees. 'And I'd promised Mehmood, "I will meet you again, brother."' His face lit up at the prospect. 'But Pammiji, I will visit you before I leave.'

Pammi watched the bedraggled Beli Ram make his way back to the refugee tents. His waddle melted her heart. She recalled the late evening Beli Ram and Mehmood had jumped in to rescue her from the clutches of the Mozang gang and deposited her home. Before Laur caught fire.

19
Hyderabad (November 1947)

'You look like a boy,' Comrade Simha grunted.

There was no mirror, or glass even, where she could catch her reflection. Jaabili fingered the thin cotton pyjama, the kurta that reached mid-thigh, and glanced at the rubber slippers – the attire of a poor Hyderabadi boy. Her hair, a crinkly cloud she always had trouble pinning into braids, had been shorn short. Under the directions of Venkateswara Rao, the leader of the Sangham, Jaabili had spent two weeks learning how to be a courier. The disguise of a boy was an essential element. It helped that Jaabili was petite with 'a bosom flat as a palm leaf', as Salamma had added dryly. Jagan was her boy name.

Without Lalitha, messages from Hyderabad city had dried up. Besides, the local unit had some exciting news to share. So Jaabili was headed on her first mission, to a city she had only heard of, with a comrade who spoke via grunts. Jaabili was convinced he either didn't like her or was unconvinced of the potential that the Sangham leader and Salamma saw in her. Jaabili had no option but to trudge behind Comrade Simha

through the forest, halt when he raised a fist, hitch a bullock
cart ride to Warangal, where they caught the late-night bus to
the city of the Nizam. Her package for delivery was in her waist
cloth covered by the kurta. Besides that, she had two other
items: sixteen annas and a sharp kitchen knife.

'Some money and a weapon for defence,' Venkateswara
Rao's guiding principle for couriers. She was still learning how
to fire a gun.

They reached Hyderabad as dawn lightened the sky. After
a quick trot through narrow lanes, where houses were stacked
like people in embrace, they stopped at a large wood door.
Comrade Simha struck the iron knocker in a distinct pattern:
tap-tap—tap—tap-tap. A while later, the door opened an inch,
an interior chain was removed and they trooped in. A courtyard,
around which a covered gallery ran, beyond which rooms lay
in shadows. The servant who had opened the door bowed and
waited. Simha headed straight for a room where the doors had
been taken off the frame. Jaabili followed.

Simha switched on a lamp. The room was occupied entirely
by a large machine. Dirty ink-stained rags were piled in one
corner. Tobacco and oil and ink, pungent enough that Jaabili
wrinkled her nose.

'Had a good journey?'

The deep voice startled her. As Jaabili whirled around,
Comrade Simha hailed, 'Lal salaam!'

The man in the doorway was dressed in a rumpled version
of her own clothes, all white unlike her mud-coloured pair. He
ran a hand through his messy hair as he greeted Simha and
took her in. 'We have a visitor,' he acknowledged with a slight
raise of his brows. His cheeks were like the hills of Warangal.
Jaabili didn't realize she was staring until Simha had occupied

the space between them and was saying, 'Jagan, this is Daniyal Khan; you have a package for him.'

Jaabili started, reaching for her waist cloth.

'Ja-gan,' the man called Daniyal was drawling as Simha explained, 'Jagan is our new courier for Hyderabad. First mission; Rao is checking he—him out.'

The package in hand, Jaabili held it out to Daniyal, who took it with a nod of his head. 'Tea,' he said, and led the way to a porch where wooden chairs were arranged around a table and an upholstered sofa in faded velvet ranged against a wall. Comrade Simha headed to the toilet. Daniyal indicated a chair and Jaabili sat down tentatively. Daniyal sat across from her and began opening the package. The house seemed strange: It had the grand size of Jagirdar Reddy's mansion, but the shabby air of a labourer's dwelling. Even the man, Daniyal, looked like he would fit better in a sherwani and dastar rather than the commoner's attire. Somehow, he looked *not*-common. His uncombed hair was not coarse like Rao's; his ink-stained fingers browsing the book that was in the package were long; his moustache was like the tipped wings of a hawk in flight—

'Why *Jagan?*' he asked, looking up suddenly from the book.

'Hunh,' Jaabili licked her lips. She had been caught staring twice. And was her disguise such a failure?

'What's your real name?' 'Don't I look a boy?' They spoke at the same time.

Daniyal laughed, throwing his head back. 'I will pretend I was taken in,' he paused and looked into her eyes, 'by the disguise.'

'Jaabili,' she blurted out, registering an unfamiliar thudding in her heart.

'Jaabili … light of the full moon …'

'Is that so?' No one had told her that her name had a meaning.

Daniyal smiled. He showed her the book. It had the outline of a woman on a deep-red background. Why had Leader Rao sent this book? Was a book important enough to dispatch a courier from ten hours away?

'Can you read?' Daniyal enquired.

She shook her head. 'But I learnt the alphabet in my two weeks of training.' Jaabili angled her head. 'Am-ma,' she read aloud. For an important book, the title was rather simple.

Daniyal shrugged. 'The heroine in this book is uneducated as well.'

A rustle of feet. Tea and Comrade Simha arrived at the same time.

As they drank tea from glasses, Jaabili listened to Daniyal and Simha. Daniyal ran a printing press and published a bi-weekly newspaper in Urdu and Telugu, *Hyderabad Khabrien*. He supported the Sangham and was a nodal point for other sources in the city, many of whom were students.

'Two of them will be here soon. Meanwhile, I will go change. Jagan, Khudabax will show you the bathroom Lalitha used.'

Inside the bathroom – gusalkhana, he had used the Urdu word – Jaabili saw a half bucket of steaming water, a mug, a bar of soap that smelled like sandalwood and a folded towel on a low stool. A bottle which she didn't recognize – she peered at it: teeth were displayed on it. Hmm ... some cleaning powder. She cast a look around. Against the far wall was a latrine. Surprisingly, there was no smell, no odour of piss or shit or unbathed bodies. Just the smell of vapours and sandalwood. So far removed from the rationed water at the Sangham, or the once-weekly trek to a nearby stream for a bath back at home. The memory of home pricked her before she turned resolutely to the bucket. Squatting down, she cupped water and began to clean up.

∽

There were as many opinions as men.

They spoke a mix of Telugu and Urdu, and Jaabili blanked out several times – regular visits to Hyderabad would teach her Urdu – but would she figure out their varied allegiances, and what brought them together and yet kept them apart? Comrade Simha and Jaabili/Jagan were part of the Sangham, which was part of the Telangana Party, which was part of the Andhra Communist Party. Daniyal Khan was a supporter. He was Muslim, but the Red Flag did not care for religion. Raj Kumar, clean-shaven like a baby, was an Arya Samaji, who belonged to the state Congress, which was working with Red Flag against the Nizam and his Razakars. So far, so good. However, Ali Hassan, the student with the neck that bulged as if a chameleon was trying to escape, was a Communist, but the Hyderabad City Committee wanted Azad Hyderabad – they wanted the Nizam out, but they also wanted to keep India out. It was all so confusing!

But Jaabili knew better than to show her confusion. Keeping her face as smooth as buttermilk, she looked at each man as he spoke, trying to comprehend despite the alien words that were thrown like bombs: freedom, bourgeois, imperialism, hukumat, azaadi, barabari …

Raj Kumar, whose face was like a spice box of assorted emotions, was speaking with much passion about a recent firman from the Nizam. 'No entry for non-Muslims in Hyderabad! What does he think his subjects are? Only Muslims? The state of Hyderabad is majority Hindu.' He shook a furious head, his fair cheeks flush. 'The cheek!'

Raj Kumar also threw most of the Angla bombs, like 'the cheek' – what did *that* mean?

'Mulki/non-Mulki is a big issue in Hyderabad now,' Ali Hassan shrugged. 'Being a Hyderabad native is important.'

'But the Nizam is not preventing the entry of non-Mulkis,' Daniyal said as he blew out smoke from the cigarette in his left hand. 'Only non-Muslims.'

'Exactly!' Raj Kumar's arm slammed the air. 'I am sure Sardar Patel will have something to say to the Nizam about that. Has the Nizam forgotten that Hyderabad is surrounded by Hindustan? And now that the British have left India, it's time His Exalted Highness descends to ground.'

India, again! Jaabili had pieced together that Hindustan was India. And Sangham's big leader was the Communist Party of India. So, what was India? Purnali, her village, was part of Warangal, which was part of Hyderabad, which was part of India. The kingdom of India was bigger than the Nizam's kingdom even. Except after the Angla left, there would be no kingdom, only country. India.

Ali Hassan bunched his mouth. 'The Nizam is not going to yield. The Razakars are getting more weapons and,' he leaned forward and the entire circle closed in, 'the news is that he's going to give his violent pet dog a very long leash ...'

Pet dog. Who was this?

As the circle digested this revelation, Daniyal blew out a smoke ring before stubbing the cigarette on the brick floor. Raising a brow at Ali Hassan, he asked, 'Your new source?'

Ali Hassan nodded. 'Still new. But in such close proximity to the Nizam's household.' He pinched a thumb and index finger together.

'Okay.' Comrade Simha, who had sat listening, rubbed his hands together. 'Let's share the action reports and plans ahead, and then we can call it a day. Jagan here,' he indicated towards Jaabili, who sat to his right, 'should be kept very busy with news and messages between the city and Sangham. The Razakars have a lot of support in the city, and this is where the state Congress and Communist Party have decided to work together to force the Nizam to integrate with India. Ali Hassan,' he pointed his beefy hand at the student, 'our common struggle is first and foremost against the Nizam Nawab, to remove him from the throne, and to establish a people's democratic state in Hyderabad within the Union of India—'

'But,' Ali held up a hand, 'we have to be aware that will mean changing Nizam Nawab for Nehru Nawab and Company.' His jaw was set.

Comrade Simha rubbed his chin. 'That matter is for the city and state units of the party to discuss and reach an agreement. Meanwhile,' he scrunched up his dhoti, 'we have to discuss the upcoming satyagraha: the demonstrations being planned, the forest laws to break, the customs posts to be targeted for attack, Razakar camps to raid ...'

৵

The group disbanded that evening. Comrade Simha left to meet another agent in Moghalpura. Upon his return, Jaabili and he would undertake the previous night's journey in reverse. Daniyal Khan invited her to the room with the printing machine, where he started to work on the machine like a doting mother on her toddler. His long fingers were handy, she observed, as he fiddled with knobs and levers.

'So, what do you think?'

'Think?' Jaabili asked.

Wiping his hands with a rag, Daniyal asked, 'You ready for this kind of work? You are much younger than Lalitha, clearly, and have no prior experience. There is,' he frowned, searching for a word, 'there is violence in this line of work—'

'No more than what happens in villages daily.'

'Hmm ...' Daniyal flung the rag onto the pile in the corner. 'You're fourteen–fifteen years old—'

'Sixteen.' Jaabili crossed her arms.

'Right, sixteen. Lalitha was a mature woman, a courier for four years, very good at her job, and yet—'

'She was caught and tortured and killed,' Jaabili finished his sentence. 'I know. You think that is the only terrible thing that can happen to a woman? What about the women who get raped by landlords and Razakars? Who are thrashed for slow work? Whose wounds are treated with chilli powder? Who become sexual slaves as soon as they get their blood?'

Caught in her diatribe, Jaabili had marched right up to Daniyal Khan and was staring up at him from under his nose almost. 'Have you ever been to a village? Seen a village? Know adi bapa? I am the adi bapa gift that escaped and ran to the Sangham. I volunteered to join. I want the promise of the Red Flag: Equality and dignity.'

'Absolutely,' Daniyal said quietly.

A flustered Jaabili started to pace the floor. Daniyal Khan examined a sheet of printed paper. In the courtyard, birdsong sounded and then the azan call floated in the air. Jaabili noticed that he did not rush to answer the call to prayer. A series of knocks on the wood door sounded. Comrade Simha must have returned.

'Jaabili, contrary to the impression I might have given, I wish you good luck.'

She turned to face him. Her anger had evaporated. She liked the sound of her name from his mouth. Which was strange because it was the same name that she had been hearing all her life …

'Lalitha was a good courier. She took all precautions, kept track of her enemies, was handy with a gun … Someone ratted on Lalitha to the police.'

Rapid footsteps could be heard. Daniyal rested an elbow on the printing machine, leaned forward and spoke softly. 'There are rats in every field, Jaabili, red or not. Watch out for the rat.'

Interlude
Delhi (December 1947)

Vallabh's dash to Amritsar on 30 September to counsel, browbeat, cajole the Sikh leaders – did it turn the tide in Panjab? The Muslim kafila got safe passage. The Pakistanis reciprocated. The east–west trudge of humanity though persisted well into the winter of 1947. The 45-mile stretch between Lahore and Amritsar was the new Kurukshetra, littered with so many corpses that overfed vultures sat idly by as dogs chose to eat only the livers of human corpses.

Dickie's Emergency Committee grappled with the chaos that had erupted in Panjab and overtaken Delhi. Security on refugee trains improved, influenced perhaps by the rumour that guards who failed to fire on assailants would be court-martialled and shot thereafter. Certainly the defenestration of passengers declined.

Jawahar realized how close they were to losing Delhi. It was morally and practically right to maintain religious harmony, protect Muslims, and avert a full-blown war with Pakistan. Yet, those very policies made him unpopular. He criss-crossed the city, breaking up mobs, rescuing people, even as Congressmen looked the other way.

But what turned the tide, really? What force *could*?

In a land which owed its name to a body of water, the Indus, and its tributaries, shouldn't the answer be obvious? The Beas alone swelled from half a mile to over 9-miles wide. You didn't know? Then listen closely to what the rivers say ...

cho

Muslim-majority Pakistan and Hindu-majority India. One got the river, the other got the name. But what of the Indus? Was she asked what she wanted? To go east or west? Her colour preference – saffron or green? Did she like the crescent more than the spinning wheel? Did she, the mighty Indus, realize she was free but divided? More importantly, did she care?

That summer of 1947, the Indus shrank. She refused to spring out of the Lion's Mouth with her natural effervescence; the bountiful white streams – that the Rigveda gushed were akin to milk cows exuberant with their full udders – was reduced instead to a trickle. The waters that 3,000-year-old Sanskrit hymns proclaimed were mixed with milk and honey were weighed down instead with blood and corpses. That summer of 1947, the mighty Indus refused to feed the Indian Ocean, which therefore could not birth the annual monsoon. The brutal summer thus unleashed was one when the heat spared no one: not the Muslim fasting in the month of Ramzan, not the English judge poring over maps in his bungalow in order to partition the country, not the Mahatma fasting yet again to restore the harmony that seemed permanently lost, not the animals that were slaughtered so their meat could be flung at the doorsteps of non- and co-religionists as provocation.

But that constant sweating – the perspiration in furrowed brows wondering whether to stay or go, the moisture mingling with blood on hacked hands and hands that hacked, the dampness beneath Jawahar's white side cap, that lined the rim of Jinnah's karakul hat, as the sun blazed and baked and burned the countryside, stewing the air with offal and rotting flesh, leaching all of that most vital resource, more precious than gems when scarce – would not go waste. Water has memory, which is never diluted. Humans have the luxury of short-term memory, but water remembers what is added to it over time.

The Indus remembered the Homo Sapiens who first wandered out of Africa and, locating her abundant waters, settled by her banks. She nurtured them. The Aryans who composed hymns in her praise, calling her the unconquered Sindhu. She tried not to blush. The Persian emperor Darius, looking to add her fertile valley to his territory, sent his emissary Scylax, who was so befuddled by her bounty that he misread her course and concocted stories about her denizens with feet large enough to serve as umbrellas. She tried not to drown that callow fellow. When vain Alexander outflanked Porus and crossed her waters, she ignored him but listened as Greek philosophers quizzed Indian sages on her bank in a war of the minds after the war of might. The British sailed upriver to launch an assault on the Afghans, and lingered on for years thereafter. She let them irrigate her water and watched her soil spring forth with mustard and millet, cotton and corn, wheat and sugar. In Harappa and Mohenjodaro, the British archaeologists were excavating her layers to glean her ancient mysteries. She might yield some.

There were so many stories the Indus could tell, of the myriad people who had waded through her for the land to which she lent her name, Sindhu, which the Persians made

Hindu, and thereby, Hindustan. Of the sage Vyasa, who sat on the banks of one of her rivers and dictated the Mahabharata to his elephant-headed scribe. She named Beas after him. Of Sufi saints, who sang about her water perfumed with musk, her waves which yielded rubies. She let their shrines dot her banks. Of Nanak, who bathed in her waters. She enlightened him. Of Bullah, who was born where her five rivers met. She nourished him such that his poetry became the vernacular of the land. Oh, the stories she could tell!

But the one story she would not tell would be the story of pious provenance. Her land as the *Land of the Pure?* Pure hokum. Her land had birthed Hinduism and Sikhism, given home to Islam and Sufism; she knew how to sweep up everything in her embrace. So when they declared the birth of a new nation and got endlessly at each other's throats over matters hirsute and penile, she decided: *Enough.*

So in the autumn of 1947, from the Lion's Mouth in the snowy mountains, she, the mighty Indus, roared and sprang forth with fury. Her rivers – Jhelum, Chenab, Sutlej, Ravi, Beas – surged with water and overflowed their banks, the ice melt from the heat of the parched summer adding to the rains that had finally arrived. The deluge swept up material, defensive and offensive, mammals, two- and four-legged, irrespective of caste, colour, creed, community. She would show what an effective cleansing really looked like.

Man had forgotten his place in the scheme of things, disregarded duty, abandoned virtue, rejected dharma. When Vyasa composed the Mahabharata, he said his aim with the epic was to instil dharma in the heart of man. To remind him that as long as he respected his individual dharma, cosmic dharma would be maintained. When he forgot, a terrible rupture would occur.

The brutal summer of 1947, one of the hottest ever, ended with a deluge, one of the biggest ever. The frenzy of killing abated in the face of the new killer on the field – almighty, all secular. Men scrambled to find a dry elevated spot where the surging waters would be below neck-level, clinging on for dear life as the roaring rivers plucked them at random, tossing them together with string cots and upended cows, marching to the Indian Ocean, determined to deposit the detritus into the sea.

She, the mighty Indus, was doing what the Mahabharata had already foretold, 3,000 years ago: The dharma, when it is protected, protects. When it is destroyed, it destroys. Wasn't Hastinapur, the capital city of the Pandavas after they won the Great War of Kurukshetra, completely destroyed by a great flood?

20
Hyderabad (December 1947)

'What about Dulhan Pasha Begum? Can I meet her as well?'

Emily Perkins cast an eager glance at Eden Bagh as the car turned into King Kothi past the police posse. The home of the Nizam's first wife was located across from the Nizam's. But distance was not the issue.

Uzma wondered how to break the news, delicately, to the enthusiastic Emily – 'Please, no "Miss",' she had insisted – that the Nizam's wife was a crazy old coot. Who had threatened to poison her daughters-in-law, newly arrived from Turkey via France to their new home in Hyderabad! And it was not an empty threat.

Anyone acquainted with the Hyderabad court understood the sterling role poison had played in politics through seven generations of rule. The second Nizam came to power via a poisoned meal his mother fed to a rival. The great Salar Jung (I) collapsed after a meal of canned oysters, convenient to the British competing with the powerful dewan for the Nizam's attention. A British resident had even feared the current Nizam's sons – Azam and Moazzam – would out-poison each other! Uzma herself was brought to the Nizam's palace to be the poison-taster for the Nizam's younger daughter-in-law, Niloufer. Those early days of swallowing haleem or khobani ka meetha, hovering at death's door … Uzma rearranged her sari pleats, giving herself time to jettison the memory. She might not know the entire history of Hyderabad's poisonings, but she was well aware of Dulhan Pasha Begum's proficiency with poisons.

If the Prince Moazzam Jah, Niloufer's husband, was to be believed, his mother routinely experimented with deadly poisons. And since he was a poet, the famed Shajeeh of Hyderabad, whose nightly mushairas were the talk of the town, he spun a limerick in illustration.

The kitties of King Kothi, ever wondered where they went?
Itty-bitties ate potions, Dulhan Pasha's experiments.

Uzma gave an indulgent smile and said, 'That is up to begum sahiba.'

'Niloufer?' Emily Perkins swung her head to enquire. With her short hair the colour of faded grass, flat chest and even flatter hips, she cut an arresting picture, nevertheless. It wasn't because of her looks, Uzma had observed, but because of the confidence with which Emily strode the world – like that of a paigah male. A woman so self-assured was completely out of place, like a lily on a scrub. 'I guess there's a protocol to meet one's mother-in-law. Well, whatever.' Dismissing it, Emily marched into King Kothi like some nobleman.

Having delayed her departure from Hyderabad for on-field research, Emily Perkins was vigorously chasing her book. She was convinced that Hyderabad was sitting on a powder keg of momentous change and, if she managed to catch some of that live, her own novel about the upheaval would yield a Dickensian saga. 'It was the best of times, it was the worst of times' – already Emily could apply that iconic line from *A Tale of Two Cities* to a newly Independent India facing the refugee crisis of Partition. In Hyderabad, she could see multiple fissures – class: the Nizam and the aristocracy versus the peasant uprisings; religion: Hindu and Muslim, the basis of India's partition; residency: Mulki versus non-Mulki … *So* much dramatic potential!

Seeing her friend's very evident enthusiasm for the book, Niloufer had assigned Uzma to ferry Emily around and act as her chaperone-cum-attendant. The writer had set up a meeting with Nizam Nawab – why not meet in person the man holding independent India to ransom?

Meanwhile, Emily Perkins would never figure Uzma's enthusiasm for the book project. It gave her a chance to travel around Hyderabad, escorting Emily across the Nizam's palaces, and occasionally guiding her to places Uzma herself was keen to visit – Irani cafes. Where Uzma had caught up with Ali Hassan, who was desperate for any information she could provide about the Nizam.

'Spy, you mean?'

'But,' the Adam's apple at Ali Hassan's throat had bobbed, 'you need to recruit a spy within the Nizam's palace … Someone who has daily access to him, a chance to overhear things; someone essential, but unimportant. Any information from such a source would be valuable, on the Razakars, on the future course for Hyderabad, on what the Nizam is planning … Just anything, really.'

Since then, Uzma had been tussling with herself. Should she be contemplating such an act at all? It was treason against the Nizam. But Uzma didn't owe him anything. She had one patron alone, to whom she owed her loyalty: Princess

Niloufer. As for the Nizam, it was his feudal system that had robbed her of her home and made a bonded labourer of her. That had placed her in a system where nubile, young females were given opium after dinner to drug them to sleep. Sleep in which their bodies could be violated, no evidence left in the morning, except for a strange fatigue in the limbs, soreness in the privates, occasional bruises. But now and then, a mishap happened. A young girl would conceive, like Uzma had, and her body would need to be rid of the life that had sprung within her belly. Ironically, it was as a poison-taster that Uzma had got a fresh lease on life.

'Why won't the Nizam stay in Falaknuma Palace?' Emily grimaced at the general squalor of King Kothi. 'Something to do with a superstition?'

'Nizam VI, the current Nizam's father, died at Falaknuma. That might have something to do with it. Also, it is built in the shape of a scorpion, I hear, which is inauspicious.'

'A fundamental design error. Why would the Nizam—Oh, I get it!' Emily clicked her fingers. 'Another palace grabbed as nazar.'

At the Peshi office, where the Nizam conducted his daily meetings, HEH was missing. Uzma surveyed the decrepit office, as Emily Perkins gasped in dismay before recovering and starting to scribble furiously in her diary as if she had stumbled upon a gold mine.

Uzma examined the decrepit office, which she was seeing for the first time: two tawdry swivel chairs, three kitchen chairs, two old tables. Two old wooden cupboards which looked set to fall apart, an antique safe, a few stacked boxes, piles of paper and no furnishings. Despite the lighting, the room was dark, surrounded by buildings outside. A foul smell pervaded.

Done writing, Emily held her nose and shook her head as if mystified. She walked to a window which looked onto an even dirtier yard.

Uzma noticed the cobwebs dangling from the dirty ceiling. The wall paint was peeling. At one end of the room, a cupboard stood instead of a wall and, Uzma narrowed her eyes, there was a gap in the cupboard wall. She walked towards it, squeezing through the opening, and stepped into an anteroom of sorts. This room was crowded with even more desks, chairs, and cupboards, as if it was a store room. But sitting incongruously amidst all the excess dilapidated furniture were three men hunched over narrow desks, at work. As if they had perched at their desks and forgotten time, dressed in dusty sherwanis, leaking cobwebs—

'Ah, there you are, Uz-ma. Charming! Now what does the Nizam have tucked away in here? Three little pigs?'

The men had looked up, three pairs of bespectacled eyes fixed on the two women. Emily dusted her hands, her clap ringing loudly in the room.

'Apologies for disturbing you, gentlemen,' Uzma said softly.

A bustle sounded outside followed by a harsh guttural command. At which the men ducked and buried themselves back into their files.

'Perhaps he's here,' Emily said, and squeezed her way out of the cupboard. As Uzma followed, it struck her that whatever the Nizam spoke in the Peshi office was audible in this outer office. The three clerks would overhear any and all secrets spoken by the ruler.

Ideal conditions for a spy.

21
Hyderabad (December 1947)

Uzma swivelled on her heels and began to address the clerks. 'Gentlemen, forgive us once again. Miss Emily Perkins,' Uzma indicated with an outstretched arm to the Peshi office to which Emily had disappeared, 'is writing a book on the Nizam Nawab. She is here to interview him as well.' She beamed as the high-pitched sound of the Nizam filtered clearly into the anteroom.

The clerks contemplated her, their hands briefly paused in perusal of the papers in front of them. The thick glasses that each wore and the black sherwanis made them look like copies of one another. Two of them were old – older than the Nizam perhaps – but one looked younger. Uzma would need to exit soon; she had no business in the Nizam's Peshi office. But in this precious interval, she had to toss the line and see if a fish would catch the bait … The men continued to eye her with dispassion.

Uzma had come of age in palaces – Iram, King Kothi, Hill Fort – and understood a thing or two about power and politics. Poison, opium, and coterie were defining features of the court, but the one that trumped them all was the harem. The second Nizam so loved his harem that he went to battle accompanied by his complete zenana. Mehboob Ali Khan, Nizam VI, had some 10,000 women in his harem. A night with the Nizam meant a life at the zenana, which spurred many fathers looking to offload daughters and curry favours with the ruler. How many wives Osman Ali Khan had nobody knew. The wives and concubines lived in two buildings behind Nazari Bagh. Customarily, the Nizam would amble into the garden outside the zenana late afternoon where the women would await him. A white handkerchief casually placed on a shoulder signalled which particular woman was desired for the night. Sex undergirded every enterprise, be it of forsaken children or zenana wives. A woman could wait for a white kerchief to be bestowed upon her or she could marshal herself such that fate willingly smiled upon her …

As Uzma approached the men, her hips swayed, drawing attention to her waist visible beneath the sheer crepe sari specifically chosen for the day. Black, with pink roses on the border, it was a gift from Princess Niloufer, especially crafted for her by the same tailor in Bombay who designed the princess's wardrobe. The roses draped on her chest highlighted the swell of her full bosom, and weaving around her covered head like a garland, they brought to focus her full lips and kohl-lined eyes. The men were riveted.

In a husky voice, Uzma began. 'I'm assisting the lady sahib, who is a friend of Princess Niloufer. Princess Niloufer, the wife of Prince Moazzam Jah, is involved in many charitable projects in Hyderabad. The prince, our own Shajeeh, is a patron of poets from across India, many of whom have found favour in Hyderabad. I work for them.' Uzma paused. The men were listening to her bosom. She cleared her throat. They looked up. She rewarded them with a warm smile.

'I would appreciate it if you could assist lady sahib with any pertinent information. You work for HEH ... you hear so much ... Maybe she could talk to you ... Or better still, you can reach her via me. I am at Hill Fort palace in service of Prince Moazzam Jah and Princess Niloufer.'

She dipped her head and waltzed out.

∽

Uzma headed to the zenana. She had quietly exited the Peshi office, bowing deep to the Nizam, who was gesticulating and talking loudly. Emily Perkins sat cross-legged in a swivel chair, seemingly absorbed. Uzma was doubtful she would net any fish from the Peshi office anteroom. Perhaps a tête-à-tête with Imrana ...

She approached the larger two-storey building, which housed the concubines. Several sepoys were pacing the boundary and the entrance was guarded by two sepoys shouldering muskets. Uzma neared them, smiled, and made her enquiry. She was directed to the interior. Rooms radiated out from a central building. She entered the communal bathroom. It was late morning and the baths were deserted.

'Imrana?' Uzma called out.

'Back here,' a reply boomed.

Her heart beating, Uzma hurried to the rear. Sure enough, dressed in the scarlet-and-blue uniform of the Nizam's guards, her long hair knotted on top so it hid discreetly beneath the shako, Imrana stood wiping her face.

Reaching her, Uzma garlanded Imrana's neck with her arms and standing on her toes, kissed her hungrily. Imrana's large hands cupped Uzma's buttocks as she nibbled Uzma's mouth. 'My guardeen,' Uzma whispered, using the common parlance for the Nizam's female sepoys who guarded the zenana. Imrana led Uzma to a secluded bathing area where vapours heavy with sandalwood and rose clung to them as they made frantic love.

Later, they strolled through the gardens of the zenana where several of the Nizam's wives stretched out on couches. Amidst the rustle of brocade and silk, the laughter of women sallied as they sat in clusters, singing, conversing, playing games.

'All the gossip that I catch,' Imrana said drolly, 'which woman is in the Nizam's favour, which is not, which wife is conspiring against which, and whether khobani ka meetha is more fattening than double ka meetha.'

Uzma laughed gaily and gripped Imrana's forearm. 'Let me know if you do hear anything remotely less entertaining.' She winked, and traipsed away.

⁂

The courtyard behind the Peshi office was in direct contrast to the pleasure garden Uzma had just departed from. Here, instead of jasmine, the waft was of char and ancient piss. After sweeping a bench with a shorn branch full of leaves, Uzma perched on it. She could faintly hear Emily inside. A pi dog sauntered into the courtyard, and left just as quickly. Uzma wrinkled her nose, one eye on the far end of the wall which housed the anteroom.

To keep from bolting, Uzma let her mind linger on Imrana. She had first encountered her a decade ago, when Imrana was a fresh recruit into the Nizam's female sepoys. Made entirely of 'Amazons', freakishly tall women who were regarded, both by their parents and society, as half-men, they found a place in the Nizam's guards. Most such women were of African stock, descendants of the first Africans recruited by the Nizams for guarding the zenana and escorting its members when travelling. Both had gravitated towards each other. The knowledge that one wasn't wanted had liberated Uzma and Imrana, both—

A hurried tread roused Uzma from her recollection. A sherwani-clad man, looking over his shoulder, nipped over. Uzma recognized him as the youngest clerk.

Raising his right hand to his brow in salutation, he launched forth. 'Begum sahiba, it would be my good fortune to be able to assist you and the lady sahib. It ... it would be an honour, really. I ... I have a great regard for your employer, the honourable Prince Moazzam Jah.' The man's mouth wobbled as he searched for more words.

Uzma looked at him encouragingly. He had bitten the bait. 'You are?'

'Moinuddeen. Moin. Pen name,' he added hesitantly.

He was perspiring in the cool morning. Uzma tilted her chin. 'Shajeeh holds a great court every night at Hill Fort Palace. Fani, Mahir, Najm, Sidq Jaisi – some of the poets who lead the mushairas. Of course, the prince also has many poetasters and several younger poets in training.'

The man's eyes hadn't stopped sparkling since she rattled off the names of the famed poets. With trembling hands, he offered Uzma a roll. 'This insignificant person also attempts to write ghazals. Perhaps ... you can lay them at the feet of Shajeeh.'

Referring to himself in third person, truly a poet, Uzma observed tartly.

'I'm afraid that would be an impertinence on my part.'

'Please, please ... perhaps you can read it in your spare time and tell me whether the offering is worthwhile of the Bold One? If not, I will share other shayrs I have tried my hand at.'

Mushaira attendees were regulars who partook lavish meals nightly, some were even paid a stipend. In return, they had to listen to poetry through the night and punctuate it regularly with increasingly fulsome praise. At the crack of dawn, the mushaira disbanded, and the prince might return to bed. A night spent reciting lamentations of love when the world's most beautiful woman lay awaiting him, Uzma snorted inwardly. A cold marital bed was Niloufer's private sorrow.

Uzma prolonged the hard-to-get game. Exhausted, the wannabe poet committed to supply her with 'things of interest' he might overhear from the Peshi office, all to aid the firangi lady sahib's book on the Nizam, of course. In return, Uzma would read the scroll and determine what stage of readiness the verses were at before they could be placed at Shajeeh's reading desk. Moin, meanwhile, must continue the good work. Saying which, Uzma made a show of pocketing the scroll in her sari blouse, patting the pallu on her chest before strolling away.

22
Delhi (January 1948)

The first new year of newly independent India. A great striving for change had brought Indians to this momentous point. But in the curious way of life, the present had begun to look suspiciously like the past. The foreign hand had departed; India was free … yet chained to an ancient myth and its violent stirrings. The Mahatma said that the Mahabharata, the story of feuding brothers, was in the blood of Indians. Now it was coursing through the blood of his two sons, Vallabh and Jawahar, whom, in the manner of a village elder, he had yoked to the governmental cart as a pair of oxen.

'One will need the other and both will pull together,' he had sanguinely remarked in 1946 when the enemy was still the foreigner.

Jawahar watched Bapu lying in the cot like a frail sparrow, weighing 107 pounds, his kidneys failing, on what could be his terminal fast. Incense floated in the air, and, on the closed porch where the Mahatma lay in the afternoon sunshine, people filed past him with lowered eyes and folded hands. His eyes moistening, Jawahar looked away. Hymns floated in the air, Margaret Bourke-White stood in the sun, examining her camera, a group of men waved black banners outside the gates of Birla House ...

Barely five months and Jawahar was thinking rather longingly of the quiet days he had had in prison. Vallabhbhai's sudden resignation had struck him with the force of a full-speed train. They were hurtling through space and time – from Lahore to Amritsar to Junagadh, salvaging Delhi, Kashmir, Hyderabad, through heat and rains and rations – arguing and debating and realizing that their fierce differences meant the oxen pair must separate if the cart was not to break. Jawahar sighed. He had offered his resignation in turn. Having thus reached an impasse, the Prime Minister and his deputy had turned to Bapu, as of old. Bapu, in turn, had responded with a fast. As of old.

Much as he had done in Calcutta recently, Bapu was fasting in Delhi in order to heal Hindu–Muslim relations. Hindu and Sikh refugees were pouring into Delhi, Muslim refugees into Hyderabad, communal violence stalked the whole country ... Bapu's weapon, though, appeared to be failing. Maulana was running around securing pledges from Muslims that they would shun violence. Rajendra Prasad was exhorting non-Muslims to vacate mosques. Indians were denouncing Bapu as a traitor: Let Gandhi die! Anonymous posters incited people to 'cut Gandhi to pieces'. The issue of Kashmir had become a lightning rod. Added to which the news of Hyderabad's recent loan of Rs 20 crore to Pakistan had convinced Indians that they were losing to their enemy, Pakistan. Vallabhbhai's speeches were fanning their fear and fervour both. Recently, in Lucknow, the home minister had given the RSS a free pass as 'patriots'. After Junagadh's surrender, addressing a large crowd, Vallabhbhai had openly threatened Hyderabad: 'If it didn't see the writing on the wall, it would go the way of Junagadh!' His remarks were most unfortunate.

Additionally, Vallabhbhai thought the Prime Minister was being indulgent of Muslims. 'Tell me, Jawaharlal, why do the Muslims not condemn Pakistan's involvement in Kashmir? It is their duty now to sail in the same boat, to sink or swim together. Indian Muslims cannot ride two horses. Select one horse, I tell them.'

'Vallabhbhai, they *have* selected. India *is* their home. Just because some of their co-religionists have gone to Pakistan, the burden is not on India's Muslims to prove their loyalty.' Delhi's Muslims were barely managing to keep their homes as Hindu and Sikh refugees were kicking them out. Jawahar sighed. The impasse between Vallabhbhai and him was almost as wide as the chasm that had opened up between the religious communities ...

A high-ranking British official had wisecracked that the Congress should split in two – a right-wing under Patel, a left-wing under Nehru – for a balanced two-party system. Would that have worked? Jawahar probed his brow. A bitter memory surged in his mind from a few weeks ago when both Vallabhbhai and he had visited Bapu who was on an indefinite fast.

Jawahar had urged Bapu to quit.

'Not until friendship of the heart returns between Hindu, Muslim and Sikh brothers,' Bapu had murmured.

Even the Rs 55 crore due to Pakistan as share of assets had been sanctioned. For which, Bapu had emotionally arm-twisted him, Vallabhbhai maintained. After all, as home minister, he had tied the disbursement to a settlement on Kashmir by Pakistan. 'We should not give them a pie even,' Vallabhbhai had reiterated. 'Why give them money so they can spend it on bullets for our soldiers in Kashmir?'

But Bapu had stayed adamant. The money had been disbursed, but Bapu's fast had continued.

Both the men had turned to him in exasperation. 'What *will* break your fast, Bapu?'

'I must achieve something,' Bapu had answered slowly, 'or die in the attempt.'

Bapu's answer was no answer. The question was the only thing still uniting his two sons. Consternated, Jawahar rose abruptly and, crossing hands at his back, he headed to the garden for a walk. The mellow winter sun lit up the marigolds in the flower beds. He pinched his tired eyes. He had been sleeping fitfully. His fingers itched for a smoke—

A commotion sounded.

Indu, Betty and little Rajiv had arrived to visit Bapu, who greeted them with a toothless smile. They sat around his cot and started to chat softly. Rajiv's laughter reached Jawahar as he watched his four-year-old grandson play with a jasmine garland. The next instant, Rajiv started to wrap the garland around Bapu's ankles. Who reached out an arm and gently caught Rajiv's hand.

'We only put flowers around dead people's feet.'

23
Hyderabad (January 1948)

Osman Ali Khan was in a quandary.

Kasim Razvi's bluster had cost him Walter Monckton. Following the October coup by Razvi's Razakars, his legal advisor had departed for London. The loss of legal advice had led to the signing of the Standstill Agreement with India, and the arrival in Hyderabad of the agent-general of India! At the memory of K.M. Munshi, the Nizam's face contorted with fury.

He had met Munshi in the presence of his Prime Minister, Laik Ali, and gauged right away that the fellow was not to be trusted. His sources had indicated that the man was a notorious character and also a dignified blackguard, besides being a Gujarati lawyer. India was being run by Gujarati lawyers ... Patel ... Gandhi ... and it was getting rid of the excess by foisting them upon states such as Hyderabad. Devils, the lot of them! Police Commissioner Jung had promised to set his spies on Munshi.

Osman pottered about the Peshi office, tapping his stick and setting off little dust devils. Ten years ago, this same Munshi was home minister of Bombay and had actively encouraged the Arya Samajis, who were pouring into Hyderabad, for satyagraha protests: Munshi provided for their food and accommodation during their halt in Sholapur. Now the fellow had demanded one of the former British residencies for his Hyderabad accommodation! Osman had lodged an official protest with Mountbatten: Munshi's request was unconstitutional and was a downright sinister plot to revive paramountcy! Osman brought his left hand down with force on a table, disturbing the thick layer of dust atop it. The slap rang out in the room. The dust stirred. A sneeze built up within Osman and exploded in a shower of droplets. A pile of papers teetered, exposing a magazine buried underneath. Sniffling, he slid it out. Buried under the grime was his own visage. He wiped the cover. *Time*, the weekly newsmagazine. 1937. Resplendent in a bejewelled mustard dastar, a grey cape over his scarlet jacket, piercing eyes, determined jaw, His Exalted Highness the Nizam of Hyderabad locked eyes with the world.

A trembling set off in Osman's body. His legs would collapse under him. He clutched the table with one hand and bent down upon his stick with the other. *Time* magazine had put his silver jubilee celebrations on the front cover of their edition. They had called Hyderabad a ... *a rich, potent state* ... the ruler ... *the sole relic of Mughal greatness in India!* Barely ten years ago ... Crushed, Osman tottered his way slowly back to a chair.

The silver jubilee in 1937 was celebrated a year late because of the death of King George V. Osman, 'Most Faithful Ally of the British Empire', had kept faith – only the British had abandoned him. To devils like Razvi and Nehru–Patel. Two-hundred-and-fifty years of Asaf Jahi rule the jubilee had marked ... 250 years from the time of Akbar ... Osman Ali Khan's rule was a rule of progress and reform. Under his direct rule, the revenue department was reorganized, judicial reforms introduced, communal harmony cemented. He had founded Osmania University, Osmania General Hospital, the new high court, built dams ... Wasn't Hyderabad the first city in India with a reliable supply of drinking water? Hadn't Nizam VII banned the slaughter of cows to assuage his Hindu subjects? Wasn't primary school education free and compulsory? Clean trains that ran on time? Streets regularly washed by water tankers? Abundant public gardens ...

Osman's head hung low, despondent, on his shoulders. He was no magician; he had worked hard for Hyderabad's progress. Devout, he regarded Hindus and Muslims as his two eyes. Like his father, Nizam Mir Mahbub Ali Khan – Peace Be Upon Him – who had first enunciated the principle that the government should have nothing whatsoever to do with the religious practices of its subjects. Salar Jung I, even earlier, had set up the Department of Religious Affairs to supervise all religious activities in the state. Osman's eyes moistened at a recollection. At a religious festival in Gulbarga, he had carried on his head the tray of offerings, of sandal and flowers, to the Hindu shrine – to the astonishment of all beholders ... That cherished harmony had endured until Hindus in the state had fallen prey to the communalism imported from outside. Bitterness pooled in his mouth at the memory of the satyagraha of 1938.

A sigh rose within him. Frugal, he abstained from the excesses of his father. Patriotic, he advocated and used local Hyderabadi goods: Charminar cigarettes, Golconda soap ... And yet, and yet!

A couplet came to him; it was his own.

All the rulers of the past are dead, Osman
The name of the Muslims survives only because of your Kingdom.

Which a nasty Razakar had amended:

All the rulers of the past are dead, Osman,
Your kingdom survives only because of the Muslims!

Such lack of decorum, such audacity ... Ittehad had
emboldened them with the proclamation of Ani'l Malik:
sovereignty, therefore, was vested not in the ruler, but in the
entire Muslim community. Osman clenched his teeth until his
mouth hurt. His enemies had not wanted him to ascend the
throne even, denouncing him as the son of a Shia concubine. He
sniffled as he recalled walking bare-headed behind his mother's
cortege – may Allah keep her in jannah – from Purani Haveli to
Masjid-e-Judi, a distance of many miles. Which his combatants
were forced to traverse, following their Nizam's lead.

The poet in him could not help noticing the tragic hero in
the Nizam. Osman Ali Khan was doomed, either because of his
own hubris, or because god had willed his ignorance, or both.

From the corner of his eye, Osman caught a blurry, bent
figure diving repeatedly to the floor. He turned his head. One
of the clerks was bowed from the waist and saluting him with
scooping gestures in front of his mouth so as not to defile the
air around the Nizam.

It was the young, fat one. 'NAME?' Osman hollered.

'Moinuddeen, Excellency!'

'What do you want?' Osman said querulously.

'Your Excellency wished to dictate a letter.'

A letter, yes. He had a letter in mind for Mountbatten,
who must be made aware he was dealing with His Exalted
Highness, agreement or no agreement! And Mountbatten must
be informed of the thuggish ways of India's agent-general. As
a personal favour, Osman had allowed Munshi the use of the
Hyderabad Residency at Bolarum for eleven days, precisely

the time needed to ready 'Deccan House'. This, despite Razvi threatening to throw bricks of the residency into the Musi river. Now, news had reached him that the devil Munshi had removed the words 'Deccan House' from the stone gate posts and re-chiselled them with the Sanskrit 'Dakshina Sadan'. He had also hoisted the Indian tricolour over the building! Would the blackguard also be firing off cannons in his own honour? A no-good writer of pulp novels of beastly quality ...

'WRITE!' Osman thundered.

A trembling Moinuddeen took dictation, head bent, eyes lowered as the Nizam's voice roared in his ears.

'... AS-tonished to see how the governor general is playing into the hands of Nehru, Patel ... Lord Mountbatten is NO more a friend of Hyderabad as we thought ... their agent Munshi ... danger of a serious situation arising ... by unwise acts of these people who are no more than DEVILS.'

24

Delhi (January 1948)

He dug his face into the soft folds of his mother's sari. The folds shifted and became the white sheet covering the prone body of Motilal Nehru. Jawahar recoiled. His father's face, eyes shut, was in repose. Around them, the gathering spoke in hushed voices, above which floated hymns, broken by sobs and sighs. A heaviness, as if someone was sitting on his chest. He tried to move. A ball arced through the air. It landed on the dais where he stood in the cold winter air of Amritsar. The crowd was restive. A man was trampling the tiranga under his feet. A policeman tackled the protestor. Another clambered to the stage and plucked the ball. It exploded in his hand—

Jawahar sat up in bed, swimming in his sweat. He threw off the quilt and tried to slow down his breathing. He was in his bedroom … York Road … night-time … It was dark outside the window, which was shut tight against the winter chill. He swung his feet to the floor, found his slippers, and started to softly tread the room. Bapu's fast was weighing on him. Bapu had always used his body as a vehicle for his message – his clothes, dietary habits, fasts – but his increasing frailty gnawed at Jawahar. He sighed and glanced at the clock.

Daybreak. His listless self would benefit from yoga, but his daily morning ritual held no attraction today. Even the smell of woodsmoke from the refugee camp stoves in the garden was delayed. He frowned. The dark outside indicated it would be a bleak day.

⁂

Vallabh had barely reached home after meeting Bapu when the screeching of car tyres sounded in the driveway outside 1 Aurangzeb Road.

'*Where is Sardar? Bapu has been shot. Bapu is dead!*'

Flinging aside his newspaper, Vallabh sprang to the door. Mani, assisting a supplicant in the foyer, scrambled to the waiting car. Father and daughter jumped in. Brij Krishna, one of Bapu's associates, was ashen-faced. 'Bapu has been killed by a bullet.' The assassin was a Hindu.

At Birla House, Bapu lay on a carpet on the floor, surrounded by women reciting the Gita. Bapu's face was calm, lifelike. Blood trickled down the side of his body. Hurrying forward, Vallabh grabbed Bapu's wrist. That was a pulse, right? Surely, the man with whom he had chatted for over an hour less than fifteen minutes ago could not be dead! The doctor attending to Bapu shook his head. Crumpled, Vallabh sank near Bapu's feet. He was conscious of Mani standing behind him. She had sat through his conversation with Bapu … His *last* conversation … Over his meagre meal of milk and vegetables, Bapu had reiterated that Vallabh could not resign from the Cabinet and neither could Jawahar. Bapu had brushed aside the acrimony of the past few weeks when

Vallabh's sharp words had drawn Bapu's tears. Abha, Bapu's grand-niece, had held up a watch to remind the Mahatma that it was 5 p.m. and time for his prayers on the lawns of Birla House. But Bapu, despite being a stickler for time, had taken ten more minutes to clear the air between them and emphasize that the breach between the Prime Minister and his deputy must be repaired. 'All three of us, Jawaharlal, you and I, will meet tomorrow.'

There would be no tomorrow.

From outside sounds of agitation were pouring in. Confusion reigned in the dim dusk light. Vallabh's mind kept straying to the past.

When it was suspected that Vallabh had cancer in 1941, Bapu had cared for him at Sevagram, administering mudpacks for forty days, feeding him meals of milk, raw vegetables and prunes. Morning and evening, the two would walk together, discussing current events, particularly Churchill's statement that the Atlantic Charter, calling for the right of all people to choose the form of government under which they live, would not apply to India. 'So democracy is only for the Europeans!' Vallabh had jibed.

Bapu, one eye always on the goal, had said, 'Remember, we are not to go until we have attained swaraj.'

Vallabh scrunched his mouth before covering it with his right hand. Devdas was pleading in his father's ear, 'Speak, Bapuji, speak.'

Bapu had broken their pact and had gone ahead. Vallabh's creaking body would follow soon. Meanwhile, the fruits of their hard-fought swaraj were still not secure. A crash sounded – glass windows broken by the pressure of crowds swelling outside – amidst shouts. He must instruct Bucher and the police chiefs to

impose strict security measures across India and not to hesitate
in saying that the assassin was indeed a Hindu.

∽

When a reeling Jawahar reached Birla House, policemen
were trying to control the vast crowd. Footwear was piling
up outside Bapu's room. Inside, Bapu's head was in the lap of
Brij Krishna, his body covered by a sheet. Vallabhbhai sat by
his feet. Manibehn was reciting the Bhagavad Gita. People sat
on the floor in silence, which was punctured by a sob, a sigh,
sniffles. Kneeling by Bapu's side, Jawahar clutched his lifeless
hand. Tears ran down his face.

∽

As his car raced to Birla House, Dickie mulled over the call
from Calcutta. Rajagopalachari had insisted on the need to take
utmost precautions to safeguard Nehru. Only two days ago, in
Amritsar, two men were arrested for carrying grenades to his
public meeting. Bapu's killing was a turbulence that could sink
independent India's lurching vessel. Near Birla House, the car
had to burrow through an enormous crowd as people peered
into the car's windows. A heap of cycles, people weaving
around abandoned automobiles, some clambering up the walls
of Birla House, crashing against the gates, being beaten back
by the police, but surging forth nevertheless. Only one spark
was needed. Inside the gates, young men were milling around
in the grounds and pressing against the French windows. A cry
rang out.

'It was a Muslim who did it!'

As necks spun, Dickie halted and in his best stentorian military voice reprimanded, 'You FOOL! Don't you know it was a Hindu?' Dickie had no inkling if it really was, but it seemed the right thing to do.

Sidestepping a mountain of footwear outside Gandhi's room, Dickie entered in stockinged feet. In the far corner lay Gandhi, surrounded by his granddaughters and grand-nieces. The air was thick with incense and the chanting of verses, followed by 'Ram, Ram, Ram'. Gandhi looked peaceful. Dickie had never seen him without his steel-rimmed glasses, behind which those eyes often twinkled with hidden mischief. Edwina, devastated at the news, was trying to get back from Madras. After a silent homage, Dickie adjourned to the next room to confer with Jawa and Patel. The two men were speaking quietly amidst a number of Gandhi's associates. Jawa was ashen-faced; Patel, grim. Meanwhile, a tidal wave of people was crashing against the windows.

'Gentlemen,' Dickie approached, forming a triangle of the Prime Minister, his deputy and the governor general. Dipping his head confidentially, he brought up his last interview with Gandhi. 'His dearest wish was to bring about full reconciliation between the two of you.'

Jawa and Patel were soon locked in embrace.

⁓

The grim winter day had deepened to night. A tin can on the lawn marked the spot where Bapu had been killed. Jawahar swallowed the lump down his throat and strode towards one of the gates of Birla House. Bapu was gone … To the last, his step was light, his smile infectious, his eyes full of laughter. He lived and died at the top of his strength and powers. Where he sat became a temple and where he trod was hallowed ground. Bapu was gone, but his mighty spirit would be their eternal guide.

People were frantic, people needed consoling, people needed to hear that the Mahatma had moved on. But Bapu had left them something: his vision of a peaceful, prosperous India for his countrymen and women to fulfil.

Thrusting a white kerchief limp with tears into his sherwani pocket, Jawahar climbed atop a gate. In the dull yellow light of the street lamp, he saw anxious weeping men, their plaintive faces turned towards him. They must hear Bapu's fresh call to duty. He started to address them.

'Friends and comrades, the light has gone out from our lives ...'

25
Hyderabad (January 1948)

Joining the Sangham was like tasting avakai on her annaprasana day: hot mango pickle that set her tongue and brain and body afire, instead of the customary soft rice and lentil mush, which was a toddler's first ceremonial solid food. Her life before the Sangham seemed like that of an infant's – learning to fire a gun was strictly adult business, no? And just as a toddler's world expanded, Jaabili's had grown to include the Russian Revolution, Politburo, Marxism, Leninism, Socialism, Communism ... and god only knew how many more 'ism's to come? Though, devudu was strictly forbidden: There was no place for god in Communism.

The party, Communist Party of India, was committed to political education of all comrades; the Sangham organized political classes where all manner of knowledge was thrown at them. Jaabili didn't understand much, but just being present amidst all that wisdom felt good. Besides, food could be swallowed as well as digested, and would still nourish the body, right? Jaabili was determined to banish her own ignorance.

Abolish zamindari!

End police zoolum!

End to levy, vetti, corruption!

Raising slogans, striking the ground with lathis, Jaabili had taken part in processions, and seen with her eyes how they shook up entire villages and put terror in the hearts of traitors. She loved singing the 'Song of Ailamma', the woman who had courageously resisted the deshmukh and refused to let him seize her land. Subsequently, the story of Ailamma's courage had spread like wildfire through the cotton scrub.

Ailamma was the heroine of the peasant movement, whose story had given them its iconic slogan: Land to the tiller! She was also Jaabili's personal heroine, to be summoned up when needed: the first time she travelled by herself, or travelled at night, or navigated the big city of Hyderabad. Jaabili had Ailamma. Just as Gorky had Amma.

A big procession was planned for Hyderabad city, and the Sangham was actively assisting Congress, city Communists, and the Mahasabha. There was also a big problem. In Hyderabad city, the Razakars were strong and were supported by city Muslims. Unlike Warangal, the city had no villagers fed up with deshmukhs and the police. It wasn't easy to smuggle weapons in; the Nizam's spies were on the lookout. And the police was raiding student hostels ...

Protests and processions, deshmukhs and jagirdars, guns and goondas – all this was men's work. The police believed that too. Which was where women like Jaabili came in.

Dressed in her cotton pyjama and kurta, a kerchief around her head, disguised as a boy, she had delivered messages. Dressed in a half-sari, she had transported a gun wrapped inside a cloth bundle to a drop point in Secunderabad, on the outskirts of Hyderabad. Today, Jaabili was on another important courier

mission to Hyderabad. In her waist cloth, she carried a single
sheet of paper, a coded message from Leader Rao that Daniyal
Khan would decode for the pamphlets to be printed in advance
of the big march. The printer was located in Secunderabad –
Daniyal Khan was too well known to be involved in directly
printing propaganda for the Sangham. At the memory of
Daniyal, Jaabili lit up.

'What slogan will you coin?' Jaabili had asked him once.

'Not what …' Daniyal blew on his cigarette. 'How?'

Jaabili sat back on her heels and listened. A couple of hours
to departure. The night air, moist from a shower, was fragrant
with night jasmine from a bush in the courtyard.

'The "what" follows from "how". Hmm. How do you expose
your enemy? Show his true self? Make him look weak? More
importantly,' Daniyal put out the cigarette in an ash tray thick
with stubs, 'how do you give people a good time?'

'Good time?' Jaabili frowned.

'Aren't you having a good time being a comrade?'

Jaabili thought about it, then nodded.

'The purpose of a protest is to make people aware, to make
them sympathetic to our cause … to give them reasons to
remember. Our protest is against the Nizam, but the way to
make it stick is to direct it at the Razakars. And Razvi. Razvi
with his flaming eyes, flaming beard and flaming rhetoric. An
excess of hot air.' Daniyal gazed in the distance. 'Don't oppose
dictators, ridicule them, as Brecht said.'

'Brecht who?'

'German writer.'

Jaabili nodded, awestruck. She had never met anyone like
Daniyal Khan. He had travelled the world using the pages of
books: Russia, Germany, England … He spoke of people who
lived in those pages like they were his friends. The large room

that served for his living quarters – a bed, a desk with chair, a sofa, cupboards, a dresser – was littered with books like they had wings and flew about and perched wherever they fancied. Khudabax tidied around them, careful not to disturb the pages on which a book had landed.

By now, she had learnt that the book she had carried on her first courier mission – Gorky's *Amma* – was a special edition copy, same as the one Leader Rao used. That copy was the 'key' that formed the basis of their secret language. The text was composed in groups of three figures, like (52, 12, 6). These were the coordinates for a particular word located on page 52, line 12 from the top of the page, word 6 in the line. Someday, Jaabili would read the entire book. As of now, she was reading books with pictures. Which reminded her of the picture on Daniyal's desk.

A black-and-white print of screaming people and animals, who appeared to be wailing too. Like a village tortured by a jagirdar's men. 'Why keep this?' she had asked.

'To remind me of what I'm fighting for,' Daniyal quietly replied. 'Peace.'

The picture, he explained, showed a scene of wartime. It was by a famous painter, Pica-Pico-something, who was also a Communist. 'Just like us,' Daniyal smiled.

And Jaabili had sighed, inwardly. If only he taught all the political education classes at the Sangham ... But the women would all make eyes at him. No! Jaabili was happy he stayed in Hyderabad city where she had him to herself.

∽

It was six in the evening when Jaabili got off at the bus stop at Charminar. The weather had got chilly and Jaabili had wrapped a shawl around herself. She scanned the bustling crowd for the clean-shaven face of Raj Kumar. A bell rang, tring-tring, and Jaabili sighted him with a cycle. He wore a cap, which was pulled over his ears, and a sweater. The plan was for them to pick up food from a roadside vendor for their meeting at Daniyal Khan's house.

Raj Kumar had a curious way of looking, as if he was seeing her for the first time, and when she returned his gaze, he looked away hurriedly. Jaabili hopped onto the rear passenger seat and Raj started to cycle. A wobble, then he steadied himself and started to pedal briskly. Her nose tickled in the cold air. The state Congress was taking the lead in planning the big procession and satyagrahis were entering Hyderabad from border camps in neighbouring states. A prominent Communist leader, P.V. Narasimha Rao, was also expected to join. Rao was one of the students Osmania University rusticated in 1938 when he sang 'Vande mataram' instead of 'God Save Osman'. He had graduated from Nagpur University, joined a border camp at Chanda, and was famed for his fearless speeches. But it was all very hush-hush to prevent news leaking to the police or the Razakars.

As the cycle made its way down Charminar market, flavourful spices and sizzling oil invaded their senses. Restaurants, cafes, roadside stalls, all engaged in the business of food, a ladle clanging here, an order shouted there, caramelized sugar and hot oil colliding with the aromas of baked bread and masalas. They halted at a food cart and Jaabili jumped down to order keema pulao. As she paid, Jaabili handed more money than the bill amount. Afzal, who ran the pulao bandi, was a comrade, who would ensure money reached the printers. After grabbing the square-shaped Munshi naan for Raj, who ate no meat, they cycled on, the packed food sitting snug in the cycle carrier. As they skirted Lad Bazaar, Jaabili became aware of a cyclist behind them. His fez with a bright red thread had caught her attention at the bus stop, then she had noticed him inspecting haleem at the stall neighbouring Afzal's, stroking his goatee as he looked at her from the corner of his eyes. Now, he was trailing them.

Jaabili changed her route and bus timings routinely to avoid being spotted by Razakar spies, who had grown in numbers since 15 August 1947. The Sangham had held a special class for couriers and comrades who needed to travel to the city to alert them on ways to spot a possible spy, and ways to stay safe. Jaabili paid special attention to the way in which students and women dressed in Hyderabad, since those were her two disguises. The women, she loved seeing, dressed in sarees without burkas, their head covered with saree pallus. Some wore burkas as well, which Jaabili had practised and stumbled about in with difficulty.

'Raj,' Jaabili hissed, 'we are being tailed.'

'What!' A wobble. 'H-how do you know?'

'I know.' Jaabili kept her voice steady despite the sudden hammering inside her chest.

'Okay. Here's what we do,' Raj said, speeding up. 'You cannot be caught. If they find your message, they might not be able to decode it, but they will arrest you. And when they realize you're in disguise ...'

Jaabili had already worked that out. 'They might be after you.' The cycle jolted. Raj was nervous. It was sundown and getting dark.

'Don't cycle to Daniyal's,' Jaabili hissed. 'Head towards Musi river. The bank is dark and will give us cover. I'll tell you where to slow down and I will jump off. You dash to Daniyal's after that, alert the others. With luck, we'll shake him off.'

'NO! I cannot leave you—'

'I have a plan, trust me.'

A bullock cart had trundled onto the road as the cycle curved left to the riverbank. It blocked them from the Razakar cyclist. '*Hurry!*' Jaabili urged.

The unpaved lane beside the riverbank lay dark, light filtering in only from houses bordering it on the right. A few people flitted around like shadows. Raj's rapid huffing filled her ears as he inclined, willing the bicycle forward with his whole body. Jaabili scoured the lane behind. Sure enough, a cycle sailed down the turn and onto the lane. Halfway between Lad and Chappal Bazaar lay a safehouse. Jaabili had spent many hours accessing it via the twisting lanes that formed a maze, which emptied near Daniyal Khan's house.

The dense green of Imliban loomed like a dark cloud across the Musi. Now!

Jaabili clamped Raj's shoulder, he slowed, and she slid off, hurrying into the mouth of the alley. It was dark, houses crowding into each other, no one about. If the Razakar caught up with her, she couldn't even call for help. Swallowing her fear, Jaabili cast a wary look behind. Nothing. She tried to slow her thudding heart to hear better. Only the sound of boatmen from the Musi and laughter leaking from a house. She turned her head, and almost cried aloud – something batted her face, feathery, furry. A bat, only a bat, Jaabili told herself as she hurried on. Sweat trickled down her back. She wanted to throw off the shawl, but there was no time.

Was the Razakar following Raj? Did Raj lose him? Her ears pricked. A tread behind her, a steady tap-tap … It was coming closer, closer … Steady, steady, she told herself, let him come close. Jaabili moved to the side, giving space to the cyclist who was now following on foot, clearly. Her right hand was within her waist cloth. He was level with her. Jaabili's hand trembled as she clenched her fist ... A goat trotted by, tossing its head.

Jaabili collapsed against the wall of a house.

A while later, she emerged out of the twisted maze onto Chappal Bazaar which was better lit. In the distance, a man was latching his shop shut. To ensure the Razakar was not lurking, Jaabili decided to go past Daniyal Khan's house and enter from the rear door.

Licking her dry lips, Jaabili struck out when a hand clamped her shoulder.

'Where do you think you're going?'

Jaabili's hand, clenched inside her waist cloth, swung up and hurled chilli powder at the Razakar. The man ducked, stumbled, his feet twisting, before he managed to steady himself. Red powder streaked his sherwani and neck, having narrowly missed his face. Daniyal Khan blinked at the mess on his chest, screwing up his eyes.

'Damn these Warangal chillies!'

26
Hyderabad (January 1948)

Raj Kumar had managed to shake off the Razakar. Or perhaps there never was a Razakar on his tail and Jaabili had panicked? They debated over keema pulao and Munshi naan – among the men, that is – as they tucked into succulent lamb and fragrant rice. Jaabili ate quietly, mortified at how easily she had got spooked. The drilling at the Sangham would make her doubt her shadow even ... But she could not shake off the image of that bicyclist eyeing her surreptitiously in the Charminar market ... Was he inspecting her discreetly in the manner of some men? But she was disguised as a man! Was this the work of the 'rat' Daniyal had warned her of? She chased these questions in her mind, swallowing the pulao like it were gruel, furious at herself for acting like a fearful girl.

The men had moved on from discussing plans for the big procession. Jaabili could hear Raj Kumar's enthusiastic detailing of a new programme that the Arya Samaj was actioning—

'Arming villagers selectively is a *good* idea?' Daniyal's wry voice roused Jaabili from her self-lashing. He had recovered quickly from being attacked, his sherwani bearing the brunt of the chilli powder. Laughing off her apologies, he removed the sherwani for the wool jacket Khudabax fetched, a well-worn item in blue–black. Which was when Jaabili realized Daniyal's eyes were indigo coloured! How strange. Only the Angla had blue eyes ...

Raj Kumar, swallowing a mouthful, shook his head. 'Arming Hindu peasants against the Razakars so they can defend themselves. How long will they continue to suffer?'

'The Razakars don't differentiate between Hindu and Muslim peasants. Their aim is to terrorize villages into submission—'

'The Arya Samaj doesn't think so.' Raj paused to allow a burp as he stood up. 'Our volunteers have gone into the villages, spoken to the villagers, and it's clear that the Nizam's police and the Razakars both are systematically targeting Hindus.' He went to wash his hands. Khudabax arrived with a jug and refilled the water glasses. Jaabili helped him stack empty plates on a tray, then proceeded to the gusalkhana. She liked calling it by the word she had first heard Daniyal use, playfully enunciating it, trying on iterations until it sounded like it had rolled off his tongue.

When she returned, the men were sitting in a cloud of smoke. The clear night sky was studded with stars, a breeze wafted, carrying with it a mixed aroma of jasmine, cigarettes, and spices. Daniyal offered Jaabili a cigarette, like always. Before she could refuse, Raj Kumar had spoken forcefully for her.

He frowned. 'It's not good for her!'

'While it is for you?' Daniyal snorted.

Raj's cheeks reddened. 'Men and women bodies are different ... women are more delicate ... Anyway, sit, Jaabili, please ...' He indicated the vacant chair next to him, smiling at her.

The more effort Raj Kumar put into showing he liked her, the more Jaabili felt like slapping him. He was like an annoying kid brother or a pesky fly.

Ali Hassan cleared his throat. 'I think Jaabili can speak for herself.'

'How about you all speak to me directly like I am here, present, instead of at the Sangham?' Jaabili asked as she sat, catching what seemed like a twinkle in Daniyal's eyes.

'Correct, Jaabili,' Ali Hassan acknowledged what she said with a tip of his head. Turning to Raj Kumar, he continued, 'I disagree strongly with what the Arya Samaj is proposing. We should keep religion out of politics. The issue at stake is inequality and injustice—'

'Yes, but when majority of the population is Hindu, guess who suffers that inequality the most?' Raj was the excited earnest calf of the herd, galloping, bucking, kicking his hind legs.

Ali Hassan scowled. 'That's not an accurate picture. Razakars are employed by big Hindu landlords too. Besides, if every Muslim peasant suffers, does it matter whether they are 20 per cent of the population or 80 per cent? And—'

'Eighty-*seven* per cent!' Raj insisted.

'—since we are all allied, Communists, Congress, Arya Samaj ... Any arming of Hindu peasants will only strengthen the charges that the Communist party and Congress represent only Hindus!' Ali finished his argument.

Raj waved his hands theatrically, words eluding him for now.

Daniyal blew smoke into the air. They were like a gathering of the neighbourhood pi dogs, all united in barking against the intruder in their midst – for now, the Nizam. Otherwise, what truck did the Arya Samaj have with the Communists? Their camps – at Ahmednagar and Sholapur in the west, at Bezwada in the southeast, at Pusad in the north, and at Manmad in the northwest – poured 'volunteers' into Hyderabad with the sole purpose of condemning Muslims. With their popular demands – Hindustan for Hindus; eight crore Muslims should convert to Hinduism or drown in the Arabian Sea; for each Hindu killed in the Nizam's state, three Muslims should be slain in British India – they were the converse of the Razakars. Money was the other thread that tied them together. Razakars were employed by wealthy Hindu jagirdars to safeguard their interests. And the Arya Samaj and Mahasabha were capitalist organizations seeking to establish in Hyderabad the rule of upper-class, moneyed Hindus. And yet, here was their representative, pretending to speak for the masses.

Daniyal leaned forward in his chair, locking eyes with Raj. 'Have you ... the Samaj, Mahasabha, considered the possibility that Hindu peasants could turn their guns on their Muslim neighbours? On provocation by the Razakars or the Mahasabha or Arya Samaj? Or because they covet their neighbour's cow or goat or daughter?' He patted the air because Raj Kumar had recovered his tongue and was bouncing to get a word in. 'Hyderabad's famed Ganga-Jumna tehzeeb isn't what it used to be. Now, a Hindu palki passing a mosque is considered a provocation, as is a Muharram procession passing a temple – leading to scuffles and rioting. It's insane.'

Raj Kumar beamed. 'But brother Daniyal, you yourself insist that all peasants are equally ill-treated, regardless of religion. Then why would a Hindu turn against a Muslim?'

Which *Hindu* was Raj Kumar talking of? Jaabili squinted at him. The jagirdars and deshmukhs were Hindu, but rich Hindus. And amongst poor Hindus, there were those like her friend Suguna, whom Jaabili could play with but never enter her house because Suguna's father was a Brahmin, poor but upper caste. And what of the 'wretched Malas and Madigas,' her father would berate because they were untouchables? Jaabili clucked. Raj had never been to a village or he would know that villagers understood jati, not religion. Try telling a Reddy that he was same as a Relli because they were both Hindu? Or a Balija, Idiga, Gouda, Kamma, Kapu, Uppara, Vadla …

'Power.' Daniyal twirled a moustache tip. 'When you arm peasants unequally, you change the power equation—'

A loud rapping on the front door quietened everybody. Khudabax hurried to the courtyard, glancing from the door to the men. The banging got louder and more insistent.

'POLICE! Open the door!'

Ali Hassan sprang up, Raj Kumar clutched his chair's armrests, Daniyal's hand stilled. The bird trapped in Jaabili's chest since early evening started to knock about frantically now.

'POL-ice! Hurry now!'

The door was being punished for their lack of action. The rattling would wake up entire Chappal Bazaar.

Daniyal locked eyes with Jaabili. 'You did not imagine the Razakar.' He indicated to Raj and Ali that they head inside, and turned to Khudabax. The old retainer understood the wordless communication as he volleyed in the direction of the door, 'Hallu, hallu. Co-*ming*, bhai.'

'You need to change clothes—' Daniyal was whispering when Jaabili clamped a hand on his right arm, lifting her left index finger to her mouth. 'Burka,' she hissed. 'My burka!'

∽

When the police entered the empty courtyard, frothing because of the delay, the posse of men fanned out quickly. Khudabax stood aside, massaging his hands and mumbling nervously. The cops began testing their batons against the furniture, flinging the sofa cushions to the floor when a burka-clad woman strode out. The shiny brass buttons on the policeman's uniform were like headlights, confounding her momentarily. Clearly, he was a senior officer. In a clear, calm voice, she called out a greeting to the men, who froze. Before they could get over their surprise, the woman addressed the man who appeared to be the leader, 'May I remind you, jemadar sahib, that you cannot enter this house at night, or without a sufficient notice. This is most irregular, you will agree?'

The jemadar, taken aback, scratched his neck. He flourished his baton at the house. 'We're acting on information and need to search the premises. The raid will be over quickly. Now, if you cooperate—'

The burka-clad woman pulled herself upright, angled her head and spoke imperiously. 'I'm invoking the Nizam's law that protects the custom of purdah! The law prohibits you from entering my house at night. I request you to obey the Nizam Nawab and leave, right now.'

The jemadar tapped the baton against his palm. His men, the raid suspended mid-action, watched him. An owl hooted, its *hooo* filling the courtyard. The jemadar harrumphed.

'The house belongs to Daniyal Khan ... who, we know, lives alone.'

'And never ever receives any visitors. No family, no friends, no companionship, female or male.' The woman tut-tutted. 'Only poor Khudabax here. Well,' she swept her hands imperiously towards the main door, stepping forward and closing the distance between the jemadar and herself, 'you're welcome to visit in the morning. I wish you a good night.'

When Khudabax had latched the door shut and secured the bolt, Jaabili nearly collapsed with relief. The imperious act over, she tugged the burka over her head. A rustle of hurrying feet. She'd barely shaken herself loose from the tent-like cover when Jaabili found herself swept up. Daniyal Khan, laughing soundlessly, holding her up high in his arms, spinning her around slowly.

How did a Sangham lesson on the Nizam's law lead to this, Jaabili wondered. In the last few hours, she had felt afraid, felt stupid, felt angry, but what she felt at that moment, she had no word for. The bird trapped in her chest had flown with her heart and she felt herself melting. When Daniyal put her back on the ground, Ali Hassan reappeared wearing a big grin. Raj Kumar looked like he was sulking in the shadows. Khudabax hummed softly as he emptied the ash tray. But Jaabili couldn't trust herself to put one foot after the next; her legs were muslin.

27
Hyderabad (February 1948)

Our story, flush with opium and harem, poison and propaganda, coterie and court intrigue, war and women, plenty and penury prophecy and slavery diamonds demagogues blood betrayal ... Our story is a story of excess. Profusion. An overflowing. And why not?

Have you seen the subcontinent? What, if anything, is trammelled here?

The Himalayas, with the peak that touches the heavens. The heat that melts roads, knocks birds off trees and whips up the scorcher Loo. The monsoons that never fall as rain but a deluge that inundates. Post-Partition kafilas: The largest migration in human history. The Nizam: The wealthiest man in the world. Golconda: The site of the world's most famous diamonds ...

It is fitting, therefore, that in this story of excess should now arrive the man whose real-life adventures went on to provide the blueprint for James Bond: highly intelligent, exceedingly cunning, reeking of machismo, with a license to kill, hung up on his martini ... During WWII, Ian Fleming, the creator of

007, met Sidney Cotton, on whom he would model his super spy. Tall, well-built, with an easy confidence, this real-life James Bond though was less a caricature but a man who epitomized Oscar Wilde's maxim: Moderation is a fatal thing ... Nothing succeeds like excess.

Any doubt he fit right into India?

∽

For a man whom the Government of India would eventually accuse of gunrunning, Sidney Cotton flew into the country in February of 1948 to scout for groundnuts. However, owing to a blockade imposed by the Indian Union, groundnuts couldn't be exported from Hyderabad – the only possible source. Cotton wasn't aware of India's geography, even less of its politics; so from his base in Bombay, he began to make enquiries. When he learnt that Hyderabad was an independent Princely State being coerced by India into joining, why, Cotton had to go investigate for himself! The man had an irresistible itch for adventure. Deep into his spy mission, Cotton's had been the last civilian aircraft to leave Berlin before the war started. Perhaps it was the Jew in him showing a middle finger to Nazis everywhere.

Sidney Cotton had taken part in both world wars. The ten-year-old Australian boy, who designed his own aircraft, the 'Cotton monoplane', had, by the age of fifty-two, flown English Channel patrols during WWI, and pioneered aerial reconnaissance photography with hidden cameras cut into aircraft wings and fuselage in WWII. In the guise of a businessman, he had taken Kesselring and Goering for a ride, flying low and secretly filming German installations as he spun the Nazi officials about in his luxurious new Lockheed. He was great friends with Ian Fleming, personal assistant to the director of British Naval Intelligence, with whom he shared a love of gadgets and women. Flying his Lockheed spy plane along the west coast of Ireland, Cotton had investigated if the strip was being used to refuel German U-boats. Cotton counted Churchill amongst his fans, but that didn't prevent him being expelled from the Royal Air Force for disdain towards authority. So when the war ended, Cotton was faced with the problem of how to earn a living again. The answer led him to a mission that could be straight out of a James Bond novel.

On 18 February, Sidney Cotton's Lockheed landed in Hyderabad, a bright rainbow arcing across the sky. He took it as a good omen as he set off to meet the Nizam's counsel. Sir Walter Monckton arranged for Cotton to meet the Prime Minister of Hyderabad.

'We have large supplies of groundnuts in Hyderabad state and we're happy to negotiate a contract, if,' and Mir Laik Ali shrugged one shoulder, '*if* you can find a way to get the goods through the blockade. You see, Mr Cotton, thousands of tons of much-needed supplies are being held up ... There is a severe shortage of medicines, chlorine even, which we need for the purification of water supplies.' Laik Ali swept a palm against his broad forehead. 'Cholera has broken out ... We fear an epidemic. These ...' he searched for a word, 'sanctions ... yes, sanctions against us are just a way to threaten Hyderabad state into submission.'

Quietly, Cotton asked, 'If it comes to war with India, what is the state of readiness of Hyderabad's forces?'

'Not good,' Laik Ali clucked. 'The Nizam, HEH Osman Ali Khan, re-equipped his army during WWII at Britain's request to help fight the Japanese. The promise made to us was that all new equipment thus provided would be replaced. Eighty-million pounds worth of equipment! And what has been returned to us?' Laik Ali held up his right hand, thumb and index finger forming a circle.

'*Zee*-ro?'

Steepling his hands, the Prime Minister said, 'Our only hope is that the British demonstrate their notion of fair play and stand by the terms of Partition of India Bill.'

'Which allows Hyderabad to choose independence if the state so desires,' Sidney Cotton concluded. Monckton had brought him up to speed and he was beginning to feel very deeply about the manoeuvres to coerce Hyderabad. The state was as large as England and Scotland put together.

'Why not manufacture fresh arms? Surely, you'd have some factory?'

'It was closed down by the British, all armaments removed.'

'That's a pickle.' Cotton walked to the window. Black clouds ringed the sky, sinister as the encircling blockade. He turned on his heel to enquire, 'Why not fly modern weapons into the state? The least it will do is strengthen your negotiating hand.'

'Impossible!' Laik Ali shook his head. 'The Indian Air Force will shoot down any aircraft attempting to cross Indian territory without clearing customs.'

'With respect, I disagree.' Cotton closed the distance with quick strides. 'It would be quite a simple operation to fly arms into Hyderabad.' Sidney Cotton then detailed how, if Pakistan would buy the arms, Cotton would carry airlifts into Hyderabad from Karachi. With proper agreements drawn up, the entire operation could be done legitimately. *Provided*, the Pakistan government was willing to help.

Abruptly, Laik Ali's face was as radiant as yesterday's rainbow. 'Pakistan government wants Hyderabad to remain an independent Muslim state. I will give you a letter of introduction to Colonel Iskander Mirza, secretary of defence. Go to Pakistan, Mr Cotton, and begin the proceedings!'

Cotton felt quite ready to defer or even abandon the groundnuts contract for the time being, if he could help it.

Laik Ali was rolling up his shirtsleeves. 'Prepare an outline plan for airlifting 500 tons of freight into Hyderabad in three days—'

'Woah, woah, slow down, Mr Ali! The average load of the aircraft I have in mind is nine or ten tons, and they'll have to carry fuel for the return journey. A large number of aircraft – twenty or more will be required for your mission ... Such numbers are almost certainly unobtainable, not to mention the crews to go with them.'

'See what you can do,' Laik Ali urged, leaning forward on his elbows. 'Realize that we need a quick operation, before India wises up to our initiative and sends its air force to stop the operation.'

The Prime Minister seemed resolved to take all possible steps to defend Hyderabad. A litmus test for his resolve?

'Twenty million pounds – that's the price of freedom. Will your government be willing to spend that kind of money?'

Laik Ali locked eyes with Sidney Cotton. 'You need not ask that question. The cost will not be counted.'

There was a knock on the door – the Prime Minister's next appointment had arrived. Sidney Cotton agreed to wait while Laik Ali dispensed with his meeting. Deciding to take a walk, he stepped outside. Large paintings adorned the walls, several of portly men wearing too many jewels. There was a crispness to the air and Cotton stepped away from the neat lawn that fronted Shah Manzil, the Prime Minister's official residence, and walked to the side where an unusual tree had staked out a large territory. The building itself was quite splendid, an architectural amalgam: scalloped arches were Muslim, the cupolaed parapets were Hindu. The tree that had drawn him had broad leaves with a pointy tip, a thick trunk and – he peered – nestled within the aerial roots was some kind of deity. Sacred, hmmm.

Sidney Cotton began to pace the walkway. The building was situated atop a hill with commanding views of the lake and the city. The clatter of horsecars rode up from the street below as a monkey cackled in some tree.

Without arms, Hyderabad was doomed to be run over. Yet, to bring them arms was to encourage them to fight. Besides, helping Hyderabad would entail grave personal risks. Five-hundred tons in three days was an impossible target. But there was the bullying act of the Indian Union, applying sanctions against a friendly and defenceless state – an outright act of aggression … From what he had seen in the past few days, Hyderabad appeared a contented and well-run country. Now, it was being blockaded by India while Britain sat on its ass! The more Cotton thought about it, the more indignant he became.

Suddenly, he felt a spotlight upon him. A brilliant white shaft of sunlight had broken through the pervading gloom of dark clouds. A hint of a smile crept up Cotton's lips. He knew very well what he had to do.

28
Hyderabad (January–February 1948)

The Nizam had a network of spies – now she had planted one on him!

Uzma could not keep the glee from her face. So she used her sari's pallu to cover her mouth, an ordinary gesture of ladylike coyness or a commoner's way to wipe away sweat, as she walked downhill from Hill Fort Palace. Moinuddeen, the Peshi office clerk-poet, had dropped notes on three occasions, tucked under the boulder beneath the ancient bargad just outside the palace gates. Hussain Sagar glimmered in the distance as Uzma looked around her. Naubat Pahad was a mountaintop meant for palaces, the inmates of which never walked about. If a servant surfaced, Uzma would don her imperious demeanour of a princess's lady-in-waiting who was paying the sacred banyan a visit. She had found saffron marks on the tree trunk on occasion, clearly some servant believed in the tree's powers. Which Niloufer counted on as well …

Uzma sighed at the thought of Niloufer's struggle to become a mother. After daily prayers and annual visits to European doctors, Niloufer had tried tying a taweez around her lower abdomen on the advice of a Pir sahib: a sacred locket in proximity with the womb. Thus far, it hadn't worked. A year ago, as the Buick neared Hill Fort, Niloufer had asked the driver to stop as she'd gazed longingly at the banyan.

'Buddha attained nirvana under this tree.'

'*This* tree?' Uzma asked.

'A banyan. Some banyan.' Niloufer shrugged. The gleaming diamonds in her ears lit up her pinched face. 'And they say Pirs live amongst its branches and listen to the duas you make.' Abruptly opening the car door, she stepped out. Uzma followed. In the shade of the giant banyan, Niloufer closed her eyes, clasped her hands and, with her head bowed, offered a silent prayer. Uzma glanced at the green umbrella of heart-shaped leaves and aerial roots searching for a Pir. Cool air riffled her sari, weaving through Niloufer's blue–black locks. As they walked back to the Buick, Niloufer smiled faintly, her brow puckered. 'As I prayed, I felt a hand on my head as blessing. Did you?'

'You know I don't believe in prayer, begum sahiba.'

'Uzma, the heretic. Though,' Niloufer snorted, 'I should have become one after a lifetime of unanswered prayers!'

Today, the air beneath the banyan was crisp, the aerial roots storing the mountain's morning mist as Uzma retrieved the folded sheet from an empty cigarette can. When Moin made a drop after huffing up Naubat Pahad after work, he tied a red scarf to an aerial root that was visible from the palace balconies facing the Hussain Sagar. All Uzma had to do was take a short walk thereafter, read the message, drop the scarf in the shady hollow at the bottom of the trunk, and replace the cigarette can for Ali Hassan. The first two drops had clearly been Moin's attempt to pass on his couplets to Shajeeh via Uzma. But Nag (Uzma's codename) was having none of it. She had returned the poems, which spoke of a lovelorn hero's struggles with the advice: Shajeeh is up to his dastar with tortured lovers, how about something on fiery revolutionaries? The drops had slowed down thereafter as Jaan (poet Moin's pen name) struggled with the mandated switch. But the third drop had information on a raid on the village Balemula to arrest Communist party leaders hiding there. Uzma had promptly hung a towel from the parapet of her room's balcony such that it was visible from the street. One of Ali Hassan's daily tasks now included cycling on Naubat Pahad every morning.

A pair of parakeets flew into the banyan and started to tweet noisily. Uzma read the note, a hastily scribbled message that needed immediate delivery to Ali Hassan. No wonder Moin had dropped it earlier in the day. But it was early evening already, and how was Uzma to get this halfway across town? Tossing the red scarf into the tree hollow, Uzma hurried back to the palace.

As Uzma began readying evening tea for Niloufer, Emily Perkins arrived like a godsend. A sliver of opportunity had opened up, like a bolt of sunlight through dark clouds. Smiling, Uzma took the tea tray to the terrace, where the women sat chatting. A strong smell of roses hung in the air. Clearly, Emily was liberal with the attar she had bought from the Charminar market. As Uzma offered her tea, Emily's head jigged in perplexed search. Of exactly what, Uzma knew as she extended towards her a plate of jeera biscuits.

On a frown, Emily asked, 'Where's my favourite, Uzma? The buttery ones?'

'Osmania biscuits? So sorry, but we've run out of them.' Uzma shook her head ruefully.

'RUN out of them?' Niloufer said in mock reprimand. 'How can Prince Moazzam's palatial kitchen be out of anything? Uzma, this speaks terribly of your housekeeping skills.'

Emily looked stricken until Niloufer dissolved into laughter and Uzma smiled broadly. There was one packet of Osmania biscuits sitting hidden in the kitchen, but what begum sahiba didn't know couldn't hurt her.

'Is it possible to send for some? Not now, with this tea,' Emily shrugged, 'but I thought I'll carry a batch with me to Delhi. The Mauliks will love them.' Emily Perkins was off to the capital of India for a couple of months to catch the action up close. Her host, the Maulik family, were industrialists, who also owned an elegant hotel which routinely hosted foreigners visiting India.

Niloufer, meanwhile, was looking at Uzma. 'Send the driver, will you?'

Uzma nodded. 'I'll go with him to make sure he gets the right ones. Emily leaves tomorrow … right? The cafe might make a fresh batch.'

'Good idea,' Niloufer said.

'But sit and have tea with us first!' Emily flapped a hand just as Uzma was getting up.

The delay wasn't good, but at least she had found a way to get to the Irani cafe. Hopefully, Ali Hassan would be there, or one of his comrades. Uzma bit the inside of her cheek as she listened to the women's conversation with one ear and sipped tea.

'*Why* this book?' Emily was saying. 'Well, why write any book … know what I mean? But yes, you are right, I *am* drawn to this subject matter. London is so terribly depressing at this time, all ruins and tattered economy. Even Delhi, with a hard-won independence, is teetering. Refugee tents everywhere … And Hyderabad … Hyderabad is on the cusp of something big … I feel like we're sitting on a volcano that will erupt anytime and, like Pliny the Younger and his friends, we'll be running with pillows on our heads as debris rains down from Vesuvius.'

'You're writing a book or a drama, Em?' Niloufer teased.

Emily shrugged and placed her teacup back on the tray. She bit into a jeera biscuit – 'mmm, nice' – before putting it whole into her mouth. 'My point is that the eruption of AD 79 is still with us because of Pliny the Younger's eyewitness account—'

'So you want to be Pliny the Youngest?'

At which both friends started to guffaw and Uzma began to gather the tea things.

Niloufer had told her that one reason Emily and she had become close school friends was because they were both pariahs. Niloufer's father had fled Turkey and Emily's parents had sent her to boarding school in Nice because her aristocratic English father with a German wife were seen as German sympathizers – which they were like so many English people, until Hitler went to war. During WWII, Emily had worked as an ambulance driver, a nurse, and a reporter. When Niloufer met her in Europe after the war, she thought poor Emily could do with a break from trying to prove her patriotism, and had invited her to visit India.

Like that man Pliny of her story, Emily Perkins had taken to wearing a cushion on her head to escape life's debris – Uzma concluded as the two women trotted to the Buick.

29
Delhi (March 1948)

B y early February, Vallabh had banned the RSS.
When Jawaharlal had termed them a fascist organization,
Vallabh had defended them as misguided patriots. But Bapu's
killer turned out to be an RSS member. And reports had
reached Vallabh that Bapu's assassination was celebrated by the
RSS at multiple places. He had also mandated Sanjeevi, head of
intelligence, to investigate whether Bapu's killing was part of a
much larger plan … Meanwhile, a drumroll had begun for his
resignation.

Vallabh pursed his mouth tightly. The Socialists were calling
for a home minister 'able and willing to curb the cult of, and
organization of, communal hate'. From the veranda of the
drawing room where he sat, he watched sparrows flit about
in the shade of the palash tree. Spring was arriving, fiery-red
buds dotted the tree, but his heart felt wintry. The campaign
of whispered insinuations and outright allegations had so
disheartened him that he had written out his resignation and
handed it to Mani to be despatched. But an aghast Vidya

Shankar, in a manner quite unlike him, had chased Vallabh to the car as he was leaving for a Cabinet meeting.

'So you disapprove my action?' Vallabh had asked his private secretary.

Shankar had bit his lip before blurting out, 'I dislike that you are submitting to this agitation organized against you!' Then, he had reminded Vallabh of the steps that he had taken as home minister for Gandhiji's security, and why he must resist the attempts to wedge him apart from Jawaharlal – if only to fulfil Gandhiji's wishes.

Vallabh sighed and reclined in his chair. The mellow noon sun warmed his callused feet. He had asked Shankar to tear the letter to pieces. Bapu's death had changed everything. Incidents of communal violence had come to a standstill, a stunned nation was still coming to terms with its profound loss. In a letter, Jawaharlal had reiterated to him his distress at the rumours about the discord between them.

'We have associated with each other for over a quarter century, and have faced many perils and storms together. Now, we face a different and more difficult world. This mischief that has magnified out of proportion any differences we may have – let's put an end to it.'

Simultaneously relieved and emboldened, Vallabh had defended himself in the Constituent Assembly. 'After the bomb thrown by Madanlal Pahwa, we had increased police presence at Birla House: seven plainclothes policemen in addition to nineteen uniformed ones, all armed with revolvers ... Left to me, I would have authorized the search of every man coming to Birla House, but Bapu wouldn't allow it.'

Which he had followed up with a public reiteration of his loyalty, as the deputy, to the Prime Minister. 'I am one with *my leader*, Jawaharlal, on *all* national issues.'

But his grief over Bapu's death was with him constantly. Mani remarked that while he had always been miserly with his smiles, he had now stopped smiling altogether. Perhaps. He had definitely aged overnight. Some days, it felt like his body was just waiting to mingle with dust again. With the soil of Nadiad, Gujarat, India. But an India that was whole ... Not one riddled with holes ... Hyderabad bothered him particularly. What a fuss that Razvi had made when a share of Bapu's asthi was to be immersed in the Sangam at Hyderabad. Earlier, that rascal had broken up a large public meeting in the grounds of the Nizam's college to mourn Bapu's death. Munshi had said that Razvi, in one of his inflammatory speeches, had also called for 5 lakh volunteers to be the liberators of Muslims of India from the yoke of the Indian Union! Agitated, Vallabh pushed himself upright, stood up slowly, and headed to the garden for a stroll. The Nizam's government was violating the Standstill Agreement, frequently changing its stance like it was the goddamn weather! They would not ban the Razakars, they would not accede, they would accede to the three Central subjects, provided all effective control over those was handed over to Hyderabad state ... Laik Ali's government would give the full cloth, only the cloth would be all holes!

Vallabh paused, short of breath.

A bee buzzed beneath the mango tree. His mind took him to Yervada Jail, where he had formed a 'club of regular spinners' of handloom with all the revolutionaries. However, he had found it difficult to spin as much as earlier, his ageing body refusing to cooperate. So he would rest where Bapu's cot used to be, under that historic mango tree, and tell himself that he was back at the place that Bapu had turned into a temple, where Bapu completed his fast, and the Poona Pact was signed ...

A raised voice filtered over from the refugees still tenting in the front lawns. The smell of cooking and smoke wafted as well. Vallabh started to walk again, more slowly.

Laik Ali had been Pakistan's representative to the UN before he was appointed PM by the Nizam, and he continued to be beholden to Jinnah, who, Vallabh's intel had conveyed, was saying, 'I require Hyderabad as an active ally – not as a neutral in such a war.' Vallabh opened his mouth and drew in a lungful of air.

He should stop fulminating.

Meanwhile, intelligence reports had come in that Hyderabad was trying to acquire more planes for Deccan Airways, so it could be linked by air to Karachi in West Pakistan and Chittagong in East Pakistan. Attempts were also being made to establish trade connections with Persia, Egypt, the United Kingdom, Canada ... A large amount of sterling had been deposited with the Hyderabad agent in the UK – for arms purchase? Razakars were increasingly trespassing into Union Territories, and smuggling arms and ammunition.

Vallabh tossed his head and resumed walking.

Apparently, they couldn't wait for Vallabh's demise in Hyderabad, which they were announcing on a daily basis. Munshi had reported that whenever the agent-general's car was sighted with its national flag, urchins at street corners would start singing: Taaza khabrein, Sardar Patel mar gaye!

Fatigue was weighing down his limbs ...

Vallabh might be gone soon, but he had reviewed the Hyderabad situation at a conference on 21 February with the chief ministers of the three states neighbouring Hyderabad: Bombay, Madras, and the Central Provinces. After which he had issued an ultimatum to Hyderabad: Responsible government should be introduced first, and the Ittehad must be liquidated.

A rustle in the veranda. Manibehn had come to summon him for lunch.

Sushila Nayar, Bapu's physician, was already seated at the table with Vidya Shankar. The four started to eat. Vallabh was sipping on the thin dal when he broke into cold sweat. His hand stilled. Pain exploded in his chest. In agony, he let the spoon clatter and clutched his heart.

'What's the matter?' Sushila was leaning over. 'Are you feeling pain?'

At Vallabh's nod, Shankar and Sushila helped him to his bed. 'Quick, call Dr Dhanda,' she instructed Shankar, 'and inform Panditji!'

In fifteen minutes, Dr Dhanda had administered morphine to Vallabh, and confirmed that the home minister had suffered a heart attack. When Jawaharlal arrived with Indira, Vallabh was shifting in and out of drug-induced sleep. He was trying to speak. Manibehn gave him a little water to moisten his lips.

'I had to go with Bapu,' Vallabh whispered hoarsely. Tears streamed down his cheeks. 'He has gone alone.'

30
Hyderabad (March 1947)

'These ancient boulders ... Look how delicately they perch atop one another.' Daniyal pointed to the rocks scattered across the vista. 'It is said that the gods were halted at play.'

Or ascetic yogis had turned to stone whilst doing their asanas. One tall pile reminded Jaabili of a children's game even, seven stones, only this would have to be the children of giants.

They sat atop a boulder, the city of Hyderabad shimmering in the distance. The landscape in between was a swathe of red soil dotted with green scrub, acacia trees, and giant rocks. 'This granite is millions of years old ... So, so old that us humans did not exist even as an idea. No humans, no petty human concerns ...'

Daniyal rested his chin on arms folded over drawn-up knees and continued to gaze outwards. They had come to Fakhruddingutta by bus, then hiked up the hillock with a parcel of food prepared by Khudabax. 'We must do a picnic,' Daniyal had insisted as the plans for the protest were pushed back, 'once the procession gets over. A break from planning and pamphlets and couriers and comrades ... A getaway!'

Jaabili didn't require persuasion: The prospect of getting away with Daniyal to a secluded place was enough. Being together with all the comrades was good for work, being alone with Daniyal was good for her. Whenever work brought her to the city – carrying messages, ferrying people – she found time to head to Chappal Bazaar at day's end. Most days, Daniyal would be busy with the printing machine. Jaabili would take old Telugu and Urdu copies of *Hyderabad Khabrein*, pick a headline, and, through compare and contrast, teach herself the Nizam's language. Daniyal had earlier given her an Urdu Qaida for kids. As Jaabili studied, the tip of her tongue sticking out, tracing curlicues and dots, she listened to Daniyal crooning as he worked, ghazals mostly, interspersed with Angla verses. From outside, where Khudabax shuffled watering the courtyard plants, wafted in birdsong and jasmine. On rare days, Daniyal would be unoccupied and they would get talking. His anecdotes and stories, ranging from Hyderabad to Hadhramaut to Helmsdale, wove in expanding spirals, interwoven with persuasions and poetry, a one-man mushaira. To Jaabili's surprise, Daniyal Khan was genuinely interested in what she thought and said. He would cock his head and listen intently. With him, Jaabili never felt less than a man. Which was funny considering she felt most alive as a woman in his presence.

A ruckus in the acacia trees nearby brought Jaabili back to the present. A monkey raced up a tree followed by another, their chattering sending a flock of birds into flight. Jaabili turned to Daniyal, who seemed lost in the vista.

She had arrived at the haveli late afternoon to find him reclining on the sofa, hands steepled on his chest, watching a pair of geckos on the porch ceiling. 'Getaway?' she had suggested.

Get away from the city, the party, the protests ... The big procession had got delayed twice: first due to planning issues with the volunteer jathas, second due to the killing of Gandhi. When the non-violent march by satyagrahis protesting the Nizam's rule and asking for union with India finally occurred, it became a violent affair – marked by blood and brawl, slogans and counter-slogans. Razakars, disguised as volunteers, had infiltrated the protest and begun pelting stones at the police.

'*Jai Hind!*'

'*Long live the Nizam!*'

'*Inquilab zindabad!*'

'*Nizam ke kadmon pe, Nehru ko jhuka denge!*'

Nehru bowing low at the feet of the Nizam was debatable. But what was certain was the success of the slogan chanted by marchers holding placards of a caricature with flaming eyes and a flaming beard serving up a platter of pulao.

'*Razvi ka khayali pulao, mat khao, mat khao!*'

Whether Hyderabad city was persuaded to not consume Razvi's pie in the sky was not yet settled. What was clear though was how catchy the slogan truly was. Three weeks later, it could almost be the takiya kalam of the protest movement, the witty catchphrase that vigorously demonstrated opposition to the Nizam, his militant Razakars, and Kasim Razvi's castles in the air! Like any popular offering, it had morphed and truncated as people co-opted it to express their disaffection. Women clapped hands to 'mat khao! mat khao!', men teased one another with a wink to 'khayali pulao', and students sang the slogan to the tune of '*Vande mataram*'.

To lighten Daniyal's mood, Jaabili opened the food parcel, laying out the khagina and the square parathas. She inhaled the rich, tangy smell of the egg and onion curry. 'Shall we eat,' Jaabili asked brightly, 'before the monkeys join us?'

'Great idea!' Daniyal stood up, stretched out his arms, before sitting cross-legged across from her and tucking in.

Jaabili could guess what was on his mind. In less than a month, Daniyal Khan had become Enemy Number 1 to the Razakars, way ahead of Nehru–Gandhi. An arsenal of newspapers and broadcasts – the Ittehad had seven daily, and six weekly, papers and access to the Nizam's radio for publicity – had reported extensively on the violent procession orchestrated by the Nizam's enemies, the 'rioting by the satyagrahis', their slanderous slogans. But Daniyal's paper had reported on how the march was infiltrated by the Razakars, and how the protesters were wounded at the hands of the Razakars and the police. Finally, what got the Razakars' fezs into a flurry was the sneaking suspicion that the popularity of the march's slogan might be due to the public's sympathy with the underdogs.

The police raided Daniyal's house, attacked the printing machine and made vague threats of jail time. Razakars had taken to hurling stones wrapped in paper – with vile threats scrawled on them – into Daniyal's courtyard. Somebody had roughed up Khudabax as he purchased groceries. Which made Daniyal Khan livid. Khudabax was the nanny who had raised the boy left bereft of his parents after an accident. An uncle had usurped the family fortune, leaving only the Chappal Bazaar haveli, Khudabax, and a paltry sum to the feringhee bachcha. The last was not strictly accurate – Daniyal Khan had only one feringhee in his ancestors, a Scottish grandmother on his mother's side.

Which explained the blue–black eyes, the toddy-coloured complexion, the tamarind-like tint of his coal-black hair, his way of thinking ... perhaps? But what could explain the restlessness he evoked in Jaabili, the desire to let his voice wash over her, the fierce need inside her to protect him?

In the end, Jaabili admitted to herself that what she felt was love; she didn't know how it fit into her life. After all, she had joined the Sangham for a better one. But gossip and scandal could wreck this new world. The party was known to expel women who lay with men in their squad. Or women who became mothers. Salamma had divulged how she had given away her newborn child because the safety of the squad was at stake. Women were equal to men, and yet, men were more equal. Jaabili chafed at the casual manner of discrimination: men were not under surveillance, men could have flings, men were not expected to cook ...

A sparrow flew daringly close, perching within striking distance, bobbing its head. Daniyal tore a piece of his paratha, nipped a scrap and laid it on the rock. In a flash the sparrow had grabbed it and flown. A robust chittering announced the arrival of more sparrows. Daniyal laughed, his head thrown back. Behind him, the sun was a glowing ball on the horizon, its evanescent light picking the reddish tinge of his hair. Jaabili felt an intense desire to rake his hair with her fingers, to plant her mouth on his, to—

Daniyal's level head was contemplating her. She flushed and looked away guiltily.

After the meal, morsels of which fed a knot of sparrows, Jaabili went to relieve herself behind a thicket. Twilight burnished the rocks, birds arced the sky, chirrups emanated from treetops. The patch of red soil was inviting. An idea struck Jaabili. She shot up, grabbed a twig, plucked the drying leaves off and began to draw on the surface. Then she wrote, hoping her rudimentary knowledge would not hamper her penmanship. She stepped back, but could not gauge the effect. Discarding the twig, Jaabili hopped onto the rock and clambered atop the granite.

Daniyal had lit a cigarette and sat blowing rings of smoke. Jaabili paused to survey her work, a heart engraved with two names, and giggled. She felt silly, light, light-headed. As she rejoined him, he offered her a smoke. She reached across to take the cigarette from his hand, and a current coursed through her. Inhaling deeply, Jaabili tried to tamp the feeling that her body was afire. Tapping the ash off, she returned the cigarette. Daniyal looked surprised, waiting to see if she would cough.

'I've smoked beedis before,' Jaabili scoffed. 'They taste better.'

Daniyal tipped his head in amused acknowledgement.

'Is that the Golconda Fort?' She pointed to the far right where a citadel rose over the undulating land. Idle talk was one way to distract her body.

Daniyal nodded. 'It used to be a mud fort. Many rulers later, the Qutb Shahis expanded it into that fortress of granite. Looks impregnable, eh? T'was. Until Aurangzeb offered bribes to the commanders of the Qutb Shahi king. One night, the western gate of the fort was thrown open and in stormed Aurangzeb's army. Which paved the way for young Qamruddin, the first Nizam.'

'So extortion is at the heart of the Nizam's Hyderabad?'

To Daniyal's raised brows, Jaabili replied, 'A peasant's life is crushed by bribes to be paid to officials. Once, a grain inspector was in our village when a peasant wrestled him down, caught his ear between two stones, and ground it!'

'Woah! Guess that inspector never showed his face again!' Daniyal held out the cigarette to her.

She inhaled deeply and was depositing the cigarette back between his fingers when she removed it abruptly, took another long draw, stubbed the cigarette out, turned, and, catching his face between her hands, clamped her mouth on his. A taste of wet ash and cloves before their lips locked in hunger. Their bodies claimed each other. Tearing at clothes, shedding some, Daniyal worrying about the rough rock surface, Jaabili drawing him down, they made frenzied love under a canopy of stars and the gaze of monkeys.

31
Hyderabad (April 1948)

On the invitation of Prime Minister Mir Laik Ali, El Edroos was en route to the Golconda Armaments Factory. Hyderabad Army was short of equipment, arms and ammunition. Units had returned from WWII without their equipment and, despite repeated requests for rearmament, the Government of India continued to take no action. El Edroos had deputized a party to head to the Kirkee Arsenal for the supply of much-needed ammunition, but they had returned empty-handed. Apparently, the arsenal was instructed by the Army Headquarters, Delhi, not to make any supplies to the Hyderabad forces.

The car swept past the rocky terrain studded with scrub. Snakes and scorpions nestled there, as did Communists, and lately, Congress raiders. Reports were coming in of camps set up across Hyderabad's borders, in Bombay and the Central Provinces, from which satyagrahis were making raids into the state, terrorizing villages, arming some of them. 'Volunteers,' the Hyderabad State Congress called them! Fitting, El Edroos snorted, considering the other set of active volunteers were the Razakars.

The image of Kasim Razvi dressed in a field marshal's uniform swam in his mind – El Edroos's mood darkened.

Razvi's damn men were running berserk in the state, upsetting anybody and everybody. Some of them had raided the house of an Arab lecturer at Osmania University, burnt his furniture and library, which had the holy Koran! They claimed the house was a part of their headquarters and the lecturer was refusing to vacate it. In turn, the Arabs raided an Ittehad camp, burnt it down and beat up several Razakars. Kasim Razvi had then gone on to make a fiery speech accusing the Nawab of Chhatari and the Nizam's Irregular Forces, which employed several Arabs, for the damage done. At a subsequent meeting to contain the conflagration, Kasim Razvi persisted with his inflammatory remarks. Which El Edroos cautioned him against. A heated exchange followed, which terminated only when El Edroos slapped him.

The major general eyed his palm. He regretted losing his temper, but a benefit was how quickly Razvi had cooled down, forgoing his fanatic outpourings for a few subsequent weeks. The Razakars, of course, had decided since that El Edroos was Enemy No. 1. He was of Arab stock too, after all.

The car slowed down to let a shepherd pass. The goats followed him in a herd, some bleating, some headbutting the others, all stinking. Razvi had organized the Razakars on semi-military lines, and since there was no Arms Act in Hyderabad, the jokers were armed with all varieties of firearms. From muzzle loaders and sports rifles to lances, spears, swords, and daggers. El Edroos stroked his moustache. He had repeatedly brought the matter to the notice of the erstwhile Prime Minister and his Cabinet, but no action was taken. Of course, with the *new* Prime Minister, the scene was completely different.

Mir Laik Ali, forty-five years old, a noted industrialist of Hyderabad, was friendly with both Jinnah and the Ittehad – qualification enough. From what El Edroos had heard, the Nizam had written to Jinnah seeking his opinion on Laik Ali's appointment. More like seeking the Quaid's blessing, considering Laik Ali was Pakistan's delegate to United Nations Organisation at that time. Mir Laik Ali had become Prime Minister in November when El Edroos was overseas trying to buy aircraft on orders of the Nawab of Chhatari, who suddenly found that he was the ex-PM!

The honk of the car brought El Edroos back to the present.

Passing through the factory gates, the car came to a halt in front of a brick building with a tall, sloping tin roof. Loud clanging filled the air, the raised urgent voices of men, the smell of gun cotton ... El Edroos was back in Palestine, WWI, the second battle of Gaza, the 15th Imperial Service Cavalry Brigade forcing the Turks to the coast in a pincer attack ...

⁓

Mir Laik Ali stood watching the workers from behind a large glass-panelled window. The men, mouths covered with rags, were drilling, hammering, gesticulating as they shouted to be heard. It was deafening. El Edroos entered, the men greeted each other and stepped outside. 'The OUTER office,' Laik Ali shouted, thumbing in the direction of an outhouse.

Because it was difficult to purchase arms from abroad, the Prime Minister had started the Golconda Armaments Factory. A bold effort, much-needed. Laik Ali had a spring in his step as he walked. 'The railway workshop at Lalaguda shifted the required machinery and equipment and we are off to a start in record time! Rifle making is coming along very well. I'll have some brought out for your inspection,' he beamed.

In the outer office was a sofa and some chairs arranged around a low centre table. Noise was muffled, despite there being no furnishings. Laik Ali sat cross-legged on the sofa. El Edroos took a chair across from him. They had barely settled down when the door swung open and in walked Kasim Razvi carrying with him fresh bluster. Perhaps their last encounter was still fresh in his mind. After Razvi had greeted the Prime Minister, he smiled cordially in the major general's direction and dipped his head. He was dressed in his military clothes, a green beret on his head, his mouth reddish from the paan he chewed constantly. Razvi took the opposite end of the sofa, draping one arm over the sofa's back, his fingers within stroking distance of the premier.

Awkward. El Edroos's smooth war veteran's face displayed no emotion. The Razakars under Kasim Razvi, with their faux military uniforms and parades in Hyderabad and other parts of the state, were a nuisance – a fact he had shared with the Prime Minister. It was plain embarrassing for the commander-in-chief of the Hyderabad Army when a rabble-rouser donned a field marshal's uniform and gave fiery speeches across town, accompanied by his hangers-on attired as aides-de-camp! But El Edroos was barking up the wrong tree, clearly. Razvi had Mir Laik Ali comfortably settled in one very large breast pocket. Whilst El Edroos had been devising ways to convince the Prime Minister of some sort of police or army action to suppress the Razakars! He'd been well and truly ambushed.

'Ah, good.' Laik Ali clapped his hands. 'Now that you are both here, let's inspect the rifles.' He instructed a man who scrambled away. The PM smoothed down his tie and smiled.

Mir Laik Ali was a civil engineer, with no training as an administrator. With his receding hairline, plump cheeks, and pleasant manners, did he realize he was overseeing the actions of a subversive whilst head of state? Would this lead to the rise of Hyderabad or its downfall?

On a broad smile, Razvi began to update the Prime Minister. 'As you know, my efforts over the past few months have been dedicated to increasing the membership of the Ittehad, and the number of Razakars. We've had great success mobilizing the local Muslim population who believe in our cause and pray for its deliverance. Additionally,' he made raucous sucking sounds, 'the Hindu untouchables have flocked to us in large numbers, guided by your minister for education in the new Cabinet, B.S. Venkat Rao.' Razvi smoothed his wispy beard like it were a favoured pet and lifted it up until it covered his mouth.

Mir Laik Ali nodded. 'Indian Muslim refugees also, I believe, have joined the Ittehad.'

'Oh, yes!' Razvi bobbed upright on the sofa, smacking his lips. 'Thousands of Indian Muslims are seeking the Nizam's protection from the violence of Partition. More than 1,500 are housed in the Nizam's palace in Delhi, and many refugees are pouring into the state, especially Hyderabad city. We have set up fifty-two centres in the entire state, each under a salar, and staffed by the Razakar corps in khaki uniforms. There, they undertake military training. I can confirm,' his eyes lit up, 'the Razakars number 2,00,000, or more!'

'Mashallah!' Laik Ali beamed.

El Edroos was feeling like the shunned relative at a family banquet. He fingered his shirt collar and tried not to show his discomfort. Ittehad propaganda had been popular with young and lower-class Muslims intoxicated by the idea of a collective Muslim sovereignty over the Deccan. But lately, Kasim Razvi's speeches of Hindus as an enslaved people and the Muslims as a nation with a great destiny to fulfil had entered the hearts and minds of many of his own acquaintances as well. And India had begun threatening an economic blockade. It was a recipe for war—

The door opened, a din sounded, and two men entered cradling rifles in their arms. Kasim Razvi jumped up in excitement and helped himself to one rifle. The men looked at Laik Ali who indicated the table with his eyes. Depositing the arms, they left.

'Major general,' the Prime Minister hailed, 'what do you think?'

El Edroos stood up, grabbed a rifle and inspected it closely. Barrel, buttstock, bolt, guard, trigger ... The workmanship and finish was very poor. On a soft sigh, he met Laik Ali's bright eyes.

'A rifle's main function is accuracy. These, I am afraid, would be dangerous to fire on a range even.'

A perplexed Laik Ali swivelled from El Edroos to Kasim Razvi.

'Let's test it then,' Razvi drawled and strode to the door.

32
Hyderabad (April 1948)

Kasim Razvi's bodyguards, who had been waiting outside, watched their boss saunter out with a rifle in hand. The men, each of whom had a gun slung over one shoulder, scrambled after Razvi. Laik Ali, hands in his pant pockets, and El Edroos followed. The crispness of early morning had yielded to bright heat, which polished the red soil to shining. A din assaulted their ears, gunpowder stung their noses, like a thousand firecrackers were going off.

Razvi stopped at a barren patch 500-metres away. Factory clamour had faded. He narrowed his eyes and examined the space. Rocks and scrub and a stunted champa tree. Would not qualify for a shooting range that the major general would approve of. Razvi could feel heat rising in his cheeks ... That stinging slap, his skin tingling for days after ... El Edroos had humiliated the leader of the Ittehad, the one party that was standing up to the might of Hindu India, that had the full support of the Muslim people, that was actively organizing the defence of Hyderabad! And what had the great El Edroos been doing? Hopping on planes to England and Europe, with bagfuls of money, to buy arms and aircraft. Where were the arms? The bombers? Razvi spat, red paan juice splattering on green tufts. Then he hefted the rifle, and positioning the butt against his right shoulder pocket, looked through the sight. He couldn't focus. Slinging the rifle, he walked on. Let the men think he was looking for the right spot while he got his mind under control.

Ideally, the major general of the Hyderabad forces should be in tight alignment with the leader of the largest Muslim party in the state. It was said that El Edroos could make an army out of a mob. He had come out of WWI with great laurels and had the potential to convert the Razakar corps into the finest fighting unit. Yet, he persisted with pettiness, afraid that he, Kasim Razvi, was usurping the commander-in-chief's role! Anyway, what was the war hero doing with his time? Playing polo and partying! Razvi kicked a clod that rolled away and sent a scorpion scurrying away, its tail upright. He paused. Best to test the rifle and get out. He beckoned to one of his men.

El Edroos and Laik Ali stood at the perimeter of the scrub, a good distance away. Razvi handed the rifle to young Idris, slapping his shoulder as he moved away. Idris had come from Oudh like him, his family fleeing after riots had broken out in August. Gangly, hot-headed, eager, he fit right in with the Razakars.

Beaming, Razvi swivelled his neck to the two distant observers, nodded to them, and turning, barked a command to Idris, 'Fire!'

Young Idris crouched over the rifle like it would run away from him – a crack split the air. It was nearly swallowed by agonized cries. The rifle clattered to the ground. Idris spun around, holding up his right hand supported by his left arm. His khaki shirtfront had bright-red splotches. The right half of his face was streaked red, his right ear was a bloodied rose, his crimson hand was sawed off.

∞

The gun barrel had exploded.

El Edroos shifted in the hot car, trying to wrench his mind from the rifle test that had gone horribly wrong. He hadn't seen a young man so mangled since his days with the Hyderabad Lancers in Syria. While Idris was bandaged and rushed to a hospital, Kasim Razvi had sat stone-faced, his posse of Razakars wan and silent. Laik Ali summoned the factory supervisor, reprimanded him, and asked to see a better specimen soonest. The Prime Minister was confident the rifles would get modified and be ready for use by the army soon.

'I doubt that very much, sir,' El Edroos had quietly dissented. 'In my soldierly opinion, the rifles are dangerous, at best, and beyond responsible use.'

Kasim Razvi, however, needed no convincing. Smoking, when not chewing paan, he declared loftily, 'We will take the rifles!' Clearly not chastened by Idris's mishap.

The car trundled back to Hyderabad. Pi dogs lay in the shade, bees bumbled in the hot sun, boulders baked. The days of long noon siestas were upon them. One could seek refuge inside, assume everything was working to its rhythm, but that would be a mistake. India was a giant, and the giant had started rumbling ... Meanwhile, El Edroos needed weapons to defend against the Communists and Congress raiders, and eventually, the Indian Army! Arms, ammunition, aircraft ...

A Halifax Bomber that El Edroos had purchased from the UK, and flown home to Hyderabad by enlisting a crew of ex-Royal Air Force personnel, was promptly returned. Why?

Because the Nawab of Chhatari who had commissioned it had become the ex-PM in the interim ...

'Don't look a gift horse in the mouth,' Wavell would say. Jerusalem was captured in 1917 by the British because Wavell's plan relied on the distrust between the Turks and their German general. Which enabled the cavalry brigade El Edroos was with to encircle and capture Jerusalem. The commanding officer entered the old holy city on foot, not horse or vehicle, to show respect ...

In a twist though, the new Prime Minister mistrusted his own commander-in-chief. He had ordered El Edroos: 'Stay out of the matter (buying aircrafts) in the future, and concentrate entirely on the armed forces and the defence of Hyderabad.'

Right. *Defend* Hyderabad. With *what* exactly?

The ramparts of Golconda Fort shimmered on a distant hilltop. He remembered escorting Lord and Lady Wavell to the fort on a state visit. His association with Lord Wavell, which had started during WWI, continued during WWII, had resumed during the Wavell viceroyalty when El Edroos was appointed as his Honorary ADC. The memory brought a faint smile to his lips. Lord Wavell had shown how well a soldierly training translated to civil duties. Of course, his campaign in Egypt as the commander of the British troops in the Middle East during WWII was legendary. El Edroos had seen first-hand how an enemy with greater strength could be outwitted with superior military tactics. At the memory of the Axis powers, Italy and Germany, a bitterness laced his gullet ...

He cleared his throat and swallowed. After the October coup, Ali Yavar Jung, minister for constitutional affairs, had confided to him darkly: *Hyderabad now has a Victor Emmanuel and a Mussolini!* Any student of WWII knew that the fascist Mussolini had ridden to power on the tailcoats of the pliant

King Victor Emmanuel. Which killed the monarchy and threw Italy into such turbulence that the nation was still to recover. Of course, Mussolini had convinced the Italians that as Il Duce, he was their saviour.

El Edroos probed his furrowed brow. The increasing fervour of the Razakars had led to Razvi's anointment as Siddique-e-Deccan. The comparison with the first Caliph of Islam had arisen after Razvi made a dramatic and well-publicized offer of all his property to the Ittehad. Which conveniently obscured the fortune he had amassed from shady dealings in Latur as a lawyer!

But Hyderabadis believed what they wanted to believe. They had vested their hopes in Kasim Razvi, and no longer felt the need to concern themselves with inconvenient truths.

El Edroos sighed and wiped the perspiration off his face. Was it time to resign?

33
Delhi (April–May 1948)

'Even if they came from a lunatic asylum, Razvi's speeches would be extraordinary!'

Jawahar snorted as he placed a book on the sheaf of papers that were aflutter in the eddies raised by the ceiling fan in his study.

The defence minister gave a slow nod in answer. 'You and I understand that, Panditji, but the public reads his speeches in the newspapers and asks why the government is not being tough.'

'*Tough* being the shorthand for going to war?'

This time, Baldev Singh's nod was swift and firm. 'Razvi knows the audience for his speeches is as much in India as in Hyderabad state. With our spring offensive in Kashmir, he thinks our troops are occupied. Razvi is counting on the Indian Army not being able to launch a parallel offensive in Hyderabad ... *if* we wanted to.'

Jawahar stood up and started to pace his study. 'We have a difficult balance to maintain. We must convince the Indian

194

public that we can solve the problem of Hyderabad peacefully, even as Razvi flings his speech grenades. We have to get the Nizam to accede, without force or coercion, but through a plebiscite which establishes the will of the people. With the ongoing action in Kashmir, our best bet is that Hyderabad honours the Standstill Agreement—'

'Which it is not.'

'Which is why we have a contingency plan, Operation Polo. But that plan has been prepared wholly and solely against the extreme emergency of Razvi carrying out his threat of murdering all Hindus with his Razakars.' Jawahar sighed. 'Meanwhile, we must continue to look for a peaceful resolution. Other methods might be quicker, but they will come at a cost we would rather not pay.'

Baldev Singh smoothed his whiskers. 'I agree. But Jinnah wants to extend the battle in Kashmir to Hyderabad. Unlike Hari Singh, the Nizam sits in his sherwani pocket. And Laik Ali—'

'—is a useful stooge.' Jawahar plucked the tin of State Express 555 from his desk, snapped it open, removed a cigarette and lit it. 'A conflict with India will be terrible for all Hyderabadis and will also have serious consequences for Muslims in the rest of India. The premier of Hyderabad should know that. But a worsening communal situation is exactly what Jinnah would like.' Jawahar sucked hard on his cigarette.

Baldev Singh cracked the knuckles of his hands. He could feel the sweat lining his turban. The air was as oppressive as an airless kitchen, despite the whirring fan. The Prime Minister had air conditioning which he seldom used. Gandhiji's killing had made the communal situation dormant, but it could erupt any time. Kasim Razvi's crazed utterances were reaching their targets in India – many of whom were still in shelters, disoriented by twin losses of land and loved ones. A memory surged in his mind from an Emergency Committee meeting last year. Panditji was complaining that the Sikh refugees in Delhi were particularly vicious. 'Their war cry is Lyallpur,' he had berated, 'every time they score a kill.'

Baldev Singh had felt compelled to remind the committee of the flight they had undertaken in September, on the governor general's plane, to view the Panjab migrations. 'We started near Ferozepur, on the newly created border, and then followed the kafilas for well over 50 miles. But we did not reach a terminus ... The kafila from West Panjab – remember? Trucks and tractors in the front and back, loaded bullock carts in the middle, armed men on horses flanking each side – the convoy proceeded with precision. At the head of the kafila were white-bearded Sikhs, some even wearing medals. The kafila looked like an army unit. Which was in sharp contrast to the kafila from east – raggedy, straggly, disordered. Why am I pointing this out? Because the kafila from West Panjab comprised soldiers who had fought world wars. As a reward, they were given the barren tracts of Lyallpur by the sarkar. They poured their blood and sweat into that land. The land of Lyallpur. Which they transformed to lush green fields. Which, at one brisk stroke of midnight, they were forced to abandon.'

The refugees had felt a great sense of betrayal at the hands of India, Pakistan, and Britain. Their inflow had threatened Delhi. What if Razvi and the Razakars set off fresh kafilas into India from Hyderabad? A new lot of refugees – this time betrayed by India?

Baldev Singh could feel the dust in his windpipe. He reached for the glass of water and drank quickly. Wiping down his moustache, he said, 'We must not become helpless spectators to the events in Hyderabad. Even Sardar thinks—'

'We are not.' Jawahar ground his cigarette in the ashtray on his desk. 'We are *not* helpless spectators, or spectators of any kind.' His chest heaved with emotion he was trying to control. He could not understand the bloodlust in his fellow citizens. What had happened to the values they had cherished, their brave ideals ... With Bapu gone, had ahimsa died too?

Jawahar cleared his throat. 'We will continue to negotiate, and we will *also* continue to examine military options. We already have infantry units present in areas not far from Hyderabad. Correct?'

The defence minister assented.

'Let's position them closer, such that an armoured brigade can be deployed quickly in case of emergency. But don't make haste. No precipitate action that might suggest we are launching war. Tell the troops to proceed in a deliberate manner. The news of such a movement will spread like wildfire in Hyderabad and convey our message: India means business.'

∽

The mercury was rising in Delhi. It was 112 degrees the day Edwina and Dickie invited Jawahar to accompany them to their Mashobra retreat for a few days of informal talks. As they drove up the hills in a bright-red open-topped Talbot, Dickie at the wheel, the air grew cooler and Jawahar's spirits rose. Depressed by Delhi politics, still suffering from Bapu's loss, he was hoping that a few days in his beloved mountains would restore him.

They quickly settled into a rhythm. A morning climb through the orchards along the terraced hillsides with Edwina; afternoon talks with Dickie; and, in the evening, as Dickie worked on his family tree, Edwina, Pamela, and Jawahar walked along the Ridge in Simla.

After tea one evening, Dickie broached the subject of Hyderabad. 'I'll admit the stalemate has been causing me much anxiety, Jawa. With only six weeks before our departure from India, amidst the whirl of farewell visits, I'd still like to bring the negotiations to a happy end.'

'The Nizam is a master of obfuscation.' Jawahar held out his hands, palms outstretched. 'He will repudiate every settlement whilst giving an impression of conceding to it. In April, as you know, following consultations with Walter Monckton, we handed over a simple list of four points to the Laik Ali government. Control Razvi.' Jawahar held up his index finger. 'Release the imprisoned Congressmen.' He continued counting on his fingers. 'Genuine reconstruction of the existing government to represent both communities. And the introduction of a responsible government before year-end.'

Jawahar held up his right hand, four fingers upright.

'What does the Nizam do? Disappoint us. As usual. He absolves Razvi, and claims *we* are *interfering* in Hyderabad's *internal* matters. Not only Vallabhbhai, the whole Cabinet is livid!'

'Hmmm ...' Dickie uncrossed a leg and stretched out. They had had little rest since the start of the year. An interminable programme included flying visits to India's states and provinces to say goodbyes, dinners, and receptions, with speeches, dancing and presentations – Edwina, of course, insisted on visiting the local sanatoriums and hospitals, and was plain exhausted. Unlike her husband, she didn't have the knack of dozing off during tiresome speeches and waking up just in time to reply. Kashmir had been referred to the United Nations, but the logjam with Hyderabad had to be broken.

'Even Walter has left for London. The Nizam's own consultant thinks good relations are impossible under the present Hyderabad government. But I think, even if the

Nizam was willing, Laik Ali and Kasim Razvi would never allow a proportionate Hindu representation in Hyderabad's Constituent Assembly.' Dickie rubbed his hands together. 'I cannot, in all fairness, let the Nizam go down that path, for I am convinced that only an agreement with India will save Hyderabad from a worse fate.'

Dickie arose and Jawahar followed him.

'I'm thinking of inviting the Nizam to Delhi for a man-to-man talk.'

'Godspeed,' said Jawahar drolly.

They started to stroll in the gardens cradled by snow-peaked mountains. 'Sometimes,' Jawahar mused, 'I wonder what the mighty Himalayas think when they watch us mortals wrestling with our difficulties. The pressing issues of our time – Hyderabad, Kashmir – must appear insignificant and temporary to them.'

'They give us permission to speak freely,' Dickie quipped.

'Mizzie, come along girl!'

The men turned to watch Edwina coaxing her Sealyham to walk. But Mizzie had flopped on the grass and was watching Edwina with equanimity. Shaking her head, Edwina scooped up the dog and joined them. Rubbing the dog's head fondly, she said, 'Poor Mizzie's grown old.'

With a kiss on his wife's cheek, Dickie excused himself to resume his genealogy studies. Edwina and Jawahar ambled together under the clear blue sky, their heads bent in conversation.

'So,' Edwina smiled, 'have the mountains ministered their magic potion?'

'You were right to suggest the retreat. I was weary and full of self-doubt ... You and the Himalayas invigorate me. I talk so easily with you; I only hope my unburdening doesn't weigh you down.'

Edwina shook her head. 'It's been so hectic that getting you to Mashobra to talk naturally and informally had become my obsession. Of course,' she looked in the distance, 'our time in India is almost over … You know, Jawa, I had not wanted to come. But after fifteen months here, I hate the thought of going home.' She sighed, long and deep.

'It's the mountains speaking,' Jawahar teased her. 'As soon as you're in Delhi, amidst the scorching dust storms, you'll change your mind.'

'I know that you know.' Edwina's eyes were moist as she shifted the terrier from one arm to another. 'I'm glad Mizzie got a chance to grow old here – she was with me at Adsdean, and through the war, but she will have to be quarantined upon our return. I hate the idea. She will pine so.'

Jawahar's palm rested on Mizzen's head as he looked into Edwina's eyes. Birdsong filled the air. Faint strains of a song floated. 'Life is a dreary business, and when a bright patch comes, it rather takes one's breath away …'

∽

After his restful retreat, Jawahar returned to the rising heat of Delhi.

At the Defence Committee meeting, the recent standoff between Hyderabad and the Indian forces following Hyderabad state's refusal to let Indian officials enter an Indian enclave within its territory, was debated. Earlier, Major General J.N. Chaudhuri had suggested that Operation Polo be postponed since the monsoons would hamper the movement of tanks. Following this, military action was postponed for four months.

Nevertheless, the army was mandated to be ready to execute the plan at ten days' notice – if the situation so arose.

Ten days later, Jawahar was at his desk writing to Vallabhbhai. He had left instructions to not be disturbed until the letter was done. Soon, however, there was a knock on the door and Mac popped his head in. 'I'm sorry, Panditji, but Baldev Singh is on the line for you – it's urgent, he says.'

Jawahar picked up the phone and heard his defence minister's update with a furrowing brow. The Hyderabad police had arrested Indian soldiers escorting a train of military stores. And, in another instance, a train from Madras to Bombay was attacked when passing through Hyderabad by a mob armed with daggers, hockey sticks, and lathis. A British field officer in the service of the Indian Union, who was in the train at the time, had informed that, while the mob attacked the train, armed Razakars stood by on the platform. Among the injured were women and children.

Jawahar's mind was in turmoil as he replaced the telephone's receiver.

Padmaja's letter had arrived that morning, bemoaning the alarming communal climate in her beloved Hyderabad. Jawahar's mind had raced back to 1938. When the state Congress had initiated satyagraha, the Arya Samaj and the Hindu Mahasabha, not to be outdone, had quickly followed with their parallel satyagrahas. Thereafter, Bapu had deputed Padmaja, a Hyderabad native, to prepare a report on the state's internal situation. She had damned the various organizations for disrupting Hyderabad's long tradition of communal harmony; the Arya Samaj, Tanzim Societies, especially, for their rival programmes of mass conversions. Thereafter, Bapu and the Congress high command had declared an unconditional suspension of anti-Hyderabad activities. But the Congress abandoning the field had left it open to the Arya Samaj and Hindu Mahasabha, who had embarked on joint agitations, delivering fiery speeches and despatching jathas from Sholapur and Nagpur to court arrests in Hyderabad and Aurangabad. The Ittehad had responded with counter-demonstrations. Khaksars, brandishing swords and guns, erupted in Hyderabad. In British India, Muslim League had responded in kind by attacking busloads of satyagrahis ...

Jawahar snorted. Competitive communalism was like a genie unleashed.

Now it appeared like the lunatics had truly taken over Hyderabad.

34
Hyderabad (April 1948)

From behind the bushes, Raj Kumar kept his eyes on the road leading out of Hyderabad to Medak. He had been waiting for over an hour now. Either Ali Hassan's information was incorrect or the lorry was held up ... Crouching, he extended his legs. Beside him, the muzzle-loader was inclined against the trunk of an acacia tree. Raj hoped he wouldn't have to fire the gun – surely the sight of it should be enough to scare off anybody, especially a lone person? Again, if the intel was correct.

He peered through the leaves across the road but couldn't discern much. Either Ali and his comrade were well hidden behind the boulders or the misty night was impenetrable. His nose was tingling. He pulled the muffler tighter around his head, covering the lower half of his face against the chill. Ali Hassan had got the message late last evening and the plan was made in a hurry—

A mechanical groaning could be heard approaching. Raj tensed and grabbed the gun. A thin light appeared around the bend, diffusing in the mist, before it became the headlights of a van trundling up the road. The next minute, a figure had jumped into its path and was hailing the lorry with a brisk flapping of his arms. The lorry slowed down. Raj watched Ali run to the driver's side and begin to talk. Either the information had not been entirely accurate – there was a passenger beside the driver – or it was the wrong vehicle. But he could see mattresses piled high in the lorry. It had to be this one. At this late hour, how many such lorries were on the road? The driver was shaking his head and waving Ali away.

The lorry was revving up again. Raj did not step away. Another figure darted out from behind the boulder and leapt at the passenger door. The passenger, following Ali's interaction with the driver, had been distracted. Until he found himself being dragged out of the lorry. He screamed. Simultaneously, Ali had grabbed the driver. The lorry was empty and ready for him. Raj sprinted forward. He pointed his muzzle-loader at the driver, who started to whimper. Ali wound a rag around the driver's mouth, then tied his hands behind his back. The lorry purred, occasionally gurgling, as Raj glanced up–down the road nervously. On the other side, Ali's comrade, Pahalwan, did not need Raj's help. A member of the college wrestling team, Pahalwan routinely settled matters by trussing up folks. Now, as Ali poked under the dhurries to ascertain if firearms were indeed hidden below, Pahalwan grabbed a few rugs upon which he deposited the gagged driver and passenger by the roadside. For good measure, he even covered the trussed-up men with a dhurrie as Raj hopped in anticipation.

With the gun in the passenger seat, Raj drove the lorry down the road to Medak. The plan was to drop off the rifles and ammunition at the village Nimmapalli where the jagirdar, with the support of Razakars, was harassing the villagers and had threatened to burn down their huts. A Communist guerrilla squad was hiding in the forests nearby. But they were short on firearms, having been ambushed by the police earlier. Raj's timely delivery to Nimmapalli was critical.

The lorry was old and in need of servicing, Raj reflected as he gripped the steering wheel like it were the horns of a moody buffalo and urged it on the road to Nimmapalli. He had learnt driving by the side of his father. A fervent Arya Samaji, Baba had ferried satyagrahis from Sholapur to camps in Hyderabad state after the formation of the 'War Council' in 1938. It was a just war, Baba would explain, as they drove under the cover of darkness, the volunteers snoring behind in the bus.

'The political existence of the Hindus in Hindustan depends on the success or failure of our dharmayuddha in Hyderabad. We must fight the Muslim oppression of centuries in a state run by a handful of Muslims.'

As crickets chirped and the bus snuck under the starry night, Baba told him stories – of the Tabligh, which was converting Hindus to Muslims to increase their numbers. And how the Samaj would seek out the converted, poor untouchables and tribals, and perform shuddhi to make them Hindus again. One time, Baba was very agitated. News had reached that a weaver in Osmanabad had refused to embrace Islam and was murdered. Protests were held in Sholapur, Nagpur, and Hyderabad where the Arya Samaj had opened branches. Twenty of those branches were in the city now. A shadow passed over his mind as he remembered his last visit to the Arya Samaj branch run by his uncle. Beside the office was a maidan, which volunteers had converted into an akhara for physical training. Lately, a large part of it had been taken over by shacks of Muslim refugees, who had been pouring into Hyderabad since India's independence. They cooked out in the open, hung their washing on the office fence, filling the air with the smell of their unwashed bodies and urine.

Raj wrinkled his nose at the recollection. Uncle complained that the stench of offal was desecrating the Arya Samaj office, which liked to maintain strict hygiene and distance from meat. But the refugees had the Nizam's protection. He was sheltering them even as Hindus were fleeing from Hyderabad. From the corner of his eye, Raj saw an abrupt movement and braked hard. The lorry groaned and wheezed to a stop.

A startled nilgai locked its big eyes with him. Raj exhaled his relief. Deer were common in the area. The nilgai paused, then bounded across the road. Raj rubbed his hands and flexed his shoulders. Opening the door, he stepped out for a quick piss. His urine steamed as it hit the misted grass. An owl's hoot cut through the static of the crickets. Hitching up his pants, Raj walked back to the lorry, his mind on the problem of the refugees.

The clever Razvi was recruiting them, swelling the size of his Razakar army. Uncle said 10 lakh refugees were already in the state ... and the Nizam had barred entry to non-Muslims ... The Nizam truly was like Aurangzeb – banning the flying of 'Om' flags from Arya Samaj temples, banning their books, curtailing their observance of festivals when these coincided with Muslim festivals ...

The Hindus of Hyderabad city were most vulnerable. In the villages, Hindus vastly outnumbered Muslims. But in the city, the entire police force was Muslim, the government machinery was in the hands of Muslims, the army of Razakars roamed the streets. Surely, Hindus of the city could do with arms for self-defence? Raj probed his chin as an idea came to him. The entire lorry load of firearms need not go to Nimmapalli. The guerrillas would have weapons of their own. But the Arya Samaj members had lathis only. In war, how would a staff work against a gun? Communists such as Ali Hassan could claim they were not concerned with religion. But it was not their co-religionists who were under threat.

The cool air whipped his muffler as the hilltop ramparts of Medak Fort loomed in the horizon. Raj would keep half of the firearms for his uncle's Arya Samaj branch. Ali Hassan need not know. Besides, how could anyone go wrong with self-defence?

35
Delhi (May–June 1948)

After Simla, Delhi felt like a furnace.

At the tall French windows, Dickie gazed upon the extensive Mughal Gardens that stretched outside. His work in India was done, bar one, and he would be back home by his birthday on 25 June. That would make Mother happy for she set great store by such occasions. And she would be relieved that, contrary to her apprehensions, he had returned not only with the family name intact, but, hopefully, burnished as well. In the dim light, the tall Ashoka trees loomed like apparitions. Broadlands, the family estate, was similarly lush, with its view of the river, but a wholly different flora. And it would need work, what with the barest maintenance during the war years. That might energize Edwina and give her something to occupy herself with—

A knock and Campbell-Johnson entered.

'Ah, Alan!' Dickie invited him in with an outstretched arm. 'Now that you're heading home, let's reminisce over Scotch, shall we, our joint fifteen-month adventure?'

The governor general's press attaché, who was departing on 3 June on a ship from Bombay, smiled broadly and accepted the crystal glass with amber liquid. 'Cheers!'

The men settled on a sofa and armchair each, and started to sip to the hum of the air conditioner and their thoughts.

'How is the document coming along, Your Excellency?'

'The aides-memoires? Chugging along, I'd say. I don't claim to be some sort of expert, but I have done so much thinking on the future of India that I felt it would not be right not to put some of my thoughts down on paper before leaving: India's relations with the Commonwealth, the future of the Princely States, the need for Cabinet ministers to take regular holidays … So, yes. But, tell me, once again, what you felt in your bones about the future of Hyderabad when you visited it recently.'

Alan was aware how keen the governor general was to bring some kind of resolution to the Hyderabad issue. Confident that he could pull off an accession agreement if he met the Nizam face to face, His Excellency had despatched his press attaché with a personal invitation for His Exalted Highness. Alan though had returned with a firm 'no' from HEH – he hated flying – and a sense that the situation in Hyderabad was deteriorating rapidly; there were some who had started to consider Razvi a moderate!

'Your Excellency, you had wanted to know where the real power lay in Hyderabad. I was underwhelmed with the Nizam's general appearance, but after the one hour I spent with him, I came away rather convinced that he is in full command of his faculties. Albeit, his mood was one of aggressive fatalism.'

'Aggressive, how?'

Alan wasn't sure if the governor general needed a rearticulation or if he had forgotten that part of the report he'd written down in length upon his return. 'Well, he did quiz me on Moharram and explained at length that it marks the commemoration of the death of the Prophet's grandson. And how the acceptance of death and loss is an inherent part of the Muslim faith. Besides,' Alan took a quick sip of the smooth single malt on ice, deliciously cool in the heat, 'I learnt that he visits his mother's grave every evening at 6 p.m. to pray.'

Dickie placed his glass on the table, the ice cubes clinking. 'I brought up the mention of Moharram with Jawa, and he had an interesting perspective. Apparently, Moharram also marks the schism between Shia–Sunni. And the Muslims of Hyderabad are Sunni, but the Nizam's mother was a Shia.'

'Hunh!' Alan was flummoxed. 'Which would imply that the Nizam is suspect in the eyes of some of his subjects ...'

'Possibly why he is so reluctant to stir out of the state, leave alone enter Delhi. Might explain his excessive concern for what his subjects might say.'

'And Razvi,' Alan added, 'could twist it any way he wanted. The man is a curious mix of Charlie Chaplin and a minor prophet! Slippery as an eel. One minute, he's against the Communists; the next he will take their support, even if the Reds are against the Nizam. He pitches himself as the servant of Muslims, though I think he sees himself as something of a saviour.'

'Hmmm ...' Dickie nodded as he reflected on Alan's statement, one part of his mind on Rajagopalachari, governor of Bengal, who was arriving in Delhi to succeed him as head of state.

'El Edroos is dismissive of Razvi,' Alan continued, despite the glazing of His Excellency's eyes. He knew the governor general would snap back to attention any time. 'Like one would be of a dangerous pest. And the air is thick with intrigue, which Munshi, of course, misses out on because he is located so far out in Secunderabad. Which made me wonder how well-informed the Indian agent-general is … I was rather reminded of something the journalist Alan Moorehead had said to me—'

'Moorehead?' Dickie enquired quizzically.

'He was commissioned by *The Observer* to write special feature articles on independent India and Pakistan.'

'Ah!'

'When I asked him his first reaction to India, he said it reminded him of Spain.'

'Spain?' Dickie interjected again.

'Hmm.' Alan sipped the last of his whiskey.

'"Men sit hating each other like the wrath of God – then, because the sun is too hot, shrug their shoulders and say, what is the use?" Moorehead thought the phrase "India's pathetic contentment" was the complete reverse of the truth. On the contrary, he felt their mood was one of "apathetic discontent". I'd go a step further and say in Hyderabad, it's zealous discontent.'

The air conditioner shuddered violently before returning to its usual rumble. Since His Excellency appeared lost in thought, Alan sat up in the armchair and made a deliberate rustling sound.

'You describe Razvi and the Razakars perfectly,' Dickie acknowledged with a tip of his head. 'The death-or-glory attitude is certainly worrying. And with Laik Ali acting as a sly procrastinator – Jawa's words, not mine – intelligence has intercepted cables that prove the premier of Hyderabad is dancing to the tune of his master, Jinnah. The Nizam doesn't really have any sound counsel. Though,' Dickie perked up, 'I'm happy to report that Walter Monckton is returning to assist the Nizam. Which means that the Nizam feels a sense of urgency and has recalled him from London, therefore. With his sane head involved, we might still get our agreement.'

With that, Dickie glanced at the clock. It was past midnight. Time to get some work done on the genealogy maps. Alan, watching His Excellency's eyes, had stood up. As he thanked him, Dickie patted him on the back. 'I should have perhaps sent you down to Hyderabad earlier. Until you went, the Nizam seemed content to not make any fresh moves.'

༄

The genealogy map was his way to unwind at day's end.

As Dickie worked, the ghost of his father watched over his shoulder. Tracing and delineating the interlocking branches of his family tree, according to an ingenious coding system he had himself devised, allowed him to reminisce in tranquillity. Dickie had made the youngest vice-admiral since Nelson, an accomplishment he was very proud of. It was another step up in the ladder to become the first sea lord. To reach the same rank his father did, from which he was sacked. To avenge Father's humiliation.

༄

Two weeks left to departure.

At 2 a.m., Dickie climbed into bed after another long day. The governor of East Punjab and Lady Trivedi had come to stay and say goodbye. Day after, 10 June, would be the last time the Mountbattens hosted a dinner for the King's birthday. Beside him, Edwina was snoring softly. The Nembutal must be helping. Besides the insomnia, she had blinding headaches from the bright sun. All amidst the hurly-burly of farewell.

He lay on his back, the day's events washed over him. A 'Heads of Agreement' was in the process of being drafted by the indefatigable VP and Walter. Dickie had been speaking with Walter in French – in case the line was tapped. In fifteen months, he had learnt that one could not be over sanguine in the affairs of the subcontinent. Walter believed the Nizam would sign the agreement. If Jawa agreed to it, which was very likely because he had kept him informed, then the only hurdle would be Patel in Dehradun.

Dickie turned on his side, and watched his wife's chest rise and fall gently. Hyderabad might just get resolved and history made. Perhaps, he would end up impressing his wife too.

36
Hyderabad (May 1948)

'You see, Mr Stetson, the Razakars are a purely voluntary force. Young Muslims throughout Hyderabad have been motivated to join us because of Hindu India's bullying. Any wonder we are 2-lakh strong!'

Kasim Razvi wore a pale-grey uniform and a green beret. Behind him were his personal bodyguards, a posse of ten men dressed in black – his Black Guards. They cut an impressive sight.

'Two *lakh*?' Roger Stetson could not keep the astonishment from his voice or face.

'Soon to be 3 lakh!' Kasim Razvi declared triumphantly as he escorted the journalist. The BBC had sent its Delhi representative to Hyderabad and Razvi wanted to put up a good show. Following which, Nehru would hear the radio broadcast in Delhi and shudder.

Roger Stetson doffed his sola topi and wiped his brow. Humidity was high, and a freak morning shower had left behind roadside puddles and perspiring bodies. Narrowing his eyes at his host, he questioned, 'Three ... lakh? Did I hear correctly?'

'One lakh,' Razvi blurted out, before pointing to an alley on the right. 'Through here, to the parade ground.'

He had organized a big parade for the BBC reporter. A Razakar showcase. He was counting upon 3,000–4,000 men to turn up. A cow ambled down the narrow lane. Razvi slapped its rump as he passed it, before his foot almost plonked into fresh cow dung. He swore loudly before remembering his companion and switching to banter.

'Careful, Mr Stetson, the cows have no regard for pedestrians!'

'Ah, yes, the sacred beast.' Stetson laughed.

Razvi muttered under his breath. Cows roaming about always got his goat. Why would the Nizam try to appease the dung worshippers by disallowing their slaughter?

'You said something?' Stetson asked. He'd caught 'gobar-parast', the common pejorative for Hindus used by Mussalmans. Stetson was aware that the Razakars had a beef with the Mahasabha, the cow being one of the objects of dissent. 'Tell me, Mr Razvi, how do you respond to the charges of loot and arson levelled against the Razakars?'

Swinging his head gently, Kasim Razvi smiled. 'Propaganda spread by the Hyderabad State Congress, the Mahasabha, and the Indian press. Puuu-re propaganda. Trying to discredit our popular revolt against Hindu hegemony, against the bullying of Raja Nehru and Sardar Patel.'

'You recall G. Ramachar's resignation?'

The Congress wala within the Laik Ali Cabinet had resigned in March. Razvi bristled at the memory of the man's outlandish pronouncements, which the Indian press had gleefully headlined. 'The Congress wanted Hindu representation. Then why did Ramachar not stay within the Cabinet and strengthen the Nizam's hands? Do you know about the shuddhi ceremonies the Mahasabha keeps performing? *Shuddhi*, you know? Purification of Muslims in order to convert them into Hindus. Such is the treachery we endure.'

'And his press interviews?' Stetson refused to be sidetracked. 'According to Ramachar, there is no security of life or property in Hyderabad because the Ittehad has declared a "do or die" jihad. A holy war to establish the Islamic State of Hyderabad.'

'"A holy war to establish the Islamic State of Hyderabad!"' Razvi gave a derisive laugh. 'Alarmist tales, Mr Stetson. Just take a look around. And, if I recall correctly, wasn't it Gandhi who gave a "do or die" call against the British? Gandhi, the Indian hero of non-violence.'

The alley had opened onto a dirt track across which a large ground was visible. Razvi hurried forward, Stetson following him. The rain had lashed the parade ground leaving it muddy. Clutches of men hung about, in some kind of uniform. Stetson sighted a khaki bush jacket on most, a tin hat or a fur cap on some, a leather belt on others. The men ... Well, not all men since he could see several boys ... no older than ten years of age ... Hmmm. At the sight of Razvi, the gathering came to life and, under the brisk commands of his Black Guards, the ragtag bunch started to fall into columns of sorts. Chatter pervaded as the men ranged, greybeards on one side, children on the other, adults between.

Kasim Razvi gave a nervous smile. 'It's the damn rain; people are delayed.' He swept his Rasputin-like beard all the way up to cover his mouth. Weird gesture, Stetson thought; apt though, for Razvi's bluster lay exposed. Contrary to the grand projection of at least 3,000 Razakars for the parade, Stetson estimated 300–400 max. The weaponry on display was a curious assortment:

muzzle-loaders, 12 bores, some revolvers and a jumble of steel-tipped lances, bamboo poles, and canes. A Black Guard took command and the parade began.

The march was sloppy, the arms drill sloppier, the P.T. plain pathetic. Razvi scowled at the men. Stetson kept a straight face as the march finally came to an end. The men dissipated, some clambering into a couple of trucks. Which they drove off, firing blanks into the air and shouting, 'Azad Hyderabad!' Others started to march off behind a drum-and-fife band, bandying slogans about the burial of Patel and Munshi …

Kasim Razvi was trying to hide behind his Black Guards. Stetson decided to put him out of his embarrassment by postponing the planned village visit to another day. He had seen all he needed to, really. In Hyderabad city, with its Mussalman-majority population *and* the Ittehad headquarters, the Razakars had cobbled together a sorry enough exhibition.

⁑

Amongst the observers at the periphery were Raj Kumar and Ali Hassan. Uzma had passed on the intelligence that Kasim Razvi was putting on a fierce parade for a foreign reporter and the two had arrived for a reconnaissance. The sorry display they witnessed made them giddy almost. As the men had lurched about in march-past, Raj's bravado increased. In the end, the disbanding Razakars appeared relieved. Reverting to form, they resumed sloganeering in the manner of their street protests. Acrimonious rants against Nehru–Patel split the air. Raj got agitated.

'Stop!' Ali Hassan hissed. 'We cannot afford to be seen. Let's go.' He gripped Raj by the elbow and started to drag him away from the ground.

'*Nizam ke kadmon pe ...*'

The slogan rang shrilly through the air. Answered by:

'*Nehru ko jhuka denge!*'

Lusty cries rent the air, the slogan was repeated over and over. A furious Raj escaped Ali's grip, raced back to the vantage point and catching a moment's lull, shouted, 'Bharat Mata ki Jai! Hindustan zindabad!'

'Fuck!' Ali muttered as a clamour burst from the ground amidst the sound of hurrying feet. Raj spun back, grinned, and the two men sped off.

They had a head start, but a group was hot in their pursuit. Raj and Ali dashed into a residential street with houses set apart with little gardens. Sighting an open gate, they scampered inside and hid behind a large bush. Ali glared at Raj as the two covered their mouths with their hands to muffle their loud exhalations. The sun beat down upon them, the cries got more raucous as the Razakars thundered up the street. Raj crouched back, and yelped as a thorn scraped his arm and drew blood. Ali glowered at him.

'Oye!' A voice hailed. Followed by, 'Catch him, catch him!'

'Why?' A puzzled voice asked. 'What are you doing? Let me go.'

'Shout slogans, will you? Say, "Azad Hyderabad!"'

'Azad Hyderabad.'

'Long live King Osman!'

'Long live King Osman.'

'Say, "Hindustan zindabad."'

'Hindustan zindabad,' the man said, sounding more puzzled.

'*See*! He's a non-Mulki! Indian spy! Kill him!'

'No ... no! I'm Hyderabadi, Mulki. Let me *go*! I fought in World War One, when all of you were running naked—'

'He abuses us, the Hindu—'

'I'm a soldier. Let me go!'

'Are you a Razakar? Why have we never seen you? You fought for the Angrez, but you won't fight for the Nizam? A Hindu soldier, soldier-spy, spy, Hindu spy ... Kill him kill him.'

Pummels, thuds, whimpers, lashing, howls, a slashing – a scream sliced the air.

It ripped through Raj Kumar and Ali Hassan cowering in the jujube shrub. As did the realization that an innocent bystander had been sacrificed because of them.

37
Dehradun, Mussoorie
(May–June 1948)

'He's seventy-three years old, you know, Shankar,' Manibehn said softly to her father's private secretary. She patted the khadi shawl folded over one arm in case Vallabhbhai required additional warmth. Confined to bed for several weeks, today was the first day he was allowed to take in the vista from a wheelchair. The hills of Dehradun stretching as far as the eye could see, topped by a clear blue sky, and the crisp mountain air was good medicine for him.

Vidya Shankar nodded his assent. Sardar had come to the hills to recuperate, but the home minister's portfolio of problems was a basket of snakes that had travelled with him. The moment they quashed one, another reared its head. The Sardar – patient, determined, practical, and astute – had continued to stay in contact with Mountbatten, Panditji and other Cabinet colleagues. V.P. Menon was on the phone with him almost daily. The demands on the Sardar's time were relentless, and regardless of his illness. He understood Manibehn's concern: She worried over her father while he worried over India.

'The attack was brought on by the grief he had bottled up in his heart.' Manibehn grimaced.

She remembered so clearly the year Father had become Bapu's foremost disciple and lieutenant. She was studying at the Government Girls' High School in Ahmedabad when Bapu asked for somebody who would give up everything and devote all his time to the satyagraha campaign in Kheda. Vallabhbhai, the successful barrister, knew there would be no going back after that. Thirty years later, here they were: Father joking that he would carry a letter for Bapu if they had one, it wasn't too late.

A light breeze rippled the folds of her father's dhoti. A bird flew out of a deodar tree to peck in the grass. It was blue-bearded with a needle-sharp beak. Mani was glad to be out of Delhi. She hadn't seen such colourful birds before. And the trees seemed to go on forever, the deodars must touch heaven even! And the air, unpolluted with vicious innuendos. Allegations that the Sardar was entirely Bapu's creation. Mani sucked her teeth, trying to down the bitterness pooling in her mouth. It was Bapu's satyagraha, that vision of a resistance which allowed a poor peasant in Kheda to lock eyes with the Raj's Commissioner and refuse to yield, which had convinced Father that here was a politics he could join. No bomb-throwing, no killing – just asserting the right to be equal to any emissary of the Raj.

As she and Vidya Shankar walked to the wheelchair, the grass underfoot was dewy from a brief morning shower. Ordinarily, Father would not miss this environment to take his usual brisk walk, Mani walking a few paces behind. She had stopped trying to keep pace with him.

'Were you always a fast walker? she had asked him once.

'It was practical,' he laughed, 'walking needed no ticket!'

In London, when attending the Inns of Court, he would walk several miles daily. He didn't have money for books either, so Father was at the Law Library every morning when the librarian opened it and left with him at closing time. He returned home to become Ahmedabad's leading criminal lawyer, attired in European clothes, stiff collars of which were sent to Bombay for laundry. Until Bapu's Swadeshi call, when all of Father's foreign clothes went into the bonfire. From that day to this, no looking back.

Mani draped the folded shawl around her father's shoulders. He patted her hand and smiled with his eyes.

∽

At Birla House, Mussoorie, Vallabh was enjoying the change from Dehradun. Everything was quieter, greener – it was called 'Happy Valley' after all. Or maybe he was in better health, thanks to the ministrations of Sushila Nayar, who, with Mani and Shankar, had been his twenty-four-hour doctor and nurse.

'Satisfied?' Vallabh asked as Sushila concentrated on the blood pressure monitor.

Nodding, she started to remove the cuff from around his right arm. 'I don't want to comment because then you will catch the next flight back to Delhi!'

'Only on the doctor's orders.' Vallabh grinned.

Sushila patted his forearm and started bundling up the machine.

'So, tell me,' she urged, 'about meeting Bapu. You were not an instant convert, you were saying yesterday ...'

Vallabh turned to her. Maybe it was part of the physician's training manual, but since their arrival in Dehradun, Sushila, along with daily medications and checks, would also make enquiries about him: his family, childhood, siblings, marriage, education, politics … Vallabh was enjoying the reminiscing, the trails down his past which led to unexpected pleasures – a memory he recollected with joy, a quarrel he remembered with remorse, a vision that surfaced abruptly from the layers of time and grime …

'You know, Sushilabehn, initially I rejected Bapu as "a queer-looking figure". And Bapu,' Vallabh chuckled, 'not to be outdone, said that Vallabhbhai was a "very stiff-looking person"!'

Sushila laughed and, cupping her chin in her right hand, leaned forward. Their chairs were placed in a corner of the vast grounds from where the entire sweep of the valley was visible.

'In November 1917, I came face to face with Bapu at the Gujarat Sabha. There are two things he did that left me surprised, and impressed. First, he tore up the resolution of loyalty to the King that all meetings were required to repeat before discussing any matters. Bapu said that councils in Britain were not required to repeat the resolution, which made it unjust for Indians. Fair enough. Then,' Vallabh's eyes were twinkling at the memory, 'Bapu asked that everyone present must speak an Indian language. "Why English?" he asked. "The broken English we speak does us no honour – rather, it shrinks us all." Bapu was convinced that swaraj would be based on peasant backing, and which peasant spoke English?'

'Fascinating,' Sushila said. 'Bapu read the pulse of India like no one else. Is that when you decided to join him?'

Vallabh probed his chin. 'I was a successful barrister then. Participating in a struggle against the Raj would mean giving up all the luxuries I had acquired after a great deal of personal struggle. Mani was in a Government Girls' High School at that point. Joining Bapu would also mean that I'd never be able to send my children abroad for education, just as I myself had …'

Vallabh's eyes roamed the vista, taking in the mighty Shivalik hills, the buzzard gliding in the sky, wings stretched wide, the koel that chirruped as if to entertain him, the langurs scrambling in the trees … The last reminded him of Delhi, where he would be back soon to rejoin the battles—

'Sardarji,' Sushila called him back to the present, 'what made up your mind then?'

'I decided I would be a good Gujarati in the manner of Gandhi.'

Sushila frowned.

'Have a higher legacy than money.'

Sushila nodded enthusiastically. 'And you were loyal to Bapu all through.'

Vallabh gave a long sigh. Shankar was hurrying down the path cradling the black telephone. 'V.P. Menon on the line, Sardar.' At that, Sushila gathered her equipment and slipped away.

Vallabh listened closely, Menon's voice crackling over the distance. His jaw set at the update.

Jawaharlal had given a four-point plan to Laik Ali for implementation. The Nizam, however, had rejected it and sent his PM back for further consultations. So Menon and Monckton were back to the drawing board, in a fresh round of redraft. Which meant that they would each be revising the other's alterations, which would result in another fruitless draft for further redrafting. This bluff had to be called!

'Menon,' Vallabh spoke in a slow and firm voice, 'listen carefully. You are wasting time producing formulas, which Monckton will keep revising and the Nizam will keep rejecting. Enough! At this point in time, all that Hyderabad deserves is one brief letter. What should the letter say? Accession, one. Responsible government, two. That is *all*.'

∽

Vallabh turned on the radio and settled into the chair. Twice-daily news was a staple for the home minister, who also held the portfolio of the minister for information and broadcasting. As he waited for the news to begin, he could see Mani hovering in the distance. He paused, stilled his thinking, and focused on his daughter. She had worried over him so constantly and for so long that it had become a fixture of his life. Lately though, the past tugged at him even as he debated the future with every fleeting breath. Mani had moulded herself to insulate Vallabh from as many discomforts as possible – she kept house, scheduled his appointments, accompanied him to jail, kept him from unwanted callers, guarded him in sickness and health ... Despite her ministrations, he was now running out of time. When he was gone, what would become of her? Would anyone know of the quiet revolutionary who gave all of herself so Vallabh could fulfil his and India's destiny? His eyes moistened. He must tell Shankar to ensure that Manibehn's diary got published – it would offer a rare chronological insight into the freedom struggle from close up—

The radio crackled.

'In Hyderabad, a war-like situation was developing after the state disallowed Bombay officials from entering Nanaj, an enclave of Indian territory within the state.'

Leaning forward, Vallabh listened intently. When it ended, he stood up and started to walk gingerly. A serious standoff was on between the Hyderabad and Indian forces ... The issue of Hyderabad had not stopped rankling him. In his last meeting with Laik Ali, he had been brutally frank. 'It is impossible for India to allow one isolated spot which would destroy the very Union which we have built up with our blood and toil.'

Laik Ali had lost his tongue then, accustomed as he was to the polite reminders of Lord Mountbatten and Jawaharlal. Vallabh, though, had pushed the rod further into Laik Ali's thick hide.

'I suggest you return to Hyderabad, consult with the Nizam, and come to a final decision so that both of us know where we stand.'

The Hyderabad Cabinet kept spinning circles around Delhi. As he had advised Menon, it was time to quit wasting time on formulas! Vallabh understood peace, but Jawaharlal should know when that option had been exhausted. The Nizam would keep asking them to sift imaginary pebbles from wheat as he delayed Hyderabad's union with India. Too much was at stake, with too little time left.

Sushila had commented that Vallabh had stayed loyal to Bapu for over thirty years. What choice did he have? He had hitched his wagon to Bapu's yatra – the yatra of swaraj, the yatra of an independent and whole India. When he was a child, he would often hear the elders of his clan remark: 'Ek guru kaa aasra, ek guru ki aas; tinse raaji rahiye, auranse udaas.' One worthwhile guru was all a person needed to repose one's faith in. His Swaminarayan family had taught Vallabh the way to be loyal. That loyalty, to Bapu, to the struggle for India, to the Indian Union, was one and the same.

38
Hyderabad (May 1948)

'Three messages in three weeks, each about a secret arms drop, despite the first two having failed ... Should we be worried?' Ali Hassan asked the little gathering, his Adam's apple bulging as he tried to swallow his misgiving. They were seated around a table in Daniyal Khan's airy courtyard. A cat sunned itself on one of the walls.

Uzma adjusted her burka. When she had caught a tonga from Naubat Hill, it was still cool. She had kept it on because she didn't plan on staying long. But it was mighty uncomfortable, and she blessed Niloufer and the Nizam for not mandating she wear one. The despot had some saving graces. Ali had instructed Uzma that the next time she had an urgent message, she should head to Daniyal Khan's haveli in Chappal Bazaar. Now, Uzma fanned herself with a burka fold and listened to the conversation.

'Considering we managed to steal the vans two previous times ...' Ali worried. His deeply furrowed brow resembled a bitter gourd. 'Why would the Razakars repeat the same step—'

'Well,' Daniyal blew on his cigarette, his fingers stained with ink, 'the Golconda factory is running full steam. Laik Ali is producing rifles faster than a Razakar can wield one.'

When Uzma had landed at his door and knocked the particular pattern she had been instructed to, tap-tap—tap—tap-tap, he had emerged wiping his fingers on a rag. Uzma knew who he was – there were very few Muslim-run newspapers which dared to criticize the Nizam or the Razakars; she just wasn't prepared for a man who looked like sheer khurma, yet worked with his hands.

Ali Hassan massaged his palms. 'But wouldn't they be suspicious?'

'It's a trap.'

Jaabili, clearly a Communist – who cut her hair so short ... unless she wanted to be mistaken for a boy? – had arrived soon after Ali. Quiet, contained, dark, she reminded Uzma of the phalsa berry. Everyone turned to her. A goat bleated outside. Which startled the stray cat that jumped into the courtyard.

Jaabili cleared her throat. 'The Sangham teaches us to change patterns frequently. A pattern means routine, habit, repetition. Easy to spot if someone's on the lookout.'

Daniyal shrugged. 'They do have a lot of rifles to distribute to their village branches. And this time, the van is headed from Golconda to Nanded, different start and drop points.' He offered his cigarette to Jaabili, who, after a moment's hesitation, took it and blew on it.

The gesture did not escape Uzma. She had seen Daniyal and Jaabili lock eyes as their fingers met. So, sheer khurma had a thing for tart berry. Sweet.

'Let this one go,' Uzma waded in. 'If there are so many rifles being distributed, you will get another chance—'

A brisk knocking on the door. In code.

'Raj,' Ali Hassan surmised. 'But he's early. Aapa,' he slid forward in his chair, 'will you please go inside until he leaves? I don't want to expose you to more people than needed.'

Sensible, Uzma thought, as Daniyal led her inside. Except, she was hoping to get back before Niloufer returned from the club. Uzma settled behind a curtained window to catch the action in the courtyard. Raj Kumar, as clean-shaven as a baby's bottom, got into great excitement at the news. His face flushed as he recounted the last two ambushes, his own sterling role in them, and the gratitude of the villagers whose defences were greatly strengthened with fresh arms. The boy was trouble, Uzma concluded. And annoying, the way he kept throwing glances in Jaabili's direction, in anticipation of applause. Pfft. Meanwhile, Jaabili stroked the cat, who had sidled up to her, and gazed only at Daniyal. The boy was also blind.

౸

Later that evening, Jaabili attempted to dissuade Daniyal again. The coded message she had brought from Venkateswara Rao, the leader of the Sangham, was the real culprit. Rao had information that a train from Madras to Bombay on 22 May would be attacked by Razakars when it passed via Hyderabad. The Razakars would very likely pin the blame on Communist guerrilla squads. Could Daniyal Khan be on the train and write an accurate report?

'The Razakars are ruthless—'

Daniyal grabbed Jaabili's flailing hands in his and gazed into her eyes. 'I hear you. Believe me, I'm not an idiot. Or suicidal.' He patted the bed where he sat. 'Sit.'

Jaabili huffed and perched on the edge. When she had started, things had been clear. The Red Flag stood for the peasants' fight against the Nizam and the Nizam's forces. Now, Razakars were spreading lies that the Communists were looking to disrupt the Nizam and Nehru both. Meanwhile, rumours had grown that the Nizam's government was making peace overtures to the Communists in an attempt to unite all factions against India. However, their Sangham leader, Venkateswara Rao, had assured the nervous comrades that such a union was out of question. Coarse millets did not sit at the same table as shami kebab. Jaabili probed her forehead. Razakars reigned by day, while Communists were cheekati doralu, kings at night – was a union between the two possible? Everything was unclear. Daniyal's calm voice seeped into her frenzied thoughts.

'If I get to observe this first-hand, I can write an eye-witness report, which will broadcast to the world the dangerous game that the Razakars are playing. The—'

'You may not live to write this report!'

Daniyal took her hands to his lips and started to kiss them softly. 'We have no time to lose.'

He was so infuriating—

His thumbs circled the insides of her wrists.

He was killing her resolve—

His lips were on her forehead. Her eyelids drooped. His mouth journeyed down her face, leaving a trail of feathery kisses.

She moaned. She would bring it up again before she left—

With his mouth on hers, he tipped her back, sweeping the bed clean with one arm. Then he made love to her.

When she awoke, it was to the smell of old books and fresh jasmine. Somewhere a dog barked. Moonlight shone on the clock. 1 a.m. A couple more hours before she headed to the station to catch her bus. After their picnic at Banjara Hills, they had settled into this routine: Jaabili spent the night at Daniyal's before catching the morning bus. Unlike Lalitha, she shared Daniyal's bed, which, to her surprise, was often littered with fresh jasmine buds.

'It means,' Daniyal had winked, 'Khudabax approves.' Then he had elaborated, 'In childhood, in summers, our beds would be covered in jasmine flowers to keep the room fragrant and cool. Occasionally, Khudabax relives those days. Clearly, he's decided your arrival is an occasion.'

Crooning an apt ghazal – *'Phir chhidi raat baat phulon ki'* – he had drawn her in. It was by Makhdoom Mohiuddin, a Communist leader and poet whom Daniyal admired. On that memory, Jaabili nestled further into Daniyal's chest. He made a contented sound; his breath stirred her hair. The Sangham had opened the world to her, but Daniyal had opened Jaabili to her. Fingertips and toes and depressions at the back of her knees, elbows, neck – all were packed with sparks that lit up on his touch. He took her on world travels with his stories. He was fearless, for himself and her, and gentle. Every time she took leave, he kissed her forehead and said: 'Be safe, you have a man waiting for you.' A warmth filled her.

Jaabili turned to her side and watched the wing tips of his whiskers soar with every breath. She began to trace his high cheekbones. Daniyal shifted, wrapped a leg and arm around her, and pulled her in closer.

39
Mussoorie (June 1948)

The terms were now so heavily weighted in favour of Hyderabad that it would be a miracle if India accepted them.

The back and forth between VP, Walter, Dickie, and Laik Ali had resulted in a revised draft and a draft firman for the Nizam to issue. On 12 June, Walter had returned with glad tidings. The Nizam and his Executive Council had accepted all proposals except two: Overriding legislation by India, and the composition of the Constituent Assembly with a majority of non-Muslims. Admittedly, these two were not the straw that would break the camel's back. They were integral to the camel's load, fundamental as they were to Hyderabad's accession to the Indian Union. But there was little chance of the Sardar accepting them, VP prophesied. Even Walter was partial to that forecast.

"'So much profitless discussion with so many Hyderabad delegations and still we are producing formulas for their acceptance,'" Jawa had quoted from one of the Sardar's missives.

Still. Dickie must make a final attempt and try to persuade the Sardar in person.

On 13 June, Dickie flew to Mussoorie, taking with him Jawa, Baldev Singh, Rajendra Prasad, Gopalaswami Ayyangar, VP, and Edwina. Since the Cabinet was not willing to sign the agreement, Dickie had proposed that he take it personally to Mr Patel. If he signed it, the others would abide by it – their understanding was that it would not pass muster with the Sardar.

Upon arrival at Birla House, Dickie sought a private audience with the deputy prime minister. Summer in the hills seemed to have restored his vigour, Dickie noted as the two men chatted in a garden overlooking the Shivalik hills. The preliminaries over, Dickie handed the draft to Mr Patel.

He read it with a furrowed brow. When he looked up, his gaze was steely, the mild sun burnishing the bald dome of his head. Finally, the rocklike demeanour cracked.

'Impertinence,' he grunted. 'I will not sign it!'

∽

Lunch thereafter was a quiet affair, overseen by Manibehn with her usual efficiency, the keys at her waist clinking as she supervised the bearers. Over lentil soup, vegetables and fresh curds, Dickie pondered how to break the stalemate. Was Patel miffed perhaps because Dickie had suggested his name for the next governor general? Unlikely. Apparently, the idea had amused him mightily. Over Hyderabad though, he remained testy. In his last letter, Patel had forcefully set forth the proper, indeed the only, course for India: Break off negotiations and inform the Nizam that immediate accession alone was acceptable as a solution! Reading which, an irate

Dickie had sought a meeting immediately with Jawa. If war came between India and Hyderabad, it would be the result of Sardar Patel! Dickie had fumed, but he also knew that an attack on Hyderabad would be vastly popular with the Indian people who were opposing the relative moderation of leaders such as Jawa ...

As the meal ended and the party broke off into groups, Dickie shrugged. He would be a free man in a fortnight's time. A fortnight in which much could still be accomplished ... Barely nine months after the massacres in Punjab had ended, could India afford a fresh round of killings? Of Hindus in Hyderabad and Muslims in India? Squaring his shoulders, Dickie approached the deputy prime minister where he sat conversing with Edwina under the shade of a tree.

'Your Excellency,' Patel hailed him with a wistful smile.

It was the Edwina effect. Were Mr Patel's eyes moist or was it the sun glinting in them ... Returning the smile, Dickie pulled a chair close and sat down.

'As I was telling Lady Mountbatten, we are grateful for your love and service. How do we repay our debt to you?'

Dickie leaned forward, the draft rolled up in his hands, ready to ambush. 'Why not sign this agreement for me?'

The Sardar was startled. He locked eyes with the governor general and enquired softly, 'Does an agreement with Hyderabad mean so much to you?'

'Yes. Because what is at stake is India's good name.'

Edwina watched the interaction, hands clasped over a crossed knee. In the deodar tree above, a bird was tweeting loudly. Smells of coffee and tea wafted in the air, mingling with the eagerness that Dickie radiated.

The Sardar nodded slowly before extending his right hand.

It was Dickie's turn to be startled as he watched the deputy prime minister initial the draft.

∽

Dickie's coup set off a flurry of activity amongst the ministers resulting in an impromptu Cabinet meeting in Mussoorie. VP, with his customary skill, produced a new draft where the proposed amendments were incorporated. These amendments provided for the deletion of the provision for overriding legislation, substituting the clause – if the Nizam's government fails to pass the required legislation with due despatch, the Nizam will forthwith pass the necessary ordinance under his own powers – and omission from the draft firman of any reference to the composition of the Constituent Assembly.

Dickie was well and truly astonished. Here he was hanging on by his eyelids ... and now it was mission accomplished! With such substantial changes in favour of Hyderabad, all that was needed was for Walter to return with the Nizam's signature. As they walked towards the aeroplane, Dickie couldn't keep his elation from his wife.

Edwina answered with a cryptic smile, which momentarily nonplussed Dickie. Did she know something he didn't? She had spent the better part of the visit in the company of the Sardar, the two sharing a mutual regard ... Had that spurred the signing? But Dickie couldn't conceive of the Sardar succumbing to sentimentality. No. Patel had signed the agreement with his own legacy in mind. He was not keeping well and a peaceful union with Hyderabad, however prolonged and contorted, would complete the integration of Princely States – a mammoth task to which the home minister had relentlessly applied himself.

On that affirmative thought, Dickie boarded the airplane.

40
Hyderabad (June 1948)

Osman Ali Khan had woken at six as usual and had his coffee, but he had no desire for the salt biscuits or the daily newspapers this morning. No desire to recline on the bolsters and watch the balcony fill up with light as a shayr or two tiptoed around. His mind was crowded instead with half-penny Indians bent upon instructing the Nizam, VII of his family, on how to run the state of Hyderabad! Mr Monckton had returned with another draft, this one midwifed by the Viceroy himself, who had snatched so many concessions for Hyderabad from under the very nose of home minister Patel himself!

But Osman did not share the triumphant mood of his legal counsel. The draft still required that the Nizam hold a plebiscite in his state, *after* he had disbanded the Razakars and arrested Razvi ...

A plebiscite! When Muslims and Hindus were like sheer and shakkar in the semolina pudding of Hyderabad. The demand that he dissolve the Razakars, volunteers in the service of the state, infuriated him! They were his defence units against

Congress jathas, the volunteers pouring into Hyderabad from across all the borders. Ah, Osman knew the game Nehru–Patel were playing ... The aftertaste of black coffee surged in his throat. Drowning it by sucking loudly, he glared at the empty demitasse cup on the table. A servant had surfaced and stood bowing in a corner. Osman ignored him and lit a cigarette.

Now if Lord Mountbatten had accepted his invitation and visited Hyderabad, he would have hosted him in his most opulent palace, Falaknuma, and taken him on a grand tour of the city, so the Viceroy could witness for himself how unparalleled Hyderabad was, a realm Mountbatten was comparing with *other* Princely States. At the Palace Below the Heavens, with its gilded paintwork – where no guest below the stature of a Viceroy was ever permitted stay – the Viceroy would have showered with scented perfume, the City of Pearls twinkling 2,000 feet below him, as he experienced the hospitality of Britain's Most Faithful Ally. How was Lord Mountbatten to appreciate that special relationship when surrounded day–night by Indian roughnecks?

Osman harrumphed, knocking over the plate of salt biscuits. A scrawny cat darted from the balcony and started to nibble at a piece. Osman was intrigued: How had this one survived Dulhan Pasha? The next instant, his wife's rat-like face morphed into that of Nehru's. Osman recoiled. The cigarette fell to the floor, startling the cat. But the picture refused to be dislodged. For that would be his fate when Hyderabad acceded to India: Nizam VII would live on the scraps doled out by Raja Nehru! Indignant, Osman reached for his walking stick, stamped out the glowing stub, and hobbled out to the balcony. But the onslaught of dark thoughts continued. Omens from Falaknuma chased him, the palace structured like a scorpion, on whose balcony Mahboob Ali Khan had drunk himself to death, where stuffed long-dead dogs stared with marble eyes when he last visited his dying father's bedside ...

Osman teetered and tottered down the balcony, which usually sat undisturbed with its treasure of months-old newspapers, flinging his left arm, raising dust as he drove the cobwebs from his mind. Lord Curzon had anointed him successor as a two-year-old when Mahboob Ali Khan was struck with cholera. Father had survived disease, but could not escape the wife who stalked him repeatedly, demanding that her son, Salabat Jah, be crowned – Osman Ali Khan was born of a Shia concubine, after all! Suspicion, jealousy, intrigue, inside his family, inside the court, in the residency, in the Indian capital ...

If Osman disbanded the Razakars to join India, he would bring down the curtain on the Asaf Jahis and thus fulfil the Pir's prophecy. But Razvi and the Razakars gave Raja Nehru something to be fearful of. A strong Hyderabad could enter into a treaty of equals with India, so why accede to it? Osman Ali Khan was pre-eminent among the princes, His Exalted Highness, Nizam VII, and *he* would be the arbiter of the Pir's prophecy.

41
Hyderabad (June 1948)

And what of Sidney Cotton, aviator extraordinaire, commissioned by the Prime Minister of Hyderabad to shore up its defences against India?

Mr Cotton, James-Bond style, had been working behind the scenes to fulfil his promise. He had concluded an agreement with Colonel Iskander Mirza, secretary of defence, Pakistan, and with the substantial advance, gone to UK seeking aircrafts for purchase. Attlee government's spies were everywhere; some of whom, fortunately, felt similarly as Cotton with regards to Hyderabad. Eventually, he had managed to buy five Lancastrians and hired the crew for each, a total of sixty people. Since the monsoon season was about to start in the subcontinent, he'd purchased wireless communications and direction-finding equipment for installation at both terminals – Karachi and Hyderabad – so his men could operate under any weather.

In early June, word arrived from Hyderabad that negotiations with India were breaking down, and they needed immediate airlift. They settled on 4 June as D-day: The first flight from Karachi to Hyderabad.

'What about the monsoon?' Laik Ali worried, his voice crackling with long-distance static.

'It will work in our favour.'

'How so?' Cotton could see the Prime Minister knitting his thick brows. It was the engineer in him.

'Good cloud cover will help us avoid Indian fighters. The Indian Air Force is equipped with Tempests, which are not much faster than Lancastrians at low altitude. Besides, I doubt if the general standard of flying … yes, *flying*, you heard me correctly … I doubt the standard of flying AND of ground equipment of the IAF is such as to make flying in monsoon conditions possible for them … Certainly, it's possible … BUT at *great* hazard.'

Another factor that Cotton was relying upon, but did not share with Laik Ali, was that Indian Air Force pilots, he had learnt, were unwilling or unable to fly at night. Cotton's crew had to land at Hyderabad shortly before dark and shortly after dawn, and unload cargo quickly. As long as they could execute that, they were safe. Cotton was betting that Indian pilots would not be able to observe or attack them on the ground without facing a night landing or take-off at their base. No, they wouldn't risk it.

On 4 June, with Captain Frewin at the helm, Sidney Cotton took off from the military aerodrome at Drigh Road, Karachi, for Hyderabad. They took a direct route rather than trying to disguise their intentions with an indirect course. The Lancastrian was fast and Frewin was a wartime bomber pilot who knew his evasive action. Soon after take-off, they went into clouds, exactly as he'd anticipated. People in Karachi and Hyderabad were sceptical about the airlift. Rumours and counter-rumours had swelled the air in London even, which made Sidney Cotton more bent upon success. The past few months had tested him as he cobbled together an air force in Karachi. As the aircraft coasted through the clouds, Cotton's mind journeyed back.

Colonel Iskander Mirza had suggested Cotton fly with him to Zurich in April to witness a test of an anti-tank gun at the Oerlikon factory. After which, Mirza had bought two guns and 30,000 rifles. To get around Swiss export regulations, which barred arms export to Pakistan, the Oerlikons were consigned to Chile via the free international airport at Bale-Mulhouse, on the Swiss–French border. It was important to Cotton that he stayed legally legitimate; therefore, he got Mirza to issue a certificate for each aircraft showing it was under charter to the Pakistan government. Meanwhile, Ghulam Mohammad, Pakistan's finance minister, with a stake in PakAir, wanted Sidney Cotton to use his planes for the airlift. However, PakAir's Dakotas were unsuitable for the task and Cotton had rejected the proposal – and gained an enemy. The Pakistan Cabinet remained committed to the operation, but the finance minister's shadow continued to loom over Cotton, who gritted his teeth at a recent memory: Ghulam Mohammad's refusal to allow use of the civilian airport at Karachi, so that Cotton could operate under cover of genuine freight schedules.

In May, flying the aircrafts and arms to Karachi, they had stopped at Bale-Mulhouse. But the Oerlikons and other armaments had been packed into cases which were far too big for the Lancastrians. There was no option but to crack them open on the airfield and stack the contents into the fuselage. Interested observers ringed them, and Cotton knew reports would be made soon. Repercussions would arrive with the tailwind.

But fate had appeared to be conspiring against Hyderabad from the get-go. First, the runway at Bale-Mulhouse proved to be a short one. So they had to take off with a light load, which mandated a new refuelling stop at El Adem, away from prying British civil airfields. However, El Adem was in the midst of a sandstorm. So they tried Rome, which was under fog. Ultimately, they had to land at Malta.

'What are you carrying, Mr Cotton?' asked the customs men.

The fight for Hyderabad could stall in the Crown Colony. With Sidney Cotton in a Maltese prison. Lie with a straight face ... or brazen it out with the truth?

Cotton grinned. 'Gentlemen, we're loaded to the roof with arms and ammunition!'

The customs men laughed, stamped their papers and waved them on to their last leg into Karachi.

That was the last time Sidney Cotton doubted his motives. India, in imposing sanctions on Hyderabad, had committed an act of war – he was fighting on the right side.

A clear patch opened up. Cotton surveyed the skies and the ground below. There was little to be seen, and certainly no other aircraft. Frewin smiled at him. Soon they were landing at Warangal, 50 miles northeast of Hyderabad. They descended to applause from Peter El Edroos and his staff. A quick unloading later, Frewin was back in the Lancastrian to Karachi and Cotton was in El Edroos's jeep to Shah Manzil.

Prime Minister Laik Ali greeted him warmly, congratulating him on the first airlift. 'The fight for Hyderabad has begun, inshallah!' However, he could not hide the dark monsoon clouds furrowing his brow. Over tea, Laik Ali laid out his concerns.

'I'm not very hopeful about our ongoing negotiations with India. Sir Walter too shares my view.' His right hand spun the air in question. 'In spite of the Standstill Agreement, a complex document which was worked upon for months by both sides and then agreed upon and signed, Mr Nehru persists in making inflammatory speeches demanding our accession. His speeches, I am afraid, are evoking a strong reaction in Hyderabad ... The people and Razakars have to respond.'

El Edroos smoothed his moustache. 'The good news is that newspapermen from all over the world are now in Hyderabad reporting on the blockade. That should put pressure on India.'

Laik Ali grimaced and shook his head. 'With Patel convalescing in Mussoorie, Nehru has gone on the offensive. Indian newspapers are quoting him with headlines of "War or Accession"! And the Viceroy ... Governor General Mountbatten ... useless though he has been, leaves for England soon. Who will rein in the Indians then?'

In the room, fragrant with milky sweet tea, the mood was sombre, if not downright negative. Sidney Cotton sat up in his armchair. 'On the bright side, you'll have your 500 tons soon. I've planned for sixteen further flights over the fortnight from now. Before the worst of monsoon—'

'Mr Cotton, you are our man of need. Our target now is 3,000 tons! How quickly can you deliver?'

42
Delhi (June 1948)

Dickie's luck did not hold.

The Nizam's year-long mushaira with India had transformed into a depressing nautanki – one that Walter Monckton could not abide with. Four days after Dickie's triumphant return from Mussoorie with Mr Patel's signature, the Nizam's legal counsel sent a one-word telegram: '*Lost.*' When Dickie updated Edwina, she gave him a wan smile. 'Had you considered the possibility that Mr Patel signed the document knowing full well that the Nizam would not?'

In his subsequent conversation with Walter Monckton, the mood was Sophoclean as the two men debated exactly how unhinged the Nizam was to have failed to grasp the hand of friendship which Nehru was extending. Walter, the Oxbridge man, summed it up in hifalutin fashion – a departure from the prosaic that the Nizam, he of the perfumed ghazals, would have appreciated – when he quoted from *Antigone*: 'Those whom the Gods wish to destroy, they first make mad.'

∽

Two days to departure.

In the garden of the Prime Minister's new residence – a switch for security reasons from York Road to the erstwhile accommodation of the British commanders-in-chief at Teen Murti – a full moon shone brightly. It lit up the sandstone house built in the days of imperial splendour, the garden, with its lush green turf, and the mirror pools in which lotus flowers floated. Those were Jawa's favourites, Edwina sighed. She was fatigued from the round of farewells, but this particular farewell dinner was weighing her down with sadness.

Indu, the excellent hostess, had laid out a spread of Indian delicacies. The air was fragrant with roasted spices and rain flowers. Pamela, tucking into the egg curry, slurped, 'This dish has single-handedly changed my conception of eggs.'

'Not surprising!' Dickie snorted as he heaped a ladleful. 'Blame the dismal British supper: a glass of milk and a boiled egg!'

Jawa laughed, in that full-throated manner of his. Their eyes met, his twinkled. It was a standing joke between them. Over several informal breakfasts with the Mountbattens, Edwina had teased him, 'You don't know how to cut a soft-boiled egg!' To which he would parry, 'Now don't tell me, Edwina. I know I do it wrong.'

Sadder and sadder. She felt as if she were being ripped apart.

∽

It was time to say goodbye.

A year ago, Pamela had been taken out of school to accompany her parents to India. During this time, she had been the chief visitor to the school on the estate of the ex-Viceroy-now-Government House. She had encouraged Pammi to start assisting at the school and, in the four months since she first shyly assisted Pamela, Pammi was now teaching daily! But the time had come to leave, and Pamela was feeling very emotional. Maybe it was because Indians were an emotional people and it was catching, but Pamela had not been able to keep a stiff upper lip the last few days.

'Namaste!'

At the quiet voice, Pamela turned and stood up from the bench where she was awaiting the class to finish. Pammi looked so different from that first time they had met at the refugee camp in Panditji's garden. She still wore long sleeves, despite summer – the tattoos inked in hatred would be a constant reminder, but Pammi was cautiously turning over a new leaf. Pamela smiled broadly and the two young women started to walk, sidestepping the puddles left by monsoon rains.

'I finally have some news about your friend, Be-li Ram.' On Pamela's pleas, General Pete Rees had worked his network to locate him. 'Not very good, though, I'm afraid.'

As Pammi looked stricken, Pamela rushed to reassure her. 'No, no, he's fine. It's just that he hasn't reached Lahore yet.'

'Not reached Laur?' Pammi recoiled in shock. 'But he left last year.'

'Yes. A case of bad luck, I hear. Either he got on the wrong train or the bus was halted or he fell sick.'

Pammi frowned. 'Where is he now?'

Pamela looked away. The chrysanthemums were saucer sized and bobbing to the breeze. Did Pammi's friend speak to flowers as well? She cradled Pammi's hands. 'He's recovering in a hospital in Ferozepur ... His mental health has suffered.'

❧

21 June. The day of departure.

Early that morning, Jawa visited Government House to say goodbye. He gifted Edwina an ancient coin, which she attached to a bracelet. She gifted him an exquisite eighteenth-century French box of enamel and gold. And an emerald ring.

A bemused Jawa held up the ring.

'If you ever need money, because you give away all your own, you should sell it.'

Seeing Edwina's solemn demeanour, Jawahar tried to keep a straight face, but burst into giggles promptly. However, he pocketed the ring solemnly and thanked her for the other gifts that had been delivered at his residence from Government House: photographs of Edwina and Dickie, and a silver engraved box.

'I might add that the spelling of my name was all wrong! In a way, I like the mistake. The inscription will remind me of Dickie,' Jawahar quipped, 'who has thus far failed to grasp completely how my name should be written or pronounced.'

The Mountbattens said goodbye to the servants and the staff, Dickie inspected the guard of honour, pictures were taken, and Rajagopalachari and Jawaharlal drove with them to the Palam airfield. 'Three guards of honour,' Dickie recorded, 'all Cabinet and Corps Diplomatique ... Fighter Escort, 33 Gun Salute. Tears all round. Left 08:20.'

43
Hyderabad (June 1948)

From the upholstered brocade sofa where she sat in a pink sari embroidered with roses, Niloufer casually asked, 'How long have I known you, Uzma?'

Uzma looked up from the long list of delicacies to be prepared for the upcoming afternoon tea with members of Lady Hydari Club at Hill Fort Palace and frowned. Of late, Niloufer had acquired a dreamy vacant look which often required Uzma to repeat herself.

'Fifteen years, begum sahiba,' Uzma replied, knowing how well Niloufer knew that count.

'All my married life.' Niloufer's eyes met Uzma's as she played with the string of pearls around her neck. 'In which, I have spent more time with you than with Shajeeh. Only fair that I tell you first.'

A hollowing in the pit of Uzma's stomach, a feeling she had not experienced since she finished with the role of official taster for the young dimple-cheeked Ottoman beauty. Uzma had been secure for so long that she had forgotten what its opposite felt like. Stricken, she watched the princess from the armchair beside the sofa.

Calmly, Niloufer said, 'I'm going to file for divorce.'

Uzma's right hand rose to her mouth, the pencil jabbing her cheek, as she gasped audibly.

'I know. That's how all of Hyderabad will react. But I've made up my mind.' Niloufer turned to look out the door that opened onto the terrace. There was no breeze coming off Hussain Sagar to lift the heavy moist air that day. The palatial house lay quiet. 'I should have filled this house with children. *We* should have … To be a mother is all I wanted. But,' Niloufer straightened her shoulders as she turned her gaze back, 'C'est la vie.'

Uzma knew that French phrase. Niloufer used it as a substitute for cussing. It was the way she had been brought up. A princess of the Ottoman and Hyderabad royals, exiled to France, then India, she had navigated everything life had thrown at her with remarkable self-possession and a bagful of French phrases. Niloufer's mother's family had ruled the Ottoman Empire. After WWII, when they fled to France, Niloufer watched her mother settle into a new life and learnt that the only certainty in life was uncertainty. Maybe it was her Circassian blood, which made her one of the most beautiful women in the world and gave her a history of displacement.

'So,' Niloufer said perkily, 'you will keep this to yourself, Uzma, because Prince Moazzam Jah is unaware. But he will not be much bothered, married as he is to his poetry and his nightly darbars—'

'But, begum sahiba,' a worried Uzma waded in, 'what will the Nizam Nawab say?'

'Abba?' Niloufer's hand paused on a pearl in her necklace. As she thought, her right foot encased in beaded slippers tapped the floor. 'I know all the unsavoury things people say about him ... He's selfish, miserly, addicted to women and opium ... blah blah ... But I can only speak for the father-in-law I know. He has been nothing but kind to me. I have all the freedoms I want ... and he's never commented on my barrenness, despite Durru's two sons. Agreed?'

Uzma nodded. The Nizam was proud of both his daughters-in-law, showcasing them at all the important ceremonies and functions. Niloufer, unlike her older sister-in-law, Princess Durrushehvar, was outgoing and social, indulging in late-night parties as well. Perhaps the Nizam was okay with that, aware as he was of his son's amorousness.

'Besides, Shajeeh is also seeking a new wife to provide him with heirs,' Niloufer concluded with the shrug of one shoulder.

Uzma's mouth wobbled with emotion. Niloufer's divorce would mean Niloufer's departure – the only family she had known.

The next instance, Niloufer had clasped her arms around Uzma and was hugging her tight. 'Uzma, Uzma, you are my only concern. You've guessed right. I will leave for Europe, but what you don't know is that I will always have you in my life. *Always*.'

When Niloufer pulled away, Uzma's tears had left wet patches on her rose-pink sari. Niloufer patted the brocade sofa and the two women sat down, facing each other. Niloufer cradled Uzma's right hand in hers.

'I want to build a hospital in Hyderabad for women and children. Not all women can afford to go to Europe for treatment, right? So I wish to bring the best gynaecological and paediatric care available in the world to Hyderabad. That is my mission. And you, my dear Uzma, will be the manager of the hospital.'

At Shaheen Irani Cafe, a popular Hindi film song sung by Noor Jehan greeted Uzma as she traipsed in. Rustom, the manager, dressed in a white coat-pant and black pheta cap, recognized her immediately. Begum sahiba's afternoon tea would be prepared in the bountiful kitchens of Fort Hill Palace. However, there were two items that Niloufer wanted ordered from the cafe: Osmania biscuits and the Irani chai. Many kinds of tea – adrakwali, elaichi, Darjeeling – would be provided to accompany sweets and savouries, all served in small portions called finger food.

Upon hearing the size of the order, Rustom excused himself to go confer with his kitchen. The cafe was packed with patrons, as usual. Through the haze of cigarette smoke and lively banter, Uzma discreetly sought Ali Hassan. He wasn't anywhere.

Which was rare. Ali roosted at the cafe, which was a Communist coop for similarly inclined students. She surveyed the cafe again, pausing to study the table at which Ali normally sat with his comrades. As if sensing her glance, a young man looked up. He was in the student attire of a black sherwani and white pyjamas. Their eyes met and held, before Uzma looked away. Meanwhile, Rustom waddled through the swinging doors, carrying with him the clang and sizzle of the kitchen.

'The cook is delighted with the honour. I will have the order delivered fresh and piping hot just in time for the tea.'

Uzma opened her purse. Rustom waved both hands in front of his chest, smiling benignly, as he started his usual ritual of outright denial then gradual acceptance of payment. While Rustom wrote the bill, Uzma watched from the corner of her eyes. The student was watching her. After making the payment, Uzma turned to glance at Ali's friend, before she stepped out of the cafe.

Uzma was on the pavement when someone hailed her.

'Mohtarma!' The young man was holding a folded piece of paper in one hand. 'Looks like you dropped this.'

A surprised Uzma was about to shake her head when she caught the meaningful glance as the man indicated the paper with his chin.

'Faqr,' the young man introduced himself with an adaab. He held up the folded sheet.

Uzma reached forward.

'From Ali,' he hissed. 'Urgent. I was to drop it beneath the banyan, but you are here.' Faqr gave a slight nod and spun away.

Uzma turned to cross the road. Evening traffic had grown with bicycles and cycle rickshaws. Waiting her turn, she glanced around. A beggar sat along the wall of the cafe on a faded cloth, a battered bowl in front of him. Was he new? His right hand sought alms as he gazed into the distance – he was probably blind. A tonga clattered down the road packed with the permissible six people. A last glance at Faqr's receding back before Uzma began weaving her way across the road, something niggling at her. She couldn't quite place it.

In the Buick, Uzma removed the pallu from her head and rearranged it. The driver turned on the ignition and a purring filled the car. Uzma settled against the seat and discreetly opened the paper. She frowned as she read. Biting her upper lip, she re-read the short note.

Lie low. Raj got arrested. It was sabotage. They know of 'Nag'!

Uzma glanced out the window as the car pulled away. The half-drawn curtain obscured her. She gasped.

The beggar in the shade of the Irani cafe was watching her intently. At least, he was studying the car. Gone was the vacant look on his face. And Uzma realized what was niggling at her. She had seen this beggar outside King Kothi, too. What had caught her attention that time was his shirt with large pockets and a stitched-on belt. A bush coat. Like something a Razakar had discarded.

The Buick slid down the road. It was no secret that the police used a network of beggars as spies. And all the beggars in Hyderabad were Muslims. But beggars also staked out their territory and didn't switch unless they had to ...

Uzma nibbled on her right thumb as she pondered on her discovery. Bush Coat was keeping an eye on the cafe, a known haunt of Communists. And he had seen Uzma's interaction with Faqr. Entirely innocent. Couldn't a man return her dropped bill? Unless the beggar was stationed there to keep a watch on her when she visited the Irani cafe ...

Her mouth felt wet. Uzma wiped her lips. Her finger was red. She had bitten through her thumb.

44
Hyderabad (July 1948)

Jaabili left the safehouse and headed towards Chappal Bazaar. Rain had made the lane slippery, which slackened her pace as she hurried towards Daniyal. Her mind was in turmoil. It was the second time Comrade Simha had not stuck to the plan. The first time, he had arrived late at the safehouse for a scheduled drop which Jaabili was to carry with her for Venkateswara Rao. This time, he hadn't shown up at all. Simha was supposed to have picked up a guerrilla squad member from across the Musi, and brought him to the safehouse so Jaabili could safely escort him to Khammam. *Aah!* Jaabili slid over a grassy patch, latching on to a tree branch as she reeled. Pain shot up her ankle. Had she twisted it? Trying not to put weight on that leg, she started to limp down the alley. Smells of caramelized sugar and piquant masalas collided in the air as iftar time approached.

Raj's capture by the police had spooked her. His Arya Samaji uncle was trying to get the state Congress to help secure his release. But Raj had been caught red-handed, with a gun while attempting to steal arms, and the police was still looking for his accomplice who had fled the scene – Ali was lying low, therefore. Jaabili winced as her right foot throbbed. Daniyal would send Khudabax for some ice—

The thought of him rose unbidden and Jaabili could not distract her mind from what was really agitating her ... Daniyal was on the train when it was attacked by Razakars and the Nizam's police. Hindu passengers were looted, injured, and several were killed that day – including women and children. The driver managed to pull out of the station just in time to prevent more fatalities. All this Daniyal had faithfully reported in *Hyderabad Khabrien*. But what really cemented his status as Enemy Number 1 was the accompanying editorial he wrote, alleging that Kasim Razvi was using the Hindus of Hyderabad as the bakra to unite Muslims behind him. Muslims should reject the Razakars and accede to India, he had advocated. Since then, Razakar newspapers had published a slanderous news report on him almost daily. *Daniyal the half-breed. Daniyal the Communist pig. Daniyal the stooge of Hindus.* Posters circulated caricaturing Daniyal as a Brahmin with a sacred thread beneath his sherwani. Rumours grew of cows birthing dead calves in Chappal Bazaar. Daniyal's ongoing scapegoating agonized Jaabili. Hyderabadis were suffering under India's endless blockade and looking for someone to blame for their hardship ...

∽

Moin had deemed the message so urgent that he had tied several red scarves on multiple aerial roots. When Uzma had glanced out of the window, the banyan appeared to be bleeding in the damp dusk light. Grabbing her burka, she had rushed outdoors. Almost time for iftar ... Uzma would be missed ...

the other maids would manage ... Thoughts scrambled through her mind as Uzma jogged down Naubat Pahad, Moin's note clenched in one hand, slipping-sliding, feverishly scouting for a cycle rickshaw, a bullock cart, a tonga ... Anything that would get her to Daniyal Khan's haveli. At the foot of the mountain, an empty tonga awaited passengers. The day's fast would end soon. Uzma clambered into the tonga, thrust a one-rupee coin into the startled driver's palm, and rattled off the address. Accustomed to negotiating for every anna, he was confused for she had given him eight times the fare.

'GO!' Uzma's shriek roused the driver.

He clicked his tongue, the whip flicked, horse hooves clattered. Uzma clutched a rail, but couldn't stop shaking.

ॐ

As Jaabili turned onto the Haveli lane, a siren rang through the air, startling her. The day's fast had officially ended—

'Get the bastard! Kill him!'

In the twilight, Jaabili saw two men dart from the shadows, a sword in one hand. Their shouts filled the air before gunshots lacerated it. A body fell to the ground. Standing over it, a man took aim. Screaming, Jaabili sped forward. She threw herself at the assailant and knocked his revolver loose. On the ground, Daniyal was writhing, his legs twitching, his chest blooming a bright red. The man tackled her, grabbing her wrists. She spat in his eyes, kneed his groin, and the two tumbled to the ground. Footsteps sounded. Gasps, onlookers, startled cries. Abruptly, she was alone. Dazed, Jaabili struggled to sit up. A crowd had gathered. They stood in a circle and watched and gesticulated as Jaabili dragged herself to where Daniyal lay. His right arm was a bloody stump … his hand had been hacked off. Jaabili's screams rent the night air. Inside their homes, people about to begin iftari meal, disturbed by the cries of an animal being sacrificed, unlatched doors and started to step out.

∽

Uzma grabbed Jaabili by the shoulders and tried to prise her off Daniyal's body. But Jaabili had become one with her man, his blood glueing her, as she whimpered and wailed and wept. Eventually, Khudabax, Ali Hassan and others started to raise Daniyal from the ground, and Uzma wrapped herself around Jaabili and rocked her back and forth. A blood sacrifice had taken place. But from the chatter around, Uzma knew it might not end with Daniyal alone. As she comforted Jaabili, Uzma gritted her teeth at the slander flying around.

'His Hindu whore. Who else?'

'Bedding her in the holy month, the heretic!'

'Writing against the Nizam day in and day out … had to happen.'

Using all her strength, Uzma propped Jaabili up. Blood roared in her ears, filled her nostrils, coated her hands. The sullen crowd parted, unsure of the burka-clad woman who shooed them away with a reprimand: 'Don't you have a fast to break?'

Together, the two women staggered to the parked tonga. The driver had waited – either intrigued by the drama or by Uzma's promise of another rupee as return fare. He dropped them off at King Kothi. Before the palace gate and the police posse, Uzma covered the comatose Jaabili in her burka. Praying not to rouse the chief policeman's curiosity, she acknowledged him with an unobtrusive adaab as she shouldered Jaabili to the zenana. Imrana would be able to offer the refuge Jaabili would need. After Daniyal Khan printed the report of the train attack, the Razakars had proclaimed: 'Every hand raised against the honour of Muslims would be cut off.'

Daniyal's public execution had scorched Jaabili.

45
Delhi (July 1948)

Since Vallabh's return to Delhi on 5 July, news of horrors coming out of Hyderabad had just been piling up like farmer's debts.

The Razakars had upped their aggression, not only against Hindus but also Muslims who were critical of them. A newspaper editor was hacked to death to set an example. Intel was that the Communists were being supplied with fresh arms because of a new alliance with the Razakars. And J.V. Joshi, the only Hindu member of the Nizam's Executive Council, had resigned in despair. The resignation letter was a litany of grievous problems, and verified from on the ground what Intelligence was saying: 'Attempts were being made to smuggle arms and ammunition into Hyderabad through an Australian by the name of Sidney Cotton.'

Vallabh had invited Jawahar and V.P. Menon over for dinner. Since his return, he had realized that with Jawahar's move to his new residence, they could not easily walk across between their homes as before to have a quick chat. A face-to-face talk was the best, but the shift to Teen Murti had disrupted things.

'Cotton's gunrunning base is Karachi,' Vallabh said, picking up from where he'd left off. 'Why are we not surprised?'

Jawahar spooned some cucumber salad to his plate. 'The Laik Ali Cabinet is under the control of Razakars – Razvi and Laik Ali himself are inspired by Jinnah.'

V.P. Menon cleared his throat. 'The Government of Pakistan has begun to cash a portion of the Government of India securities which the Government of Hyderabad had offered to them as loan. This, despite Laik Ali's solemn promise that no portion of the securities transferred to Pakistan would be cashed while the Standstill Agreement is still pending.'

'That money is being used to procure arms and ammunition.' Vallabh grunted. 'What are our options, Menon?'

'The Government of India can issue an ordinance declaring that any Government Securities held by, or on behalf of, the Nizam, the Government of Hyderabad and the Hyderabad State Bank, are not transferable without the approval of the Central government. Also,' Menon chewed thoughtfully, 'the currency chests of the Government of India in Hyderabad can be withdrawn.'

Vallabh nodded. 'We will prohibit the export to Hyderabad of gold, silver, jewellery, and Indian currency. The Nizam's purse strings though …'

A thunderclap rent the air, followed swiftly by a downpour that slapped the windows. The sky had darkened and Manibehn switched on more lights. A bearer entered with fresh puffed rotis, which she served to the men, their heads dipped over thalis with bowls of light dal, sweet kadhi, chopped beans, papad, and fluffy rice. Jawahar refused a second roti, being the spare eater he was. Manibehn kept an eye on Father's plate.

There was a time when he had stopped eating rice to mimic Bapu's diet. The stay in Dehradun had brought some of his appetite back. VP was the only one at the table who seemed to be relishing the meal.

'There's the blockade as well.' Jawahar reached for a glass of water. 'Except for essentials such as food, salt, and medicines, all other articles are denied entry into Hyderabad. Hopefully, this swings public opinion our way.'

Vallabh listened as he chewed slowly.

'But Jawahar, the public is criticizing us for adopting an appeasement policy. And you will agree that the Indian public is very alarmed at the daily news of cross-border raids into our provinces from Hyderabad, and the massacre of innocents within the state.'

'Talk of appeasement is absurd! You know that. We are preparing for military action, but such a move should be our last resort. With our large army, India is assured of victory … But at what cost?' Jawahar shook his head forcefully, his mouth pursed.

Vallabh's face stayed impassive. He recalled the time he had had to shave off his moustache after a surgery to the nose in 1936. With his whiskers gone, he looked like any of the smooth upper-lipped Socialists, he had quipped! The bogey of large-scale communal violence was repeatedly served up by the Socialists within the party. Did the naysayers really believe that the Muslims of India would rise up against the invasion of Hyderabad? Or that Jinnah would come to the aid of the state with his Pakistan Army? Laik Ali would be on the first plane back to Pakistan! Wasn't the Pakistan Army tangled up enough in Kashmir? And where was Jinnah exactly? Intelligence reports indicated that he was unwell.

'Our cause is not helped by the horror stories that the refugees are bringing into the neighbouring provinces from Hyderabad. A complete reign of terror prevails in Parbhani and Nanded districts, Munshi tells me—'

Jawahar sat back in his chair. 'Munshi is an alarmist, Vallabhbhai ... you know that as well as I do.' The choice of a novelist for agent-general had been an unfortunate one. Munshi's imagination having soared in Hyderabad, he was being prolific at manufacturing scenarios and composing fictions ... 'Indeed, his lack of diplomacy is one thing that hasn't helped the situation in Hyderabad. Walter Monckton had complained to Lord Mountbatten in March that the Indian agent-general was openly hinting at the probability of military intervention in Hyderabad. Not satisfied by the reaction, he was even naming various dates for D day!'

'Munshi is a useful thorn in the side of the Nizam.' Vallabh chuckled to cut the tension which had settled upon the dining table like grease. 'A reminder that he cannot keep postponing the settlement of Hyderabad.'

His mood was buoyant. By rejecting the final Heads of Agreement, which Lord Mountbatten had staked himself on, the Nizam had cleared the road for them. Their conscience would be clear when they invaded Hyderabad. After His Excellency's departure, Munshi had telephoned that Hyderabad was hopeful that the last settlement offered by India could still be worked on.

'Settlement? What settlement?' Vallabh had asked.

'The Mountbatten Settlement,' Munshi had replied.

'Tell him the settlement has gone to England!'

Jawaharlal was in agreement with him, the question was of timing: He wanted now, Jawahar wanted later. The years had turned, yet, here they were, still differing in their approach. But this very policy of drift was what the Nizam had successfully managed thus far. There should be no more vacillation. But a Cabinet sanction was essential and Jawaharlal had to be co-opted soonest. It helped that Rajaji felt similarly—

Menon had finished eating. 'The Nizam is now keen to take a plebiscite in Hyderabad on the basis of adult franchise. Under the supervision of some partial and independent body.'

'*Now* he's keen!' Jawahar spat out. 'After all the concessions we have made for his state! A long period of grace for accession, a Standstill Agreement without accession, and a final offer that didn't even demand accession, only certain limitations on the Nizam's sovereignty ...'

'Another delaying tactic,' Menon quipped. 'Because he also wants an arbitration clause overriding all Heads of Agreement as in the Standstill Agreement.'

'Or madness,' Vallabh said wryly. 'Only a madman would have tossed out all the gains of the Mountbatten Settlement. Well, that's that then.'

'Sardar, Panditji,' Menon looked from one man to the other. 'Hyderabad is being duplicitous. They have breached the Standstill Agreement, which alone should be cause for firm and definite action. Not to mention the gunrunner landing planes nightly in Bidar and Warangal.'

With his acumen and loyalty, Menon was an asset to the states ministry, Jawahar knew. And Vallabhbhai was right: Between war or accession, the Nizam had chosen the wrong option. 'We are heading for a major conflict, I know,' he sighed. 'My worry is that war creates more problems than it solves.'

∽

A few days later, Mac entered Jawahar's study with a telegram.
It read:

Prime Minister Nehru, Delhi.

*I am sorry to hear over the radio of the rough time you had
in Congress today. In order to make it easier for you, this
will inform you that I am taking off for my return flight to
Karachi at 3 p.m. tomorrow afternoon, local time.*

Sidney Cotton

An annoyed Jawahar flicked the telegram aside.

On 2 July, a complaint had been made to the Pakistan
government on the nightly flights from Karachi to Hyderabad.
But Cotton was continuing with his flights under the charade
of 'mercy' missions – each well publicized with cameramen
awaiting him at Hyderabad's airports. Thomas Elmhirst, the
commander-in-chief of the Indian Air Force had warned Baldev
Singh that if the gunrunning aircraft were loaded with bombs,
he would be powerless to intercept them with the Tempest
aircrafts at his disposal.

Jawahar directed Mac to pass the telegram on to Elmhirst
for appropriate action.

∽

The next morning, Sidney Cotton's telegram appeared in print
in *The Statesman*, a pro-British newspaper. And Krishna Menon
rang from London about a newsreel titled 'Hyderabad Mercy
Flight', which was shown on the evening Movietone News.

Evidently, Cotton the buccaneer was not done promoting
himself, for he had flown a Lancastrian to London to personally

deliver the film to Movietone Laboratories. The Indian high commissioner in London had tried to stop the showing, but failed. Rapid barks sounded from the garden and Jawahar trooped to the window to watch. One of the golden retrievers was giving Rajiv a chase around the mirror pool. He smiled. Teen Murti was developing quite an informal zoo: parrots, pigeons, peacocks, a deer even ... The memory of Cotton surfaced to wipe off his smile.

Cotton's propagandist film would go down well with the British public, Jawahar reckoned. A section of the British press had been hostile to India since independence. Churchill, meanwhile, could not stop frothing about the injustice being done to Hyderabad state.

To avoid trouble was often the mantra for inviting it. Jawahar was trying to steer India away from war, but the countdown had already begun.

46

Hyderabad (late August 1948)

At Shah Manzil, the premier wore the look of a man whose bowel motion was causing him some trouble. El Edroos was not surprised. Mir Laik Ali had dashed to Pakistan on one of Sidney Cotton's Lancastrians for an urgent consultation with the Quaid. But, if rumours were to be believed, Governor General Jinnah was quite unwell. His marked absence from the first anniversary of Pakistan's independence celebrations had set the subcontinent speculating on his impending demise. Had Laik Ali even managed to meet the Quaid? Rumours also alleged that Mr Jinnah had shifted base from Karachi to Quetta to convalesce … Or die …

'We can count on Pakistan air support in case Indian Union troops entered Hyderabad; I have assurances.' Laik Ali clasped and unclasped his hands.

The whole idea of air support from Pakistan was absurd. Hyderabad had no petroleum for its own vehicles, leave alone the special type of petrol required for aircraft. Moreover, there were no ground crews to maintain the planes and no anti-aircraft guns to defend the aerodromes. But El Edroos had already shared his misgivings with the premier. Indeed, the Military Appreciation Plan, that he had submitted to Laik Ali in early August, had been returned. And Laik Ali had clarified: 'I'm the best authority in this vital matter, leave it to me.'

When El Edroos stayed silent, the premier reiterated, 'You really think we will find ourselves isolated? Do you think we have no friends?' He shook his head vigorously. 'If it comes to a fight after all, Hyderabad will not find itself alone. Besides, I do not expect an Indian invasion until late November ... After the one-year Standstill Agreement has expired.'

El Edroos maintained his upright posture, speaking in a firm, clear voice. 'Respectfully, I must disagree. Indian armoured units stationed along our borders tell a different story. India's stranglehold on Hyderabad has only tightened. They have banned Deccan Airways from Indian airspace. Their trains now bypass our state. Hyderabad has been isolated from the rest of the subcontinent. And the economic blockade continues. In short: We are facing a siege.'

Laik Ali glowered. 'The Razakars will be able to hold the Indian Army at bay ... Cotton has been able to airlift sufficient arms and we are equipped.'

El Edroos did not doubt the thousands of .303 rifles and Sten guns; he doubted the Razakars. Bravado did not win battles, strategy and bravery did.

'The Razakars need to hold the Indians for a month ... Plus, Pakistan will help ... And the United Nations, inshallah, will come to our aid.' The premier tilted his chin at his commander-in-chief, challenging him to object.

A delegation appointed by the Nizam had indeed flown on one of Cotton's Lancastrians to submit Hyderabad's case before the UN. But wasn't that the equivalent of riling up an already agitated India? The rumbling Indian elephant was being constantly goaded by the bullhook of Kasim Razvi, whose speeches were carried proudly in local papers, including Pakistan's *Dawn*.

'*Hyderabad can take it ... people are determined to shed their last drop of blood to safeguard the honour, integrity and independence of their country.*'

What fool's paradise was that joker living in? Even the Nizam had not disagreed when he had asked El Edroos's opinion: India can walk into Hyderabad whenever she wants to!

El Edroos smoothed his moustache. It was pure statistics. The average Hyderabad village was 5 per cent Muslim population at most. With the first appearance of an Indian uniform, the villagers would surrender. The Hindus of Hyderabad were Hindus first, as the Razakars had repeatedly reminded them. And the average villager was afraid to tangle with authority – be it the Nizam's police or the Razakars. Besides, it wasn't the tradition of a poor peasant to resist invaders. The best Hyderabad state could do was to try to make a stand on Hyderabad city, Aurangabad and Gulbarga, the three largest cities, and hope to hold out for a few days ...

'Sir, if I may.' El Edroos cleared his throat and tried once again to sway the premier's mind.

The Prime Minister and his Cabinet had decided upon a dispersal of the armed forces of Hyderabad as a strategy for defending the state. El Edroos had objected strongly and submitted his resignation when they refused to listen. However, they had rejected his resignation and told him to direct the army. They would take charge of the overall defence of Hyderabad and organize the Razakars.

'Our best defence lies in withdrawal of troops from the borders to within 3 miles in order to avoid any clashes with the Indian Army concentrating on our borders. Sending the Razakars—'

'E-*nough*!' Laik Ali held up his right palm. 'Do not attempt to teach me my job, El Edroos. You have your orders, follow them.'

❧

In his office, El Edroos stood pondering the large map of Hyderabad hung on one wall.

An old military story played in his mind, from the Peloponnesian War between Athens and Sparta. The small island of Melos wished to stay neutral and independent. It resisted Athens with logic and dialogue, but to no avail. Faced with invasion, the Melians put their faith in god, the Spartans and their small army. After a long siege, Melos surrendered to Athens. The men were killed, the women and children enslaved, the island colonized.

Landlocked Hyderabad was encircled by India; the Indian Army would follow an encirclement strategy too. Several pins popped on the periphery of the state, zones where Indian Army units were already positioned. Preparations had been on for the last three months. The Indians were expecting stiff resistance. '*El Edroos could convert a mob into an Army overnight*!' – a senior British officer advising them had warned. Tch!

Annoyed, El Edroos swivelled away from the wall and started to pace.

The Indians believed that he was training the Razakars, some 2–3,00,000 of them, according to Kasim Razvi's fantastic figures! And Munshi had been fanning the flames of Razvi's speeches all the way to Delhi. The result was one giant bluff. The

Hyderabad Army numbered 24,000, of which fully equipped and trained troops were no more than 5–6,000.

The recent clash between Indian troops and Razakars at Nanaj should have been illustrative. A unit of Indian Army, on a routine move from Sholapur to Barsi, an Indian enclave in Hyderabad, was fired upon by the Razakars. A fight broke out, and the Indian Army captured Nanaj and was now occupying it. Some days later, a squadron of the Poona Horse of the Indian Armoured Corps had entered Hyderabad territory from the east and moved 13 miles inside where a squadron of the First Hyderabad Lancers with armoured cars was camping. The Indian column took the Lancers by complete surprise, made them all prisoners, and carried them away in broad daylight!

El Edroos started to crack his knuckles – something he did in private when perturbed.

The Nizam was the one person who could still arrest this downward slide. A recollection from their last meeting came to mind. Osman Ali Khan looked feebler, his long bony fingers shook as he gripped his stick. Perhaps he was tired from the letter writing: The Nizam had been firing off missives to Attlee, Churchill, the British King, Attlee again. But the deputy high commissioner for Great Britain in India had recently visited El Edroos from Delhi with a request to ensure the safety of British nationals in Hyderabad. After which the commissioner counselled, 'India is a Commonwealth country, as you know. So, if the British officers in Hyderabad Army fight against India, they will be fighting against the British Crown. Understand?'

The Nizam might think he was a scorpion with a sting in the tail for India, but he reminded El Edroos of the native star tortoise with elaborate patterns on its shell: A shell into which he could retreat from troubling realities.

A consignment of anti-tank guns was stuck in Cairo, the hands of several of his officers were tied, India was periodically demonstrating its military might. Meanwhile, the Ittehad promised blood sacrifice, the premier warned about a hundred bombers he had hidden in Saudi Arabia, and the ruler scribbled away ... El Edroos was responsible for the defence of Hyderabad. He was also responsible for the safety of his men. A hardened veteran, El Edroos contemplated the conflicting demands before him.

A parakeet chittered and whistled outside, enjoying its own opera. Pausing at the window, the general scanned the foliage which was full to bursting in monsoon. Sure enough, a red-ringed bird with a flashy red beak and green plumage strutted on the branch of a large banyan. He was reminded of a green beret. On a scoff, El Edroos returned to the map.

The Indians were concentrated in Sholapur (west), Nagpur (north), Bezwada (east), and Hampi (south). He had divided the state for the purposes of defence into four sectors: the Northern, the Eastern, the Western, and the Southern. The three airports in the state's territory were located at Warangal, Bidar and Hakimpet. The Indians held Hyderabad state's Peacock Airborne Division in high esteem. His sources indicated they were worried about Hyderabad Air Force. Good.

One of the oldest military principles was to try to mystify, beguile, and deceive the enemy. El Edroos had learnt well from General Wavell during the Battle of Jerusalem ...

47
Hyderabad (August 1948)

The morning drizzle made the banyan's leaves shine like large emeralds. Which was why Uzma missed seeing the red scarf hanging limp from a branch. It was so early in the day that she had to assume the drop had happened the previous evening. At a late hour though, because she had checked the banyan at dusk and seen nothing. When she retrieved the hastily written note, Uzma knew she was carrying a bomb in her hand. If caught, she would be executed. A bloody image of Daniyal popped in her head. Or she'd be tortured in jail. Uzma sucked the bitterness pooling in her mouth and walked to the royal kitchen.

The tart smell of tamarind stung her nose as she looked for the khansama amidst the banging of ladles and lids. Several cooks were at work, chopping, stewing, stirring. Mirchi ka salan bubbled in an open pot, and Uzma inhaled deeply its nutty aroma as she tried to settle her nerves. Moin's message was succinct: *He had been outed.* The police had come into the Peshi office and questioned the clerks. Who all visited the office,

when, why? One of the older clerks had mentioned Emily
Perkins. Emily who? Who accompanied Emily? Had the clerks
heard of a 'Nag'?

Uzma exhaled. Since Raj Kumar had snitched about 'Nag',
the cops had been on the lookout for a man. And Uzma had
been scrupulous about not meeting Ali or his comrades at the
cafe. But Bush Coat, the beggar, had been consistently staking
out Shaheen Irani Cafe. As soon as the cops put together the
facts of Uzma's visit to the Peshi office and to the Irani cafe,
she would be outed as well! The sweat beads sprouting all
over Uzma were because of the humid kitchen, an onlooker
would assume. With the corner of her sari, Uzma patted her
forearms and face. Hyderabad state was sweltering. Daily,
there were reports of lathi charges in bazaars and colleges. Ali
kept her updated through notes: Osmania University students
were teargassed when they were protesting police brutality.
The Indian tricolour was being hoisted in so many places that
Section 144 was imposed to keep people inside their homes.
Two days ago, when Uzma and Niloufer were in the Buick,
the police, in shiny helmets and black sticks, had turned them
back since the Tank Bund road was swelling with Arya Samajis
shouting anti-Nizam slogans. Niloufer said the blockade was
destroying Hyderabad, but Abba was refusing to surrender to
India, and had appealed to the United Nations and the King
of England.

War was coming. And, in the battle between elephants, ants
would get crushed.

Uzma was near the tandoor where fresh naan was being
cooked for breakfast. The khansama, overseeing the nihari,
sighted her and raised his brows in question. Uzma swept
forward and rustled up a request on Niloufer's behalf. It
was Emily Perkins's farewell lunch, and the poor thing was

dehydrated. The khansama, with whiskers like a buffalo's horns, said he would send a pomegranate and green mango chutney as accompaniment which would help with rehydration – the infrequent drizzle and sizzling heat was killing more than everyone's appetite. 'Here,' he scooped a dollop of chutney on a plate and indicated the tandoor. 'Try it with a fresh square naan.' His gaze lingered on her.

She looked dewy as a marigold after a drizzle, Uzma knew. On a smile, she inclined her head and waltzed to the tandoor. As she chatted with the cook, who was plucking out the bread with a long-handled prong, she quietly fed Moin's folded note to the blazing fire. It vanished in a blink.

⁊

Emily Perkins was finally getting out of India. In a year, she had witnessed so much and collected so much raw material that her version of A Tale of Two Cities could run as a weekly series on newly independent India, à la Mr Dickens's tome. She had flown in aboard an aircraft that was ferrying British citizens to safety out of Hyderabad. Military action was imminent and, much as Emily wanted to stay behind and catch it, the high commissioner for Great Britain was not willing to guarantee the safety of 'reckless British nationals'! So Emily had snuck in to bid a quick farewell to dear Niloufer and dear-old Hyderabad before flying home to London.

As Uzma supervised lunch for the two women, she plotted her one final visit to Shaheen Irani Cafe. 'Nag' was a curious spy name that had risen unbidden to Uzma's lips. Her life had been one of constant transition: from a little girl in Faizpur, to the discarded one, to the young girl impregnated at Iram Manzil, to the poison-taster at King Kothi, to a princess's lady-in-waiting, to a spy girl. Now, with Niloufer relocating to Paris, Uzma would become a manager. It was time to shed one skin and grow another.

Ceiling fans valiantly attempted to create a breeze as Uzma supervised the dessert bowls being filled with khobani ka meetha, stopping the server when the bowl was three-quarters full. Niloufer said a container filled to the brim was plain gauche. French for lacking in tehzeeb. Clenching her stomach, Uzma beamed as she carried the tray to the dastarkhan. When she was made to miscarry and her body was racked with raw pain, an old matron fed her khobani ka meetha as a reward for not howling. Unlimited dessert was compensation for the loot of her little girl's body. The dessert revolted Uzma now; its thick unctuousness reminiscent of the cloying opium-scented air of Iram Manzil. Uzma couldn't cry aloud, couldn't scream, couldn't thrash about. So she turned her attention to discreetly teaching a new parakeet, that had been gifted to the zenana, to speak. In time, the parakeet started to greet arrivals with the choicest Hyderabadi cuss words. Because he wouldn't stop singing, the bird was put down. He paid the price for Uzma. Better him than her.

Uzma had learnt that there was no accounting for karma, taqdeer, fate for people such as her. It was always the poor, the vulnerable, the defenceless who paid the price. So Uzma did all she could to hoist herself out of that camp. Grooming, manners, make-up, hygiene – she mastered it all through quiet observation, staying in the shadows – in order to attract the eye of some paigah noble. She landed Niloufer.

As the ladies bantered, a smiling Uzma served them dessert and backed away to emerge from the shadows when summoned. All Uzma could do was secure herself, her body, her only possession. Imrana was safe in King Kothi, Uzma was safe in Hill Fort. Only Bush Coat had to stop singing.

∽

The car ride to Shaheen came about because Uzma dropped into the women's conversation a seed: Perhaps Emily would like to carry a Hyderabadi souvenir back home? It sprouted quickly. Emily clasped her hands in delight. 'What better than Osmania biscuits with English tea over which to recount my grand Hyderabad adventure?'

Uzma duly noted Bush Coat's presence as the two women stepped into the Irani cafe and she patted her purse. They placed the order and waited. Emily chatted gaily about Delhi, the tension in the air after Gandhi's assassination, sighting the handsome Pandit Nehru in Connaught Place, the fears of the Anglo-Indian community ... Uzma waited for the right opportunity to introduce the next set piece which would require Emily's cooperation. As they left with a large box of biscuits, Uzma touched Emily's forearm and, indicating the beggar, said, 'Please wait. I'd like to give alms.' From her purse, Uzma removed a cloth napkin, nestled within which was one square nan and a couple of Osmania biscuits.

'Hey,' Emily said, 'let me get some more food from the cafe. What,' she wondered, hands at her waist, 'do I get?'

'More biscuits? That will complete the circle?'

To a frowning Emily, Uzma elaborated, 'Remember your first visit to Banjara Hills? When we were returning and you saw a dead cow and—'

'Fed Osmania biscuits to the hungry children!' Emily snapped her fingers. 'Tell you what. I'm going to get a box of biscuits and feed every beggar we sight en route to Hill Fort!'

When Emily gave food to the blind beggar outside Shaheen, Uzma made sure to include the nan and two Osmania biscuits from her purse. Which had been doused with a colourless, tasteless fine powder. At Iram Manzil, folks consumed datura flowers as love potion. Occasionally, they died. In King Kothi, Uzma's life had been at stake with every meal. Nevertheless, she persisted.

In the long history of poisoning at the Hyderabad court, the humble datura had served for love potion and witch's brew. Through both, Uzma had persisted.

48
Hyderabad (September 1948)

At the Mozamjahi market, oil lamps had come on. The hot humid air absorbed smoke from the lamps and made the place look ghostly. Jaabili sat at the base of the platform with other vendors of humble produce: spinach, cluster beans, green chillies. In her four weeks at the market, by day's end, Jaabili earned just enough to ensure the vegetable wholesaler continued to employ her. The effects of the economic blockade were visible in the market: no Bombay mangoes, no Kashmiri apples, no Nagpur aubergines ...

A customer asked for the price of spinach.

Hearing Jaabili's answer, he started to haggle. Having learnt the game, she joined in the back and forth. It was the menfolk who came to buy fruits and vegetables for their womenfolk to cook. Which was one reason Jaabili, ex-courier, was now a vegetable woman. The market was close to the bus station, and from her humble perch, Jaabili had a view of passengers exiting and arriving. Another reason for her to be at Mozamjahi.

The man bought a sheaf of spinach, paid ten pies, and shuffled off. The floor was streaked green with torn leaves and stalks.

Spinach was all she could swallow in the days following Daniyal's killing, a gruel of spinach with tuvar dal that Imrana made sure Jaabili finished. The safest place to hide is in the enemy's lair. Using that dictum, Uzma had smuggled Jaabili to a basement in King Kothi, where guards who protected the tarpaulin-covered trucks agreed to shelter Imrana's sickly cousin. What trouble could the poor woman be? All she did was lie in bed and moan, sitting up only to be force-fed? Uzma brought news of the outside world to Jaabili. Daniyal's murder had horrified a section of the population, but with war with India looking certain, and Razvi's inflammatory speeches continuing, Hyderabadis were locking doors and huddling at homes. The Communists and Razakars had gotten into bed with each other against their common enemy – so easily had the Sangham betrayed Daniyal! It was fury that made Jaabili get out of bed. She would mourn him all her life, but now was the time for revenge. On Jaabili's prodding, Uzma also brought Ali Hassan's intel on Daniyal's assassins. The Razakar who wielded the sword was a refugee who lived in a shanty beside an Arya Samaj office. The Razakar who shot Daniyal was a recruiting agent who travelled daily by bus to Razakar camps in the state.

Around her, vendors were starting to pack up. A cow was wandering on the platform, chewing greens from the floor.

The first thing Jaabili did upon leaving King Kothi was to stake out the safehouse. She started to shadow comrade Simha. And understood that he was practically married to the Razakars! When Jaabili learned that the guerrilla squad member whom Simha was supposed to have ferried from across the Musi had been ambushed by Razakars as he lay awaiting, she took the overnight bus to meet Salamma. Who divulged that all Telangana Communists did not support the new alliance with the Razakars. Indeed, Venkateswara Rao had decided to follow the lead of Makhdoom Mohiuddin, the leading Communist figure who had rejected the Nizam's feelers. Hearing which, Jaabili's eyes filled up. Mohiuddin was Daniyal's ideal, a committed Communist and a poet, whose ghazals Daniyal had crooned to her. Salamma fed Jaabili maize rotis with red-chilli chutney and promised her that Simha would pay the price of his treachery. She also loaned Jaabili a revolver.

A few food carts sold naan and murukku outside the Muslim shanty that housed refugees. These refugees bought the remains of vegetables at day's end from Mozamjahi. The Razakar would buy something every evening. His teeth were very yellow, which he picked with a fingernail. He didn't look like he could wield a sickle, leave alone a sword … Did women, who used knives daily, look like what they were capable of, Jaabili wondered. After Mozamjahi, Yellow Teeth stopped at one of the carts outside the shanty. There, Jaabili made sure to show up around the same time twice, a come-hither look in her eyes. The third time, he followed her as she entered a narrow alley. Turning to smile at him, she branched into a dark passage littered with goat droppings. When Yellow Teeth entered, a lascivious smile on his lips, Jaabili embraced him. She dug her knife into his abdomen as she clamped his mouth shut with her left hand. His back against the wall, Jaabili twisted the knife inside him.

The large clock in the Mozamjahi market struck the hour. 7 p.m.

Thursday evenings, the Recruit-Razakar travelled from Hyderabad to Mangapet, a forest area Jaabili was intimate with. Unknown to him, she had accompanied him once, sitting on the seat behind him. His breath was sour; he sweated constantly. Jaabili had to control the urge to throttle his thick neck. To remind herself, she touched the cloth bundle that nestled against her bosom. It contained the soil stained with Daniyal's blood that was clenched in her hand when she arrived at King Kothi.

Now, Jaabili tied up the basket, returned it to the wholesaler, pocketed her earnings and purchased a bus ticket. Dressed in a half-sari, and smelling of sweat and old vegetables, she looked like any vegetable vendor. Except for the waist bag, and the revolver tucked within.

The bus reached Mangapet past midnight. Sour Breath would walk a short stretch before he reached the outpost where he retired for the night. He covered the distance in seven–eight minutes. Additionally, he was big and beefy. If it came to combat, Jaabili would stand no chance. What was in her favour was the thick forest canopy that Sour Breath had to cut through. When Jaabili descended the bus after him, he noticed her, furrowed his brow, but paid no attention otherwise. A mere woman. Then he dived into the forest. Quiet as a forest animal, Jaabili trailed her prey, overtaking him at some point. When Sour Breath reached a copse so thick that he had to go around it, Jaabili stood facing him, gun drawn, still as a deer. He started. A woman in a half-sari with a gun? He was slow to draw his own revolver. Jaabili had wanted to face him as she shot him dead. She kept firing until her revolver was empty. Men underestimated women all the time. Even in the Sangham, they wanted the women to do all the cooking. *Housework. Women's work. Women and the kitchen.* Men had no idea of the violence inherent in a kitchen, the domain of knives, scythes, sickles, pounding rods, rolling pins, chillies, fires, hissing fat, spitting oil, butchering meat …

Jaabili returned to Hyderabad city to bid goodbye to Khudabax and Uzma, before she disappeared into the refuge of dense forests. After the war between India and the Nizam, the victor would hunt down Communists. It was time to go underground.

49
Delhi (August–September 1948)

Parson ki tughyani. The Deluge of the Day before Yesterday. That is how Hyderabad recalled the Great Musi Flood of 1908. The river that ran through Hyderabad like its lifeline breached its banks, washed away three bridges and killed 50,000 people. It changed Hyderabad forever. Tughyani Sitambar. The Deluge of September.

Forty years later, a deluge would arrive again, in September; it would shatter lives and change Hyderabad forever, once again. Listen closely, you will catch the incipient rumblings swiftly swell to a spate. Tughyani Sitambar.

∞

19 August: Laik Ali announced that Hyderabad would place the dispute with India before the United Nations.

23 August: V.P. Menon advised Hyderabad that India regarded the dispute as a purely domestic issue and did not

consider that Hyderabad had any right in international law to seek the intervention of the United Nations Organization or any other outside body for the settlement of the issue.

24 August: It was announced from Lake Success, New York, that Hyderabad had formally asked the secretary general of the United Nations, under Article 32 of the Charter, to consider its grave dispute with India. (A delegation from Hyderabad had earlier snuck away on one of Cotton's planes to New York.)

In the meantime, Prime Minister Attlee and the King of England had responded to the Nizam's calls for help with regret, and with hope and prayers for a peaceful solution.

∽

By end August, Jawaharlal had come around to the view that if the mounting brutality of the Razakars was not stanched, there might be a state of lawlessness throughout Hyderabad. He sought assurances from the premiers of Indian provinces about the possibility of communal troubles – no particular likelihood, they answered. The statesman was aware that good intentions by themselves, without power behind them, could do nothing. Jawahar was no Chamberlain. 'Grave decisions have to be made by us, and the alternatives between which we have to choose are equally undesirable,' he forecast grimly.

'So, as often in life, we search frantically for the lesser evil.'

∽

31 August: Following a Cabinet meeting, C. Rajagopalachari, India's governor general after Mountbatten, sent an ultimatum to the Nizam: Ban the Razakars, and allow Indian troops to be stationed in the state.

The Nizam took a week to reply. Umbrage and defiance were his answers: India had a very wrong impression, and stationing Indian troops was out of the question!

The *Dawn*, 10 September 1948, quoted Kasim Razvi, hysterical as ever: 'The people of Hyderabad are determined to shed their last drop of blood to safeguard the honour, integrity and independence of their country.'

The next day, India telegraphed its ultimatum as answer: The Nizam's government appeared determined to regard facts not as they are but as they wished others to believe them to be ... the only law that now prevailed in the state was the law of the jungle by which the Razakars and their allies preyed upon a large majority of helpless citizens ... the Government of India regarded themselves as free to take such action as they considered necessary.

That night, Jinnah died. India marked it by lowering the tricolour on 12 September.

∽

The Nizam, noticing the wind had changed to a tempest, shot off another of his telegrams designed to delay Indian action.

Vallabhbhai, fed up with the to-ing and fro-ing, wanted to send a brusque reply: 'Repeated denials cannot alter facts. I have nothing to add.' Jawahar and Rajagopalachari however wanted a longer text that stressed the goal of peace that India had in mind in wishing to send troops. Next, Vallabhbhai despatched V.P. Menon to Rajagopalachari's house at 10 p.m. They debated the draft of the telegram for three hours. The next morning, Rajaji complained to the Sardar about the arguments that ran late into the night. But Menon had argued his way into history: By delaying the telegram, he had denied the Nizam a chance to change stance before troops crossed the border, and scored a goal for Vallabhbhai.

At 4 a.m. on 13 September, Operation Polo began. In pre-dawn darkness, villagers in scrubby border areas awoke to the ground trembling beneath them, the sky howling above. Cowering in their huts, they watched as Sherman and Stuart tanks swept past Hyderabad's borders and Tempest fighter planes sliced its air. The military invasion was a domestic issue.

A paradox in urgent need of a fig leaf must reach for a euphemism. Police action.

Anyone familiar with the history of Hyderabad would have offered something more apt. Tughyani Sitambar. Redux.

50
Hyderabad–Delhi
(September 1948)

The Indian Army attacked Hyderabad at five strategic points simultaneously as Operation Polo began.

Advancing eastwards from Sholapur, the 1st Armoured Division swept into Osmanabad district. Their first target was the vital Naldurg bridge, 12 miles inside. The wet red–black soil, that grew cotton and Communists, offered resistance by making traction difficult. From inside their hutments, petrified people watched as twilight was obscured by columns of clanking machinery. Their brothers had come to rescue them. Monkeys sat still in treetops, their scampering suspended. Stray dogs hid in the dusty cotton fields. Except a pup. Curious, wanting to stick its nose and paw into the wheelie monster, it toddled onto the road. A young soldier with a covering of fuzz on his chin and cheeks was the only one who noticed it. He strained his ears for the inevitable. But a pup's yelp, if it did make one, would not rise above the rattle and clatter of tanks. Still. He had to see. Glancing back quickly, he saw the small pool of smashed flesh and blood before the following Sherman squished it. The soldier averted his eyes.

∽

By 7 a.m., Deccan Radio sputtered with fiery exhortations. Civilian officers, Hyderabad Army, Razakars – all were inundated with orders: 'Fight to the last man and the last round!' Martial music poured forth, punctuated by jubilant songs. 'We got Pakistan with a smile; we'll get Hindustan fighting!' Premier Laik Ali projected confidence. He was expecting a consignment of anti-tank guns to arrive at any moment. Unfortunately, these had been held up at Cairo airport, but the bungling had been sorted out and the guns would arrive any minute. Then, they would be devastating! The plan was to use them against the Indian tanks when they approached Hyderabad city. Emergency was proclaimed in the state, all lights out at night.

∽

The 1st Armoured Division crossed the crucial Naldurg bridge on schedule, and captured a British officer employed by the Nizam's army. Lieutenant T.T. Moore, his jeep laden with explosives, was planning to destroy the bridge. If he had succeeded, it would have added one extra day to the schedule and lengthened Operation Polo beyond the planned 100 hours. The Company of the Pathans under Hyderabad Armed Forces refused to withdraw at Naldurg and suffered heavy casualties. Tuljapur fell next, the Infantry Company withdrawing into Hyderabad city. Resistance to the advancing Indian columns crumbled quickly as Tamalwadi and Aljapur fell. Other units of the Indian Army attacked along the Bezwada–Hyderabad route. The aerodrome at Bidar, where Sidney Cotton had landed his Lancastrians, came under heavy bombing from Indian Air Force planes.

∽

The commanding officer of Osmanabad district, Major Mohsin Ali, knew his men, armed with .303 rifles and ridiculously low amounts of ammunition, were no better equipped than civil defence forces. Nevertheless, he made efforts to boost the men's morale. As he began burning official papers, he muttered repeatedly under his breath, 'Where were the guns Hyderabad had been importing all these days?'

Civilian officers fled their posts, the rank and file of Razakars was alarmed, and panic spread throughout Hyderabad. As the Indian Army continued its march to the Nizam's city, Razakars discarded their uniforms and ran. Their weapons, they cast into wells and lakes all over the countryside. Deccan Radio broadcast that the Hyderabad forces were advancing everywhere, and had captured Masulipatnam. Rumours flew that after capturing Goa on the west coast, the Nizam's forces were marching to Delhi.

∽

In Hyderabad, Mir Laik Ali and Kasim Razvi scoured the skies for signs that Pakistan's Air Force was coming to their aid.

The promised air support never arrived. No Pathan tribesmen marched into Delhi from the hills either. The pan-Islamic jihad that would defend the Nizam remained hazy in the hot humid air of Deccan. Razvi, losing some of his bluster, contemplated: 'Shall we be destroyed? That's up to them. Shall we be defeated? That's up to us.' Laik Ali vainly talked of breaking the encirclement and surrounding the Indian forces in turn when they came a little closer to Hyderabad. But the Swiss-made arms, expected to arrive any minute, had vanished into the air, fragrant with champa from the morning shower. Indeed, Sidney Cotton, with his James Bond–ian sixth sense, ensured that his last Lancastrian flew out of Hyderabad just before Indian Tempests started to strafe the airfield. Wooden replicas of planes that El Edroos had built and camouflaged had fooled India into thinking that Hyderabad actually possessed an air force. But the game was over: The bluff of entire Hyderabad state had been called.

The United Nations was scheduled to hear Hyderabad's case on 20 September.

'Can you hold out for three days?' Laik Ali asked Major General El Edroos.

'Not three hours.'

The Hyderabad armed forces were ordered to fall back. Deccan Radio switched to playing film songs. Smoke rose from Shah Manzil's back lawns as important papers were burnt.

∾

Operation Polo ended on the evening of 17 September when Major General J.N. Chaudhary, commander of Indian forces, accepted Hyderabad's sword of surrender. Earlier, India's agent-general in Hyderabad, K.M. Munshi had asked Vallabhbhai if the Indian and Hyderabadi generals should meet face-to-face for a gracious end to the hostilities.

'This is a surrender,' Vallabhbhai had caustically remarked. 'This is not a tea party.'

India's victory was swift and all out.

∽

In Hyderabad city, released from curfew, residents started to step out. The bazaars soon filled with jubilant Hindu men. The tricolour was in hands, atop cycles and rickshaws and cars. Slogans rent the air: 'Jawaharlal Nehru ki jai! Sardar Vallabhbhai Patel ki jai! State Congress zindabad!' Muslims stayed indoors, dazed and defeated. Their leaders had promised to hoist the Asafia flag on the Red Fort. Instead, their rabid rhetoric left Muslims cowering behind closed doors as killings started across Hyderabad state ...

51

Hyderabad (September 1948)

The vultures had resigned. Osman Ali Khan's fingers trembled as he handed Laik Ali's resignation letter to K.M. Munshi.

'Your Excellency,' Munshi said, 'it is time you make a broadcast welcoming the police action, and inform Hyderabad that you are withdrawing your complaint to the United Nations.'

The Nizam's pale, thin face was turned to a mounted portrait on the wall. Munshi followed his gaze. Sharp nose, pointed beard, bejewelled dastar, a white angarakha overlaid with pearl necklaces up to his waist. One of the earlier Asaf Jahs, no doubt, Munshi reckoned. He snuffled, trying to clear his nostrils of the thick cigarette smoke that pervaded the room. With effort, the Nizam turned, his eyes boring into India's agent-general.

'How … does one broadcast?'

∾

His Exalted Highness, Nawab Sir Mir Osman Ali Khan Siddiqi, Asaf Jah VII, arrived at the radio station to make a speech to his people. It was his first visit to the station. No red carpet was laid out for him, no formalities were observed. Dressed in his customary threadbare sherwani, limp jodhpur trousers, and fez, the Nizam looked no different from when he was a sovereign.

There had been no preamble to his speech except for the announcement at 4.30 p.m.: 'A royal proclamation will be read out by the Nizam at 7.30 p.m.' In his high-pitched voice, Osman Ali Khan spoke in English. Skittish, he bungled some words. Only a cave dweller would be unaware that the Nizam was broadcasting a public apology.

The essence of the speech came early on: 'We have decided that the state of Hyderabad shall accede to the Indian Union.'

After the broadcast, Osman Ali Khan drove back to King Kothi. His battered old Ford Tourer wound down the streets filled with excited people shouting slogans in support of India, Nehru, Patel, the Indian Army … Gaiety rippled from one jubilant knot to another. Osman kept his face straight and looked forward.

∽

The following day.

He punctured a shaft of sunlight as he tottered across the room, speaking to himself. He tossed his left hand, his slender fingers arguing with the air. A word, a sigh escaped loudly every now and then. His Arab Guards watched him from behind the heavily curtained doorway. The Indian Army was advancing slowly, waiting for the Nizam's forces to clear the mines laid along the way. The surrender ceremony had got postponed from noon to 4 p.m. Osman paused at the table littered with papers.

His decked-up portrait stared back at him. From his silver jubilee celebrations on the front cover of *Time* magazine. His right hand bore down upon the walking stick. Pressured, it creaked where it was tied with string. His left hand smacked the magazine pile and sent the *Time* issue flying to the floor. Heaving, Osman clutched the table, the knuckles of his left hand white.

A crumpled ball of paper slid towards him. Distracted, he started to pluck apart its folds. A lime-sized gem lit up in his hand. A memory shifted in his mind. His father, Mehboob Ali Khan, Peace Be Upon Him, believing the diamond was accursed, had wrapped it in a dirty rag and tucked it away in the table's drawer. Osman had retrieved it and made an innocuous paper weight out of it. But, no more, no more ... The diamond was not secure on the table any more.

Clutching the diamond in his left hand, Osman wove his way to the locked cupboard. Opening the lock, he dragged out the jar of biscuits and deposited the gem inside it. Having secured it, he locked the cupboard, tugged at the lock to verify, then tottered back to his chair. Settled, he started to puff a Charminar.

A ghazal raised its head ...

He would put his turmoil in words ... as always.

He grabbed the foil of the cigarette packet and smoothed it on his thigh with his right palm. Satisfied, he plucked a pencil and gazed at the distance. From the corner of his eye, he registered a shift. From his profitable perch on the wall, Qamruddin had turned and was peering over Osman's shoulder. On a sigh, Osman started to write a qasida of the kulcha.

Kulcha on their flag, the Asaf Jahs drew,
Paean to their Pir, the bestower of bread
and Princely rule over the Deccan plateau
For a full seven generations ahead.
Now the day dawns, the prophecy comes true,
The Pir's blessing, finally on death's bed:
Seized by Raja-e-Hindustan Nehru
Glorious Hyderabad is gallows led.
All must change in the paramountcy new,
So all can stay the same, Osman piped.
It's the way of the world to bid adieu:
To renew, all that is old must be wiped.

The cigarette had burnt to ash in the tray. Through the stained-glass window, evening light cast the room in dappled shadows as a drizzle fell gently upon King Kothi. Osman glanced up from the ghazal he had scribbled. It wasn't his best, but it was the truth. Pursing his mouth, he wedged the wrapper against the base of the Victorian statuary of mother and child, grabbed his walking stick and rose with effort. Time to head to Masjid-e-Judi to pray at his mother's grave.

Today would be longer, he felt it in his bones.

Postlude

Over the next few days, policemen vanished from the roads. Smoke rose from the refugee shanties which had been attacked, tattered clothes and meagre possessions tossed into bonfires. Hindu mobs broke into prisons and set convicts free. Surrendered Razakars were slaughtered in many instances. Muslims shops were looted and set afire. Muslim men were killed, their women and children reclaimed as Hindus. Lest they forget, the women had their new Hindu names tattooed on their foreheads and forearms.

With Hyderabad's collapse, its women's bodies became the new battlefield.

⁊

Much as Jawahar had foreseen, violence erupted in the wake of Operation Polo. Only, Jawahar had worried over the potential for communal violence in the Indian Union. What he had overlooked was that violence that would come from within erstwhile Hyderabad state.

After the initial euphoria, news started to trickle in of the widespread killings following India's police action. For months after, passengers on trains travelling between Hyderabad and Aurangabad reported seeing vultures feeding on corpses scattered in the fields. A concerned Jawaharlal sent a fact-finding commission to the state.

The Sunderlal Report concluded: 'At a very conservative estimate ... at least 27,000 to 40,000 people lost their lives during and after the police action.' Armed villagers had turned upon their Muslim neighbours, as Daniyal had foreseen. Indian soldiers and volunteers from border camps were implicated. Vallabhbhai declared the report showed the enquiries 'lack balance and proportion'. It was considered damaging enough that it disappeared from view. Until it resurfaced in 2013. And was reproduced in full in A.G. Noorani's 2013 book, *Hyderabad Reborn*. (The report is currently held at the Nehru Museum and Memorial Library in New Delhi.)

∽

And what of our primary actors?

Kasim Razvi was imprisoned. It was one thing to talk of shedding blood, every last drop of it – quite another to actually fight. Unsurprising then, perhaps, that one of the worst incidents of violence occurred in his hometown, Latur. In what might be a fitting denouement, Laik Ali escaped to Pakistan – in the guise of his begum. The Nizam was made the governor of Hyderabad state and continued to reside in King Kothi. Princess Niloufer found Niloufer Hospital, a maternity hospital still functioning in Hyderabad, moved to France, and remarried. El Edroos

was charged with the gradual disbandment of the Hyderabad
Armed Forces. The Communists went underground, many
were imprisoned, until the Telangana peasants' armed struggle
was withdrawn in October 1951. The people of Hyderabad
state finally became citizens of India in 1955 under the Indian
Citizenship Act.

∽

As in Punjab and Bengal, there was a large-scale exchange of
populations in Hyderabad, with upwards of 12 lakh people
moving in and out of the state between July 1947 and September
1948. Seven lakh Muslims crossed into Hyderabad seeking the
Nizam's protection, while 5 lakh of Hyderabad's non-Muslims
left for the Indian Union.

The foundational violence of India, which Vyasa filled
reams with writing his cautionary Mahabharata, which the
Mahatma sacrificed his life for, reared its head at the accession
of Hyderabad into India. Brother against brother. Redux. Did
we learn well from our colonial masters? Or did we know it
already in our veins?

What was destroyed? What prevailed?

How history is lived, and how it is made?

What history is remembered, and what is lost?

The questions dangle in front of us.

What is undeniable is this: Hindu–Muslim harmony as a
facet of Hyderabad was gone. As one Communist wistfully
remarked: 'We got what we wanted, but we lost what we had.'

Acknowledgements

This book is a pandemic baby. In the first week of its writing, my daughter's school shut down, my husband was advised to work from home, then New York City clamped down. We staked out a separate room each in the apartment and hunkered over our laptops – which totally threw the cat who was used to packing off two humans at 7 a.m. and then lolling on the writer's desk! She staked out the corridor to keep an eye on each one of us.

The city that never sleeps paused and muted, its surreal silence punctured with sirens. We ferreted out for groceries, masked and muted. Our world collapsed to our computer monitors. I was luckier, in a sense. My job *is* WFH: From my desk, in my pyjamas, I get to travel the world as I write. Writing *Hyderabad* became a gift as I journeyed to the Nizam's palaces, picked my way through the boulder-strewn landscape, witnessed the peasants' struggle, eavesdropped on the rabid elements, walked through newly independent India's corridors of powers in Delhi …

Hyderabad was a complex book to write. In *Lahore*, the stakeholders were split between Delhi and Laur, political leaders and common people; in Hyderabad, they multiplied: the Nizam, a Lear-like figure with enough contradictions to fill a book; Razvi and the Razakars; Hindu Mahasabha and Arya Samaj; Telangana peasants' struggle; varied Communist groups … Everyday, the book challenged me and made me write better.

One benefit of the lockdown was that courtesy the New York Public Library, research material was arriving home by post, and for extended loan periods. I could not be more grateful. And to all the writers whose wonderful books on Hyderabad aided my understanding of a complex chapter in our history. I have been able to mention some of them in the Select Bibliography.

Thanks to my brother-in-law, Praveen Someshwar, for sourcing an elusive manuscript that was absolutely critical to my research. My sister-in-law, Kavitha, for her steadfast support of my writing career and for being the first person to read each of my published books and write a review – ab kya misaal dun main tumhari. Minoshka Narayan, wonder child to a wonderful woman, who researched this trilogy of books and continues to be a first reader of drafts – so much love. The gorgeous covers for the trilogy are the excellent work of Devangana Dash whom I so admire.

My gratitude to the entire team at HarperCollins India, especially the wonderful Udayan Mitra, Prema Govindan, Paloma Dutta, and Jaseya Fazili. I could not ask for better collaborators in my storytelling.

None of what I do would be possible without the love and support and cheerleading of my family, Prasanna, Malvika, Nyx – mere jaane jaans.

Select Bibliography

Azad, Maulana Abul Kalam. *India Wins Freedom: An Autobiographical Narrative*. Bombay: Orient Longman, 1959.

Benichou, Lucien. *From Autocracy to Integration: Political Developments in Hyderabad State, 1938–1948*. Hyderabad: Orient Longman, 2000.

Birkenhead, Frederick. *Walter Monckton: The Life of Viscount Monckton of Brenchley*. London: Weidenfeld & Nicolson, 1969.

Bourke-White, Margaret. *Halfway to Freedom*. New York: Simon and Schuster, 1949.

Brown, Judith M. *Nehru: A Political Life*. Yale: Yale University Press, 2003.

Campbell-Johnson, Alan. *Mission with Mountbatten*. London: Hamish Hamilton, 1951.

Carter, Lionel, ed. *Partition Observed: British Official Reports from South Asia*. 2 vols. New Delhi: Manohar, 2011.

Chaudhuri, Nirad C. *The Autobiography of an Unknown Indian*. London: Macmillan, 1951.

———*Thy Hand Great Anarch! India, 1921–1952*. London: Chatto and Windus, 1987.

Chopra, Prabha, ed. *Sardar Patel and the Partition of India*. Delhi: Konark, 2010.

Collins, Larry, and Dominique Lapierre. *Freedom at Midnight*. New York: Avon, 1975.

Corfield, Conrad. *The Princely India I Knew: From Reading to Mountbatten*. Madras: Indo-British Historical Society, 1975.

Cotton, Sidney, with Ralph Baker. *Aviator Extraordinary: The Sidney Cotton Story*. London: Chatto & Windus, 1969.

El Edroos, Syed Ahmed. *Hyderabad of 'The Seven Loaves'*. Hyderabad: Laser Prints, 1994.

French, Patrick. *Liberty or Death*. London: Flamingo, 1998.

Gandhi, Indira, and Jawaharlal Nehru. *Two Alone, Two Together: Letters between Indira Gandhi and Jawaharlal Nehru, 1940–1964*. Edited by Sonia Gandhi. London: Hodder and Stoughton, 1992.

Gandhi, Rajmohan. *Patel: A Life*. Ahmedabad: Navjivan, 1990.

Gopal, Sarvepalli. *Jawaharlal Nehru: A Biography*. 2 vols. London: Jonathan Cape, 1975–1979.

Guha, Ramachandra. *India after Gandhi: The History of the World's Largest Democracy*. New York: HarperCollins, 2007.

Hajari, Nisid. *Midnight's Furies: The Deadly Legacy of India's Partition*. New York: First Mariner Books, 2016.

Hodson, H.V. *The Great Divide: Britain–India–Pakistan*. Karachi: Oxford University Press, 1971.

Hutheesing, Krishna Nehru. *We Nehrus*. New York: Holt, Rinehart and Winston, 1967.

Hyder, Mohammed. *October Coup: A Memoir of the Struggle for Hyderabad*. New Delhi: Roli Books, 2012.

Khan, Yasmin. *The Great Partition: The Making of India and Pakistan*. New Haven and London: Yale University Press, 2007.

Khilnani, Sunil. *The Idea of India*. London: Penguin Books, 2003.

Khosla, G.D. *Stern Reckoning: A Survey of the Events Leading Up to and Following the Partition of India*. New Delhi: Oxford University Press, 1989.

Krishna, B. *Sardar Vallabhbhai Patel: India's Iron Man*. New Delhi: HarperCollins, 1996.

Luther, Narendra. *Hyderabad: A Biography*. New Delhi: Oxford University Press, 2012.

Mathai, M.O. *My Days with Nehru*. New Delhi: Vikas, 1979.

Menon, V.P. *The Story of the Integration of Indian States*. London: Longman, Green, 1956.

———*The Transfer of Power in India*. New Delhi: Sangam Books, 1981.

Moon, Penderel. *Divide and Quit*. London: Chatto and Windus, 1964.

Moraes, Frank. *Jawaharlal Nehru: A Biography*. New York: Macmillan, 1956.

Morgan, Janet. *Edwina Mountbatten: A Life of Her Own*. London: HarperCollins, 1991.

Mountbatten, Pamela. *India Remembered*. London: Pavilion, 2008.

Munshi, K.M. *The End of an Era: Hyderabad Memories*. Bombay: Bharatiya Vidya Bhavan, 1957.

Nehru, Jawaharlal. *The Discovery of India*. Delhi: Oxford University Press, 1985.

———*Selected Works of Jawaharlal Nehru*. 1st series. 15 vols. Ed. Sarvepalli Gopal et al. New Delhi: Orient Longman, 1972–1982.

————*Selected Works of Jawaharlal Nehru.* 2nd series. 55 vols. Ed. Sarvepalli Gopal et al. New Delhi: Jawaharlal Nehru Memorial Fund, 1985–.

Noorani, A.G. *The Destruction of Hyderabad.* New Delhi: Tulika, 2013.

Pandey, Gyanendra. *Remembering Partition: Violence, Nationalism and History in India.* New Delhi: Cambridge University Press India, 2003.

Shankar, V. *My Reminiscences of Sardar Patel.* Vol 1. Delhi: Macmillan India, 1974.

Sundarayya, P. *Telangana People's Struggle and Its Lessons.* Calcutta: Desraj Chadha, 1972.

Talbot, Ian. *Divided Cities: Partition and Its Aftermath in Lahore and Amritsar, 1947–1957.* Oxford: Oxford University Press, 2006.

Talbot, Ian, and Gurharpal Singh. *The Partition of India.* Oxford: Oxford University Press, 2002.

Von Tunzelmann, Alex. *Indian Summer: The Secret History of the End of an Empire.* New York: Henry Holt and Co., 2007.

Wolpert, Stanley. *Shameful Flight: The Last Years of the British Empire in India.* Oxford: Oxford University Press, 2006.

Ziegler, Philip. *Mountbatten: The Official Biography.* London: Collins, 1985.

Zubrzycki, John. *The Last Nizam.* Sydney: Macmillan, 2006.

About the Author

Manreet Sodhi Someshwar is a bestselling author of eight books, including the award-winning *The Radiance of a Thousand Suns* and the critically acclaimed *The Long Walk Home*. Hailed as 'a star on the literary horizon' by Khushwant Singh and garnering endorsements from Gulzar for two of her books, Manreet and her work have featured at numerous literary festivals. Her articles have appeared in *The New York Times*, the *South China Morning Post*, and several Indian publications. Manreet lives in New York City with her husband, daughter, and cat.